THE COUNTDOWN

TWO MINUTES TO MIDNIGHT

CONTRITION

ANTOWON GOWDY

NEWMAN SPRINGS PUBLISHING
320 Broad Street
Red Bank, NJ 07701

First originally published by Newman Springs Publishing 2024

Note: All references to Scripture are taken from
the King James Version (KJV) of the Bible.

ISBN 978-1-63881-313-2 (Paperback)
ISBN 978-1-63881-314-9 (Digital)

Printed in the United States of America

To Frances Gowdy
My grandmother, who always told me to chase after my dreams.
I wish she were here with me to see my dreams come true.
I miss you, Granny, and I love you.

CONTENTS

CHAPTER

1

My name is Antowon Anderson. My brother William and I grew up together in Houston, Texas. I was sixteen, and William was fourteen. We both grew up as Muslims and served Allah as our god. William and I both went to Austin High School. One day, William and I were walking to our sixth-bell class when four strangers walked up to us and asked us our names. I told them that my name was Antowon and that my little brother's name was William. The four kids introduced themselves; there were two boys and two girls. The first person who introduced himself was Eric Robinson, and he said that he was fourteen. The next person was Brittany Brown, who was sixteen. She was the oldest of the group. The third person who introduced herself was the youngest of the group; her name was Jasmine Washington, she was thirteen. And the last person was Daniel Peterson, and he was fifteen.

Eric asked us what religion were we, and I told him that my brother and I were Muslims. Jasmine said, "Have you ever heard of Jesus Christ?"

William said, "No, I have never heard of Jesus Christ. Who is he?"

Eric said, "Jesus is God. He came to the earth to save us from our sins."

I yelled, "That's enough." I told William to leave and go to class. I told Eric and all of his friends that they were not allowed to talk to my brother about their religion, that we were Muslims, and that we would not stop being Muslims. Then I went to class. Later on that day, William saw me in the hall, and he came up to me and said, "Bro, what was that all about with them kids earlier?" I told him that those kids were trying to turn us away from the true god, Allah. "Do not let what anyone says take you away from the truth." I asked William what class he had next. He said that he had math next and asked me what class I had next. I told him that I had social studies. William said, "I will see you later, bro." I told him that I would see him later and left.

After school, I asked William what he learned in school today, and he said that he learned the quadratic formula. He asked me what I learned, and I told him I learned about the Revolutionary War, and he said okay. I asked him if he was ready to go, and he said yes, so we left school and went home. That night, William came up to my room and saw me looking up the Bible. He closed the door and said, "Antowon, what are you doing reading the Christian Bible? I thought you told those people at school that we are Muslims."

I said, "Yes, we are, but I'm curious about what they believe. Those kids at school seemed to really want us to convert to their religion." I went to Google and typed in "Is Jesus the only God" and hit the search button, and about a thousand different results came up. I clicked on this website called JesusIsTheMessiah.com. When I got to the site, the first thing I saw was a picture of Jesus with the world in his hands, and underneath it was a message that said Jesus is the light of the world and that we should believe in him and accept the gift of salvation.

William got mad. He said, "I can't look at this anymore." After he left, I went to itube.com and looked up videos about Jesus. I watched a video on this girl comparing the Bible to the Quran, and when I finished with the video, I sat back in my chair, thinking, *What if those kids at school are right? What if Jesus did die on the cross to save me from my sins? What if he did come back from the dead with all power in his hands? Would that mean that everything I was ever taught about Allah being god was wrong? No, I can't believe that. Allah is god, and I will serve him for the rest of my life.* I went downstairs and saw

William watching TV. I told him not to tell our parents what I was doing on the computer; if our parents found out that I was looking at another religion, I would be in very big trouble. I would be disowned. I could even lose my life.

William said that he would keep my secret, and I said, "Thanks, bro." At dinner, my mom asked me how school was, and I told her it was good and that I learned about the American Revolutionary War and how the United States beat the British to win independence. She said that was good, and Dad asked William what he learned. He said he learned the quadratic formula. Dad said okay, and we continued eating. That night, I couldn't sleep. I kept on thinking about what I read on the Internet.

The next time I saw Eric and his group, I went up to them and told them that I had gone on the Internet and looked up everything they told me about Jesus, but I still didn't believe in anything they told me. They said, "Sit down." I sat down, and Eric pulled out a Bible. He said, "Do you want to know how we know that Jesus is Lord? This is how." The first scripture he showed me was **Revelation 1:8**, which said, "I am the Alpha and the Omega, the beginning and the ending, saith the Lord the almighty." The next scripture he showed me was **John 3:16–17**, which read that God so loved the world that He gave His only begotten Son, that whoever believed in Him shall not perish but have everlasting life, for God did not send His Son into the world to condemn the world but so that through Him the world would be saved. When Eric finished, he told me that Jesus lived a sinless life but was killed like a common criminal. He was dead for three days, then on the third, He rose from the grave with all power in His hands.

Brittany said, "He died so that we can have eternal life. Eternal life is a gift that He made possible by dying on the cross for your sins. That's how much God loves you. You can have eternal life if you accept Him as your Savior and mean it in your heart." I thought about it and said, "Okay, I want to accept Jesus as my Savior." Eric, Brittany, and the rest of their friends prayed with me. Eric led the prayer, and I repeated it. "Lord Jesus, Savior of the world, You died for me. You were beaten for me to save me. Today, I accept what

You did on the cross, and I accept You. I ask You to come into my heart and be my Savior. Cleanse me from all of my sins. I pray this in Jesus's name. Amen." When we finished, Eric hugged me, and the rest of the group embraced me. Daniel said, "Welcome to the family of Christ," and I said, "Thank you, but you cannot tell my brother that I have accepted Jesus as my Savior. If word gets back to my parents that I have converted and become a Christian, they will disown me. They might even kill me."

They all said that they would keep my secret and said one more time, "We welcome you into the family." I left.

I was going to class when I ran into William in the hallway, and he asked me how I was doing. I told him, "I feel alive, more alive than I have felt in a long time."

William looked at me and said, "There's something different about you, but I can't make it out." I thought to myself, *It's a good thing you don't because you wouldn't like it.* Later that night, William and I were watching TV when our parents came into the room and told us, "It's time to pray to our god Allah," and I told them that I wasn't feeling well. William helped me to my room. He asked me, "Will you be alright, or do you need me to stay here with you until you feel better?" and I told him that I was alright, then William left. After he left, I prayed, "Lord Jesus, help my brother, mother, and father find and accept the truth."

About two hours later, William came up to my room and asked me how I was feeling. I told him that I was feeling good. He said, "That's good," and I asked him how was prayer, and he said it was good. He also said it helped him get closer to Allah, and I said okay. I said in the back of my mind, *Lord Jesus, please break the cloud of darkness that is covering my brother and keeping him from the truth, and help my parents too.* William said, "Well, bro, I'm going to bed." He hugged me, and I hugged him as he was leaving the room. I said, "God bless you," and he said, "The same to you, brother."

When he left, I locked the door and got down on my knees and said, "Lord Jesus, thank You for dying on the cross for my sins. I want to thank You for sending Eric and his friends to tell me the truth. I pray that my brother William receives Your word and accepts You as his Lord and Savior, in Jesus's name, I pray, and I thank You, Lord. Amen." After I prayed, I unlocked the door and went to sleep. The next thing I knew, William was jumping up and down on my bed, telling me to get up; it was time for school.

When I got to school, Eric, Brittany, Jasmine, and Daniel all said hi to me, and William said, "What was that all about?" and I said I didn't know. Later on, Eric, Brittany, and Daniel came up to me while I was talking to William, and William said in a mean tone, "What do you want?" Daniel replied, "We want to talk to your brother." I asked William if he wanted to stay or if he wanted me to catch up with him later, and he said, "I will stay."

Jasmine said, "Antowon, we have a present for you. We will give you the present later." I said okay, and Brittany said, "May He bless you in your good times and bad times," and I said, "Thank you, and the same to all of you." Eric asked me if we could speak in private, and I said okay. We went to another part of the school, and Eric said, "We have a Bible class after school, and we would like for you to join us. It's in room 240." I asked him what the group was called and where it was at, and he said, "The group is called CROWN. Christ Rules Our World Now."

I told Eric that if I come, I will have to bring my brother. "And I do have to pretend to disagree with everything you say even though I will agree with everything you say."

Eric said, "Okay, I will see you there."

Later on that day, I saw William in the hall and I told him that I wouldn't be coming home after school. "I have something to do." William asked me what it was, and I said, "I have a club to go to." William said, "I want to come," and I said, "Are you sure?" and he said yeah, and I said okay. After school, William and I went around the school looking for room 240, where the meeting was going to take place, and while we were looking, we ran into Daniel. Daniel yelled, "William! Antowon!" We both turned around and looked at him. He told us to follow him. Daniel took us to a classroom. When we walked in, we were shocked that there were a lot of people in the room.

Eric was talking when we walked in. He stopped in the middle of his sentence and said, "We welcome William and Antowon to our meeting," and everyone clapped. Eric continued from where he left off. "Well, after He was arrested, He was taken to the high priest for a trial and was accused of crimes that He never committed, and one of the high priests asked Him if He was the son of God, and He said, 'I am,' and the high priest took Him to the Roman governor Pontius Pilate. Pilate told Him that he had the power to free Him or to crucify Him, and He replied that he had no power over Him if it wasn't given to him from above. Pilate said, 'Who are you?' The man said, 'Anyone who listens to Me and believes in Me will understand the truth.' Pilate said, 'What is truth?' Pilate had the man whipped, then he crucified Him on the cross. Three days later, He rose from the grave with all power in His hands." I looked at William, who seemed to be very interested in the story. I prayed silently that he would receive the word of God and accept Jesus as his Savior. William asked, "Who is this person who went through all this pain and died just to rise from the dead three days later?" Brittany said, "His name is Jesus Christ." William got mad and said, "Antowon, why did you bring me to a Christian meeting? You know that we are not Christians. We are Muslims."

I said, "Yes, I know, but you asked to come," and Eric said, "I asked him to bring you here so you can hear another side of the argument and make up your mind without being biased." William said, "My mind is made up. I serve Allah now and forever." William looked at me and said, "I'm ready to go." I told William that I would meet him outside. When William left, I told Eric, "I'm sorry for the way my brother acted. Thanks for keeping my secret. I'm praying for him and for my parents." Eric said, "God bless you, my brother." I told him, "The same to you," then I left. When I got outside the school, I got on William. I told him that he was wrong for going off on them and that they were trying to help. He said, "I know they were trying to help, but I don't want to hear anything they want to say." I said, "Tomorrow, William, you will apologize to them when we get back to the school."

We walked the rest of the way in silence. The weekend came. William and I went to the movies and saw destruction. When we left the movies, we went to the mall, where we saw a sign that said, "Jesus can return at any time. Are you ready for that day?" I said in the back of my mind, *I'm ready for that day, but my brother isn't. I'm afraid.* We went into a store called Game Freeze, and I saw a movie called *The Crucifixion and Resurrection of Christ.* I grabbed the movie and bought it. William said, "Why are you getting *The Crucifixion and Resurrection of Christ?*" I told him that I had never seen this movie before and wanted to know what the movie was about. William said, "You are one of them, aren't you? You are a Christian." I said, "No, I'm not a Christian. I just want to see what this movie is about." I went home and put in *The Crucifixion and Resurrection of Christ* and started watching it when William came in and sat down. I paused the movie. I turned around and asked him what he wanted, and he said that he wanted to watch the movie with me.

I asked him, "Why do you want to watch this movie with me? I thought you didn't want to read, watch, or listen to anything they believed in." William said, "I can't dislike them or disagree with them unless I know exactly what they believe in." I turned the movie back on, and we kept watching, and halfway through the movie, I started to cry. William saw me crying; he turned around and kept watching the movie. After the movie ended, William walked out and closed the door. I prayed again and then took the movie and hid it under my bed just as my parents came into the room and told me to come on because it was time to go to the mosque to pray. I said okay and got up and got in the car. They drove us to the mosque. When we got there, I slowly walked up to the mosque, then waited until my family was almost inside. I slowly backed away and went around the corner. I saw a church and went inside. I saw the inside of the church for the first time and was shocked to see what it looked like. The church was a medium-size building with a few rows of pews and a cross in the front of the church. I sat in the third row of the pews and saw a Bible. I picked it up and started reading it. I was halfway through Genesis when Eric tapped me on my back and said, "Antowon, I'm happy to see you here in the house of the Lord and King Jesus Christ." I said, "Thank you, I'm happy to be here."

He asked me how I got away from the mosque since my family is Muslim, and I told him that I had to sneak around the corner, and when I got around the corner, I saw the church and saw people coming in, so I decided to follow them and came in. Eric said, "Well, we are glad to have you here, and you are welcome here anytime you like." I said, "Thanks. You know I will be back." Eric sat down next to me, and we read the Bible and enjoyed the service.

When church was over, Eric helped get me back over to the mosque without being caught. Eric went into the mosque with me and took off his shoes, and I asked him what he was doing, and he said that he was helping so my family wouldn't find out that I was a Christian. I told him that he didn't have to do that, and he said that he is my brother in Christ, and when a brother in Christ is in trouble it's his job to help. I said thank you, and then I told him that when we get in there to do exactly what I do and that when we pray that we will be the only ones praying to Jesus, and he said okay. We both got on our faces and prayed to Jesus while everyone else in the mosque prayed to Allah.

When we were done, we went outside, and I was talking to Eric when William and my parents approached me. My parents asked me who I was talking to, and I told them I was talking to my friend Eric. He said hi to my parents, and then we moved away and kept our conservation going. We started talking about Jesus.

Eric said, "How long do you think you can hide being a Christian?" I told him, "I don't know. It's hard because everything I used to do, I don't do anymore, but I think my brother is catching on, or I think he knows, but he's not telling my parents, which is a good thing." William screamed, "Antowon, it's time to go," and I screamed, "Okay, I'm coming." I shook Eric's hand and told him that I would see him at school on Monday, and he said okay.

I said, "God bless you, my brother," and he said, "Same to you, my brother." I ran and caught up with William, and he said, "I've noticed that you and Eric have been hanging out a lot lately. What's up with that?" I told William that it's nothing; "We just hang out and talk." William said, "Something is different about you, but I can't put my finger on it no matter how hard I try. I can't figure out what's different about you." I told William, "Soon, very soon, you will figure out what's wrong with me." We hopped into the car and went home. As we were walking through the door, Daniel came around the corner and said that he needed to talk to me and that it was urgent.

I got off the steps and followed Daniel around the corner. He told me that Brittany and Jasmine were hurt; they were in the hospital and needed our prayer. Daniel and I both got down on our knees and prayed, "Lord Jesus, You know our needs better than we do. We pray that in Jesus's name that You will take care of our friends in their time of need. We pray this in the only name that has the power to heal, in Jesus's name, we pray. We thank You, Lord. Amen." While we were praying, William saw us. Then when we got up, William quickly and quietly went back to the house. I told Daniel to keep me updated on their conditions and that I would see him at school Monday, and he said okay. I went into the house and to my room. I locked the door and spent thirty minutes praying for Brittany and Jasmine.

When I was done, I turned the TV on Channel 28 News. They were talking about the wars in the Middle East and how they were getting worse every single day. I looked in the Bible to **Matthew 24:6** where it said, "And ye shall hear of wars and rumors of wars. See that ye be not troubled for all these things must come to pass, but the end is not yet." I continued to read until I got to verse eight. "For nation shall rise against nation and kingdom against kingdom and there shall be famines and pestilences and earthquakes in diverse places. All these things are the beginning of sorrows."

When I finished, I was in shock at how the events on the news were following the Bible. I had really made the right decision by accepting Jesus as my Savior. Crime rates were higher than they had ever been in history. The news anchorman said different countries were at war. Libya was at war, China was at war, and Iraq was at war. I looked up in the Bible **Ezekiel 38 and 39**, which talks about the war of the end days. I also looked up **1 Thessalonians 4:16–18**, which said, "For the Lord himself shall descend from heaven with a shout with the voice of the archangel and with the trumpet of God and the dead in Christ shall rise first; then we who are alive and remaining shall be caught up together with them in the clouds to meet the Lord in the air, and so shall we ever be with the Lord. Wherefore comfort one another with these words."

When I finished reading the scripture, I started crying. I said, "Thank You, Jesus, for leading me to the truth. Now I pray that You lead my brother to the truth that You are God and that You are God alone and that there is no other God but You." I started crying, "Lord Jesus, I thank You for dying on the cross for my sins. I thank You for shedding that blood for me. I love You, and I want You to guide me. In Jesus's name, I pray. I thank You, Lord. Amen." I went outside, and William was standing outside my door. I said, "Hey, bro, what's up?" William said, "I knew it, I knew it." I said, "You knew what?" He said, "I knew you converted from our religion and became a Christian." I pulled William into my room and said, "How did you find out that I was a Christian?" and William said that he had his suspicions. "Then I saw you praying with Daniel, and when I heard you outside praying to Jesus, you confirmed my suspicions."

He said, "When did you convert and become a Christian?" I said, "I converted and became a Christian a couple of weeks ago, and I'm happier now than I was back then. William, I want you to be happy, and the only way you can be truly happy is to accept Jesus as your Savior." William said, "I will never accept Jesus. Allah is my god, and I will serve him and no one else."

I said, "William, look, I thought Allah was god too, but I was wrong. Jesus is the Messiah." William said, "I can't accept that." I said, "If you don't accept Him, then I need you to do me a favor," and he said, "What?" I told him that I needed him to keep this secret between us. "Our parents can't find out that I'm a Christian or they could have me killed." He said that he would keep my secret, and I told him thanks. I told him that I would pray for him that he would accept Jesus as his Savior, and he said, "That will never happen."

William said, "I'm happy that you are happy, but I can't turn my back on Allah. I will keep your secret, bro." Then William walked out and closed the door. I got on my knees and started to cry. I prayed, "Lord Jesus, help my brother. I want him to know that You are God alone, and You alone are God." I went to Google.com and typed in "How to convince a person who is a Muslim that Jesus Christ is Lord" and hit the search button. Three thousand results came up, and I clicked on the first link. It took me to a site called JesusDiedForMe.com. The first thing I saw was a testimony from a former Muslim named Muhammad Hussad.

He said that he was born in Iraq. He attended service at the mosque every week, and he was taught to kill anyone who didn't believe in Allah. The story went on to say how he had murdered thousands of Jews and Christians in the name of Allah. One day, he was going on a suicide mission when he ran into a Christian on the streets, and he said for some reason he listened to the man speak. The man was telling the crowd that God loved them so much that He sent His Son to die on the cross for our sins so that we can have eternal life. Muhammad said that he went home and thought about what the man had said. At first, he got down on his knees and asked Allah why he let him hear what the guy on the street was saying because he was speaking against what Allah said in the Quran. He said to Allah, "If you are real, speak to me," and he didn't hear anything. He thought since he had questioned Allah, he should kill himself.

He was about to kill himself when he heard a voice calling his name, and the voice told him not to kill himself. Muhammad said, "Who are you?" The voice said that His name was Jesus, the Alpha and the Omega, the Beginning and the End. Jesus told him, "I knew you before the creation of the world. I knew you before I formed you in your mother's womb."

Hussad said he got on his knees and cried out to Jesus and asked God to forgive him for all the murders that he had committed. Then Hussad went looking for the guy who told him about Jesus, and he found him. He went up to the guy and introduced himself. He said, "My name is Matthew," and the other guy said, "My name is Luke."

The two talked and got better acquainted. The story ended with the former Muslim, Matthew, saying, "Any Muslim reading this, Jesus is Lord, and if you accept Him, it will be the best decision you have ever made. You will have a friend that will never leave you, and you will have peace."

I said, "I can't give up on my brother. I just can't."

CHAPTER

2

Cierra Jackson hated church. She liked how God used different people to solve problems. Her parents took her to church every Sunday, and she had to listen to the pastor talk about salvation and escaping hell. She always said, "I have plenty of time to get saved. All I want to do now is have fun." Cierra Jackson was fifteen. She went to Abraham Lincoln High School. Cierra used to hang out with her friends who were Christians, but when she turned thirteen, she decided that she wanted to hang out with the cool kids, so she started drinking, smoking, and staying out late. Every Sunday when her mom came to wake her up, she would get an attitude with her mother.

One day, her mom came to wake her up, and Cierra yelled at her. "Why do I have to go to church? I can be a Christian from home." Cierra's mom said, "I'm not going to argue with you, but if you do not go to church, you are grounded for the weekend." Cierra grumbled and got dressed. Cierra went to church, sat down, and tuned out everything the bishop had to say. When Cierra's family wasn't looking, she would go to sleep.

One day, while Cierra was in her room her mother came up to her and said, "Cierra, why don't you believe in Jesus anymore?" Cierra replied, "Believing in Jesus isn't cool anymore. Believing in Him was cool when I was a little kid, but I'm not a kid anymore. I'm a teenager now, and most teenagers don't believe in Jesus. The ones that do are stupid." Cierra's mother started crying and said, "Cierra, you are wrong. Most teenagers love Jesus, and they want to have a closer, personal relationship with Him." Cierra got mad and said, "I don't care if I go to hell because it's going to be one big party there. Plus, all my friends will be there."

Cierra's mother ran out of the room crying very hard. Cierra was sad that she was mean to her mother, but she felt that she was right. Later on, she wanted to apologize, but then her mother would feel like she was right and Cierra was not. After a while, the guilt was gone, and Cierra told her mother that she was going to the movies and that she would be there for a while. Her mother asked her if she needed any money, and Cierra said no, she had money. Her mother asked what time was she coming back. Cierra didn't answer; she closed the door and left. Instead of going to the movies, she went to her friend's house, and she and her friends drank and smoked until they passed out.

Later that night, Cierra sneaked back to the house. Cierra's mother heard her come in, but instead of yelling at her, Cierra's mother got on her knees and prayed that Cierra would see the light, that she would change her life around, and that she would accept Jesus as her Savior. Cierra heard her mother praying, and tears started falling down her face. Cierra walked into her room and sat on her bed in silence.

She thought to herself, *Why am I so mean? All my mom is doing is trying to help me, and I keep snapping at her.* Cierra went to sleep, feeling sad and guilty. Cierra woke up early the next day. She went into the kitchen and saw her mom reading the Bible. She went up to her and said, "Morning, Mom. What are you doing?" Cierra's mother replied, "I'm reading **Romans 10:13** and **Romans 10:9**. **Romans 10:13** says, 'Whosoever calls upon the name of the Lord shall be saved.' And **Romans 10:9** says that if 'thou shalt confess with thy mouth the Lord Jesus and shalt believe in thine heart that God hath raised him from the dead thou shalt be saved.'" Cierra got up from the table, and as she was leaving, her mother asked her what was wrong. Cierra said, "I'm going to leave because I don't want your religion. I'm doing fine by myself." Then Cierra left and went to her room, and her mother sighed. The next couple of days, Cierra's mother and Cierra didn't talk much. Cierra went about her normal business, and her mother went about her normal business. One day, she was walking when she ran into one of her friends whom she always drank and smoked with. Jenny Thompson ran up to Cierra and asked where she was going, and Cierra said, "I was on my way to your house to get drunk and high." Jenny said, "I don't drink or get high anymore." Cierra looked at Jenny crazy and asked Jenny, "Why don't you smoke or drink anymore?" Jenny said, "I haven't had a drink or a smoke since last week. I accepted Jesus as my Savior."

Cierra said, "What? You accepted Jesus as your Savior?" Jenny said, "Yes, and I feel better than I have ever felt in my life." Cierra said, "If that works for you, fine, but don't be getting all religious on me. I'm doing fine without Jesus. I don't need Him." Jenny sighed and said, "Okay, but you do need Him." Cierra said, "No, I don't. Now can we drop this already?" Jenny said, "Okay, let's go to the mall," and Cierra said okay. When they got to the mall, they saw a man standing outside preaching, saying, "Jesus can come back at any time. **First Thessalonians 5:2–5** says, 'For yourselves know perfectly that the day of the Lord cometh as a thief in the night. For when they say peace and safety then sudden destruction cometh upon them as travail upon a woman with child and they shall not escape. But ye, brethren, are not in darkness that that day should overtake you as a thief. Ye are all children of light and the children of the day; we are not of the night or of darkness.'" Crowds of people were crowding the man as he kept preaching repentance. He also quoted **Matthew 24:42**, "Watch, therefore; ye know not what hour your Lord doth come." The man said, "If you hear the sound of my voice and want to receive Jesus Christ as your Savior, repeat this prayer. Lord Jesus, Savior of the world, You died for me, shedding Your precious blood to save me. I accept You, Jesus. Come into my heart and be my Savior. Lead me the rest of my days. I pray this in Jesus's name, amen." When Cierra looked, a lot of people were on their knees, accepting Jesus as their Savior. Cierra was close to receiving Jesus herself, but she said she would do it later. Jenny and Cierra went into the mall.

Jenny asked Cierra if she received Jesus as her Savior when they were outside, and Cierra said yes. Jenny hugged Cierra, and then Jenny said, "Isn't this great? Now we can be assured of heaven when we die, and we won't be left behind," and Cierra said, "Yep." After Cierra got home, she went to her room and closed the door. She sat on her bed and thought about what the man at the mall had said. "Do I really need to receive Jesus Christ as my Savior?" Cierra thought of Jenny. Jenny used to drink, smoke, and do everything Cierra did, but after she accepted Jesus as her Savior, her whole life-style changed.

Jenny stopped drinking and smoking; she even started going to church and read the Bible more than she used to. Cierra was happy for her, but she figured that accepting Jesus wasn't for her. Jesus was only for people who needed Him, and she didn't need Him. She was doing fine on her own, but she did promise herself that if she ever needed help, He would be the first person she would go to.

When Cierra went back to school, she ran into Jenny, who was talking to some of her friends when Cierra walked up to her. Jenny turned around and said hi, and Cierra asked Jenny what she was doing. Jenny told her that she was telling some of her friends the good news. Cierra said, "What good news?" and Jenny replied, "The good news of Jesus being God in the flesh and that He is the Messiah, and that He is coming back soon, so if they want to go with Him when He comes back, they need to accept Him." Jenny continued to talk. "And all of my friends received Jesus as their Savior. I'm so happy because when they die, they will go to heaven to be with Jesus." Cierra said, "Jenny, can we stop talking about religion so much?" Jenny said, "What are you talking about? Being a Christian isn't a religion. It's a relationship with Jesus. People need to know that the Bible says in **Acts 4:12**: "Neither is there salvation in any other for there is none other name under heaven given among men whereby we must be saved.' **John 6:47** says, 'Verily, verily, I say unto you he that believeth on me had eternal life.' Also, **Hebrews 8:12** says, 'For I will be merciful to their unrighteousness and their inequities will I remember no more.'" Cierra said okay and started walking when Jenny said, "Don't ignore Him. You can feel Jesus tugging at your heart, but it's your choice if you want to let Him in and open the door, or you can reject and keep the doors closed. This is the last thing I'm going to say about it. Whatever choice you make, it will have a consequence. It can either be positive or negative, but the choice is yours." Then Jenny walked away and went to class.

After school, Cierra walked home. She thought about what Jenny said, but the more she thought about it, the more she resented it. The next day at school, Cierra confronted Jenny and told her that she didn't want her talking about Jesus to her or around her ever again. Jenny said, "If that's what you want, then I won't talk to you about Jesus or talk about Him when you are around."

Cierra said thank you and that she would see her at lunch. At lunch, Cierra ordered tacos. Then she saw Jenny reading the Bible. When Jenny saw Cierra coming, she stopped, put her bookmark in her Bible, and closed it. Cierra sat down and said hi. Jenny said hi, then she said, "What are you doing?" and she said she had just came from social studies class where Mr. Smith was the teacher. Jenny told her that she came from English class that Mr. Johnson taught. "He's a good teacher, and he's a Christian. He incorporates what the Bible says to the English that he teaches us, and it helps me understand the Bible and his English class."

"I have that class next after lunch," Cierra said, "and I'm not in the mood to listen to a teacher preach. I have my own beliefs, and I'm sticking to them." Jenny said, "You can't be narrow-minded. You have to open your eyes to the truth and give Jesus a chance."

"I gave Him a chance, and He failed me. Why would I give Him another chance to fail me again? He didn't save my cousin from dying in a car accident, and He didn't save my grandfather from cancer when I was ten years old. If He couldn't do these two things for me, why would I trust Him to do anything else for me?" Jenny said, "Cierra, Jesus didn't take your family away. The Bible says in **John 10:10–11** that the devil came to steal, kill, and destroy, but Jesus came so that we may have life and have it more abundantly. 'I am a good shepherd; the good shepherd giveth his life for the sheep.' Just trust in Jesus." Cierra said, "I can't do that," and she left.

A couple of weeks later, Cierra was in the car with some of her friends, and they were all drunk. Cierra's friend Ben lost control of the car, and the car went into a ditch.

Cierra was whiplashed into the back of her seat, and she was slowly passing out. With all the strength she could muster, she crawled out and yelled, "Jesus, I know that I don't deserve for You to save me from dying, but if You show me mercy and save me from dying, I will stop smoking and drinking. I will stop arguing with my mom, and I will start going to church more." As Cierra was mere seconds from passing out, something happened that she couldn't explain. A white light appeared in front of her. The light was so bright that she had to close her eyes. She heard someone walking toward her, and she said in a raspy voice, "Who…who are you?" The voice told her, "Fear not, for the Lord has sent me here to rescue you."

Cierra laid on the ground unable to move, and instantly, she went from the ground into the air, then she was ten miles down to the ground again. The next thing she remembered was the big explosion from where she once was. She looked back at the flames, then passed out. Two weeks later, Cierra woke up in Xavier Hospital with a first-degree burn and a concussion. When the nurse came in and saw that Cierra was awake, she called the doctor. The doctor came in and asked her what her name was. She told him that her name was Cierra Jackson. The doctor said hi. He said that his name was Dr. John and that he would be her doctor until she checked out.

She asked Dr. John about her other friends who were in the car with her; she asked when she could go see them. Dr. John said that she could never see them, and she asked why. He told her that all of her friends were knocked unconscious from the crash, and the explosion killed them. "I'm very sorry, Cierra. We will leave you so you can get some rest. We will check on you later." Cierra sat in her room, crying. She asked herself, *Why did Jesus protect me? I know I asked for Him to protect me, but why couldn't He protect me and my friends?* Cierra thought, *What kind of God would protect one person but not everyone?* She was angry and sad at the same time. She decided that she would never follow a God that wouldn't protect everyone.

The bright light appeared again, and Cierra said, "Who are you?" and he said, "I'm Michael the archangel. I'm an angel sent by the Most High Jesus Christ, the Creator of the universe, the King of kings and Lord of lords." Cierra said, feeling scared, "Why did He send you here?" Michael said, "He sent me here to tell you that everything works for good and that your friends' dying wasn't His fault." Cierra yelled, "Whose fault is it, then, if it isn't God's fault?" Michael responded, "It is the fault of our adversary, the prince of the air, the accuser of the brother, Satan. The Bible says in **John 10:10** that 'the thief cometh not but to kill and destroy. I cometh that they might have life and that more abundantly.'" Cierra asked, "Michael, how can we live the abundant life when there is so much evil and violence and destruction in the world?"

"Jesus gives the world a choice to either serve Him or to serve the devil, and most people have chosen the devil rather than Him."

Cierra said, "This has to be a dream. There is no way I'm lying in a hospital bed talking to an angel." She closed her eyes and reopened them, and Michael the archangel was gone. She said, "It was a dream, but why did it feel so real?" No matter how much Cierra tried, she couldn't get the thought of Michael the archangel out of her head. She kept asking herself, why didn't Jesus protect all of her friends? She cried out, "God, why didn't You save my friends? They deserved to live just like I did. I know we shouldn't have been drinking, but they still don't deserve to die." She said angrily, "I will never serve You, Jesus. I won't serve a God that allows people to die."

Two weeks later, Cierra was released from the hospital, and she was told to make an appointment for a follow-up as soon as possible. Cierra went home, and Jenny came over. Cierra told Jenny what happened. Jenny started crying and said, "I wish they had listened to me when I told them not to drink and when I tried to tell them about Jesus." Cierra said, "Jenny, what are you talking about?" Jenny said, "Before the car accident, I tried to tell them not to drink or to ride in the car because Jesus told me something was going to happen, that's why I didn't ride along with them." Cierra said, "You mean to tell me that if they had listened to you not to drink or go driving, they would still be here right now?"

Jenny sighed and said, "Yes. I'm sorry, Cierra, but they are gone." Cierra screamed, "No, this has to be a dream. They can't be gone. Tomorrow, I will walk by, and I will see them, and they will say hi, and then we will go out and chill."

"Cierra," Jenny said, "come with me. I'm going to take you somewhere." Cierra followed Jenny to a brick building two stories high. Jenny led Cierra into the building, and Cierra looked around as she walked. Jenny led her to a door, opened it, and walked in, and Cierra followed her. Once they were both in the room, Cierra closed the door, and they both sat down in some chairs. Ten minutes later, a guy walked in and sat behind a desk.

He introduced himself. "My name is Eddie Brown, but everyone calls me Dr. Brown. I'm with the city morgue. I have been told that you have come here today to see the remains of your friends who died in that car accident." Cierra got up and said, "No, I didn't even know we were coming here. She tricked me." Jenny grabbed Cierra and told Dr. Brown to take them to the remains. Once they were in the other room, Dr. Brown uncovered all eight of her friends, and Cierra dropped to the ground and started crying very hard. She turned to Jenny, still crying, and said, "Why, why did you bring me here? I knew they were gone, but you had to bring it home by making me see the bodies. I was dealing with them dying by pretending that they were still here so I wouldn't be in so much pain."

"Cierra," Jenny said, sitting next to her. "There is only one person who can heal you, and His name is Jesus."

Cierra pulled away and said, "Do you know what, Jenny? I'm tired of hearing about Jesus. He has done nothing for me but cause me trouble. I don't believe in Jesus, and I never will. I am an atheist. I know that there is no god. If there was a god, why am I going through all of this? Can you explain to me why my life is a living hell? My mother is a religious nut, and my father died in the war in Iraq, and now all of my friends are dead."

Jenny replied, "We all have had a rough life. We had to deal with the pain and suffering of this life, but we have a plan, and He has a plan. Who do you think has the better plan?" Cierra said, "I don't care about His plan. All I care about is mine. Now leave me alone." Then Cierra ran.

Two weeks later, Cierra was on the Internet when a pop-up appeared on her computer. The message said, "**Matthew 5:3**: Blessed are the poor in spirit for theirs is the kingdom of heaven." Cierra looked puzzled, then another message that had a scripture popped up, and the scripture was **Romans 10:10**: "For with the heart man believeth unto righteousness and with the mouth confession is made unto salvation." Cierra turned off her computer and sat in her room in silence, thinking why everything in her life was going bad. She had a perfect life with the exception of her mother and her religion. Everyone liked her. She was the most popular person in her school. In one day, her life was turned upside down. All of her friends, with the exception of Jenny who had accepted Jesus and wasn't in the car, were dead.

She said that if she was low in spirit, then she needed someone or something to bring her spirits back up. She sat down on the floor and started to meditate on the good things in her life and not the bad. The next day, she went to the library and checked out a book called *Karma*. She started reading the book, and when she finished the first book, she went and checked out six more books on karma. Once she got home, she went to her room and kept reading more on karma. Soon she was spending all her free time reading books on karma. She was on the Internet reading, and she was meditating more than usual.

Cierra started praying to Buddha, asking Buddha for advice on how to deal with all the pain and suffering she was going through. She prayed three times a day. Soon she was doing and saying things she thought Buddha was telling her and what she thought was right. On a warm, sunny day, she was walking to the store and ran into one of her friends whom she hadn't talked to for a long time because he had been one of her friends that was a Christian, and she considered Christians uncool and fun crushers. His name was Michael Lynn. When Cierra saw Michael, she was about to turn when Michael ran up to her and said hi, and she said hi back. Michael asked Cierra how she was doing, and she said fine, then she asked him how he was doing, and he said fine. Michael told Cierra that he was still going to church and was still serving the Lord. Cierra said, "That's good for you." Then she told him that she believed in karma now and that there were two forces fighting each other, one good and one evil.

She also said, "I believe that when you do something good, you receive good karma, but when you do something wrong or evil, you receive bad karma." Michael said, "There is no such thing as karma. There are blessings and curses. The two forces at work here are spirits. One spirit is God, and the other is the devil. God is the Creator of the world. He created us to be perfect, but when Adam and Eve sinned, that made us imperfect." Michael opened up the Bible and gave it to Cierra. He told her to read **Romans 3:23**, and she read it out loud. "For all have sinned and come short of the glory of God." Then she read in verse 24, "Being justified freely by his grace through the redemption that is in Christ Jesus."

Cierra looked at Michael and asked him what he meant by that. "He said that we cannot get into heaven by our own works, only by being perfect. But since we all have sinned, there is no way we can get into heaven. That's why Jesus came to die so we can get back into heaven. When the Father looks at us after we accept Jesus as our Savior, He doesn't see the sins. He sees the perfection of Jesus. God even said in **Jeremiah 31:34**, 'And they teach no more every man his neighbor and every man his brother saying, Know the Lord, for they shall know me, from the least of them unto the greatest of them, saith the LORD, for I will forgive their iniquity, and I will remember their sin no more.'" Cierra said, "I'm sticking with my karma. My karma has never let me down, and it never will."

Michael sighed and told Cierra that she could keep his Bible, and she said, "I don't need your Bible. My mom has a Bible, but I will never read the Bible." Michael put his Bible in his bag and said, "Okay, but if you don't read the Bible, how can you ever know what's going to happen in the future to the world and what will happen when you die?" Cierra said, "Nothing is going to happen to me after I'm dead. After we die, we rot in the ground. That's it. There is no heaven or hell."

"Cierra," Michael said, "what you believe is irreverent to the facts that there is a God. His name is Jesus, and there is a heaven and a hell." Cierra said, "No, there isn't. Stop talking to me about it." Then Cierra walked away. Michael sighed and said, "One day, she will learn, but I hope she learns before it's too late before Jesus comes and she is left behind."

CHAPTER

3

Jake Summers was born in Cincinnati, Ohio. His mother and father taught him a religion called Chrislam. Chrislam was a religion that merged Christianity and Islam. Jake went to a church that practiced Chrislam. He and his family prayed to Jesus and Allah even though all his friends were Christians and told him that worshipping two gods was wrong and that Jesus was the light and Allah was the dark. They also told him that light and dark cannot mix. Jake still didn't listen to them. One day, he was walking when he ran into one of his Christian friends. His name was David. David was twelve, and Jake was eleven. David invited Jake to come to his church, and Jake said that he would come. David went to the Truth Christian Church. Their pastor was Michael Hardy.

Bishop Hardy always preached on the rapture of the church and the coming seven-year tribulation. "Won't that be a great day for us when Jesus comes back, and a day of sorrow for those who are left behind to deal with the lawless one and the coming one world government." The day Jake came to the church, the bishop was preaching on why Jesus is the only way and why we cannot compromise or join with other religions. The first thing Bishop Hardy said was that the first reason we know that Jesus Christ is the one true God is that in **John 14:6**, Jesus said, "I am the way, the truth, and the life. No man can come unto the Father but through me." Bishop Hardy continued, "In that same chapter, in verses one through five, it reads, 'Let not your heart be troubled, ye who believe in God also believe also in me. In my Father's house are many mansions. If it were not so, I would have told you. And if I go to prepare a place for you, I will come again and receive you unto myself that where I am there ye may be also.'" He told the church, "I know you are wondering what this means. These scriptures mean that Jesus ascended into heaven and that He will come back again. No one knows when, but the only way you will meet Him when He comes is to repent of your sins. Anything that is not lined up with the word of God is a sin. Will you repent of your sins?"

Jake thought, *How can I repent of my sins when I've never sinned? At my church, they don't preach on sin.* Bishop Hardy said, "If you want to receive Jesus Christ as your Savior, then come up front. Or if you are too nervous to come up here, repeat this prayer. Lord Jesus, Savior of the world, You died for me, shedding Your precious blood to save me. Today, I accept You as my Savior. I ask You to guide me for the rest of my life. I pray this in Jesus's name, amen." Bishop Hardy said, "If you just repeated this prayer and meant it in your heart, then let me be the first to congratulate you on being saved and being assured of heaven when you die."

After the service, David asked Jake, "What did you think about the service?" and Jake said, "I enjoyed the service, but there were a few things that I didn't agree with." David said, "Like what?" Jake said, "At my church, there are no crosses. My pastor preaches that we don't need the cross to go to heaven because there are many paths to god. Jesus is one of the ways to get to heaven, but He's not the only way." David said, "Jesus is the only way. We all have sinned and fallen short of the glory of God. That's why Jesus had to come to die to reconcile us back to Him. In **1 John 5:12**, it says, 'He that hath the Son of God has life, and he who hath not the Son of God hath not life.' That means if you accept Jesus as your Savior, you will have eternal life with Him in heaven, but if you do not accept Him, you will never enter into heaven. You will enter into eternal darkness." Jake said, "I have a question to ask you," and David said, "Shoot."

"Why didn't Jesus find another way to get us into heaven?"

David said, "There's no way to enter into heaven unless you are perfect, and none of us is perfect, so Jesus freely gave His life up for us. Without blood, there is no atonement for our sins, and since Jesus is perfect, He was the perfect sacrifice to save us from our sins. **Romans 8:32** says, 'He that spared not his only Son but delivered him up for us all, how shall he not with him also freely give us all things?' Jesus isn't going to force us to follow Him. He gives us free will to do whatever we want and to choose if we will follow Him." Jake said, "I don't believe what you are saying." David said, "Can't you believe in the truth?" and Jake said, "I know the truth, and the truth is I believe in Jesus and Allah. I pray to both gods. I believe that Jesus Christ is God, and I believe that Allah is god."

David said, "You are breaking God's first commandment, which is 'You shall have no other gods before Me.' Also in **Matthew 6:24** and in **Luke 16:13**, it says, 'No man can serve two masters, for either he will hate the one and love the other or else he will hold onto one and despise the other. Ye cannot serve God and mammon.'" Jake looked at David, confused, and said, "What does that mean?" David said, "That means that you can't serve Jesus and Allah, and you can't follow Chrislam. Jesus is the light of the world. He is God alone, and He alone is God. You can't mix light and dark together. The only way you can get the freedom and peace that the world can never give you is by accepting Jesus as your Savior, and you better do it before it's too late."

David started to walk away when Jake said, "Wait, what do you mean before it's too late?" David turned around and said, "Jesus is coming back soon, and no one knows when, but when He does come back, all those who have accepted Jesus Christ as their Savior will be raptured, which means they will disappear, body and all, but their clothes and all of their earthly belongings will be left behind, and many people will not know what's happened because no one will see Jesus coming except for the ones who are saved." Jake said, "Let's get this straight. When Jesus is supposed to come back, all the ones who accepted Him as their Savior will be raptured, and no one who isn't saved will be able to see Him or know what has happened." David said, "That's right."

Jake said, "And you actually believe this?" and David said, "With all of my heart." Then Jake said, "You have the nerves to call what I believe crazy? There is no way that people will disappear." David said, "Actually millions from all over the world, all at one time." Jake said, "Okay, answer me this question. What will happen next?" David said, "The whole world will be in chaos, and a world dictator will emerge before the world. He will claim to have all the answers to the world problems, and the world will believe him. Next, he will merge the whole world under a one world government, and the world will be divided into ten regions, and he will use false peace to destroy the world.

"The Bible reads in **Daniel 8:24–25**, 'And by his power shall be mighty but not by his power, and he shall destroy wonderfully and shall prosper and practice and shall destroy the mighty and the holy people. And through his policy also he shall cause craft to prosper in his hand, and he shall magnify himself in his heart and by peace shall destroy many. He shall also stand up against the Prince of princes but shall be broken without hand.'" David said, "If you are confused about what I just said, Jake, it means that the world leader who will be the antichrist will make peace treaties and contracts and never keep them, and he will use the idea and banner of peace to hide his true motives. Also, it says he will be defeated without hand, which means no human hand will defeat him. When Jesus comes back after the seven-year tribulation, He will defeat the antichrist and his right-hand man, the false prophet. A lot will happen in between the antichrist's rise to power and his ultimate fall from power. The only way you can escape all of this, Jake, is to accept Jesus Christ as your personal Lord and Savior."

Jake said, "I don't know. It's a lot to take in. If what you are telling me is true, that means everything I have known and learned is a lie. I have to go home and search my heart because I am starting to believe what you are telling me is true, but something is holding me back." David said, "What's holding you back?" Jake said, "What's holding me back is what my parents will think if I leave our religion, become a Christian, and turn my back on Chrislam." David put his hand on Jake's shoulder and said, "It doesn't matter what your parents think or what anyone else thinks because it's His opinion that matters most of all."

"I'm going home to think about what you said," Jake told David. "And I will ask Jesus what to do." David said okay and started to walk away, then said, "By the way, I want you to read **John 8:32**. It might help you make up your mind," and Jake said okay. Jake went home and found a Bible. He went to **John 8:32**, which read, "And ye shall know the truth and the truth shall set you free." Jake said, "What should I do? I need some advice."

Jake heard a voice that he had never heard before saying, "I am He that was, is, and is to come." When Jake heard the voice, he trembled and said, "Who are you?" The voice said, "I am Jesus Christ, the King of kings and the Lord of lords." Jake asked Jesus, "What do You want from me?" and Jesus said, "You asked for advice, and I'm here to give you advice. If you want to know the truth, you have to put your faith and trust in Me." Jake said, "How can I put my trust in You when I don't know You?" Jesus said, "All you need is the faith of a mustard seed to believe, and I will take care of the rest." Jake thought about it for a while, then said, "I do trust You, Jesus, and I do accept You as my Savior. I ask You to come into my heart and guide me for the rest of my life. I pray this in Jesus's name. Amen."

The next day, Jake saw David walking, and he ran up to him and said, "Guess what, David," and David said, "What?" Jake said, "I accepted Jesus Christ as my Savior." David said, "Praise the Lord. It's good that you have accepted Jesus as your Savior. If you want to continue your education, you have to get into a church that teaches on the Bible only, and you need to read the Bible, and whatever you don't understand, you can ask the Lord what it means." When David asked Jake how he got saved, Jake said, "I asked out loud for advice, and Jesus came to talk to me. He convinced me that He was the truth and the life, so I got on my knees and accepted Him as my Savior."

David asked Jake if he would be seeing him in school, and he said no because he was homeschooled by his mother. David said, "Okay, if you have any questions that I can answer, I'll be happy to answer them if I know them," and Jake said okay. Two weeks later, David went to the Truth Church. When David got into the church, he was tapped on the back. He turned around, and it was Jake. He asked Jake what brought him to the church, and Jake said that he was coming to the service and that the Truth Church was his home church now.

Bishop Hardy got on the podium and welcomed everyone to the Truth Church. He said, "Today we are starting a new series called 'The Signs of the Times.' The series will be six weeks on the future." Starting off the sermon, Bishop Hardy said, "We all have seen on the news how there are famines, pestilences, and wars, but the Bible warned us that this was going to happen in **Matthew 24:7–8**. It reads, 'For nation shall rise against nation and kingdom against kingdom, and there shall be famines and pestilences and earthquakes in diverse places. All these are the beginning of sorrows.' Also, we read in **Luke 21:11** that 'great earthquakes shall be in diverse places and famines and pestilences and fearful signs shall there be from heaven.' Also, the wars that are happening are in the Bible too. If you turn your Bibles to **Matthew 24:6**, it reads, 'And you shall hear of wars and rumors of wars. See that ye not be troubled for all of these things must come to pass, but the end is not yet.' The reason I'm explaining this," Bishop Hardy said, "Is because if you are a true believer in Jesus and are a true Christian, you don't have to worry if you're going to eat the next day or if all of your bills are going to be paid. You might say that it's impossible to get all of your bills paid, but Jesus said in **Matthew 19:26**, 'With men this is impossible, but with God all things are possible.'"

Everybody in the church got to their feet and praised God, then Bishop Hardy said, "If you know that all of your needs will be supplied according to **Philippians 4:19**, which says, 'But my God shall supply all of my needs according to His riches and glory by Christ Jesus,' give the Lord some more praise." The whole church gave praises to God, and Jake said, "I'm happy that I have accepted Jesus Christ as my Savior." David said, "Yeah, I'm happy too." David asked Jake how his parents were taking to him becoming a Christian, and Jake said that his parents were mad that he had turned his back on Chrislam and embraced Jesus as his Savior.

The last scripture that Bishop Hardy read was **Psalm 37:25**: "I have been young and now I'm old, yet have I not seen the righteous forsaken nor his seed begging bread." As Bishop Hardy closed the service, he asked the church, "If there's anyone who has heard the message of Jesus Christ, that He is the only way and that He is the messiah, and they want to receive Jesus Christ as their Savior, come up front." Over three hundred people came up and prayed the Sinner's Prayer and received Jesus Christ as their Savior.

After service, Jake told David that he had a good time and that he was coming back every week. Jake continued to go to the Truth Church, continued to get the Word of God, and continued to get closer to God. One day, Jake's parents came into his room while he was reading his Bible. He was reading **Daniel 12:4**. His parents asked him what he was reading, and he said, "**Daniel 12:4**." His parents asked him what it said, and he said, "But, O Daniel, shut up the words and seal the book, even to the time of the end, many shall run to and from, and knowledge shall be increased." Jake's parents looked at him, confused, and asked him, "What does that mean?"

Jake said, "That means we are living in the last days before Jesus comes back. Technology and intelligence will grow and advance in every form possible." Jake then said, "We are the generation that will see the coming of Jesus Christ. Our generation will not pass before Jesus comes back. The Bible says in **2 Thessalonians 2:1**, 'Now we beseech you, brethren, by the coming of our Lord Jesus Christ and by our gathering together unto him.' Also, in **1 Thessalonians 5:2–3,** it reads, 'For yourselves know perfectly that the day of the Lord so cometh as a thief in the night. For when they say peace and safety then sudden destruction cometh upon them to travail as with a woman with child, and they shall not escape.' What that means is that after Jesus comes back, this great leader which will be the antichrist will sign a seven-year treaty with Israel, and when he does, the world will say peace, but there will be no peace. Things will get a whole lot worse. The Bible says in **Matthew 24:22**, 'And expect those days be shortened; there should no flesh be saved, but for the elect's sake, those days shall be shortened.'

"Also, in **Matthew 24:23–24**, 'Then if any man shall say unto you, "Lo, here is Christ," or there, believe it not. For there shall arise false Christs and false prophets and shew great signs and wonders insomuch that if it were possible, they shall deceive the very elect.'" Jake's parents looked at him, stunned, and he said, "If you want to escape all of this before this takes place, and if you want to leave when Jesus comes back, then you have to accept Him." Jake's parents asked him how, and Jake said, "Repeat after me," and Jake's parents bowed their heads and prayed the Sinner's Prayer. "Lord Jesus, Savior of the world, You died for me. I accept You. I ask You to come into my heart and be my Savior. In Jesus's name, I pray. Amen." Jake asked his parents how they felt, and they said, "Great."

Jake brought his parents to the Truth Church. Bishop Hardy continued his six-week series, "The Signs of the Times." The next earth-shattering event is the rapture of the church. That's when Jesus comes back to take the ones who accepted Him as their Savior and takes them to heaven. "Won't that be a great day for us and a sad day for the ones who have rejected Him?"

After the rapture, this world politician, who will be called the antichrist, also called the beast, will come out of the European Union, and he will say he has come to save them from destruction, that he has the answers to the world's problems, and that he knows what has happened to the ones who have been raptured. The world will believe him. He will come as a man of peace, and they will accept him because of his peace treaty.

The Bible says in **Daniel 8:25**, "And through his policy also he shall cause craft to prosper in his hands and he shall magnify himself in his heart and by peace shall he destroy many. He shall also stand up against the Prince of princes, but he shall be broken without hand." Bishop Hardy said, "Many of you might be wondering what all of this means. What this means is that the antichrist will have a seven-year peace treaty that will grant Israel peace from her enemies, but three and a half years into it, the peace pact will fail because the antichrist doesn't intend to keep the peace pact.

"During the forty-two months of peace, a Jew who finds out who has accepted Jesus Christ as their Savior finds out who the antichrist really is and what he truly is about, and he shoots him in the head and he makes a recovery because Satan enters into the antichrist. **Revelation 13:3–4** says, 'And I saw one of his heads as it were wounded to death and his deadly wound was healed, and all the world wondered after the beast, and they worshipped the dragon which gave power unto the beast, and they worshipped the beast, saying, Who is like unto the beast? Who is able to make war with him?'"

Bishop Hardy said, "All of this means that the antichrist will be killed, and Satan will indwell in this trusted and respected world leader, and he will assume to have come back from the dead. He will force everyone to receive a mark on their right hand or forehead. Without it, you can't buy or sell. That's **Revelation 13:16–18**: 'And he causeth both small and great, rich and poor, free and bond, to receive a mark in their right hand or foreheads and that no man might buy or sell save he that had the mark of the beast or the name of the beast or the number of his name. Here is wisdom: let him that hath understanding count the number of the beast, for it is the number of a man, and his number is six hundred threescore and six. All who refuse the mark will be killed.'"

A lot of people gasped. Bishop Hardy continued, "This is why I'm telling you this. If you accept Jesus Christ as your Savior, then when Jesus comes back, you can escape what is about to happen upon the earth. If you accept Him, He can change you from the inside out. He doesn't want anyone to perish and go to hell. He wants all of us to come to the acceptance and love of God. As I close this service, I ask that anyone who wants to give their lives to Jesus and receive the gift that Jesus gave when He died on the cross to come up here now." Twenty-eight people got up and went up front to receive the gift of salvation. They repeated the prayer, "Lord Jesus, Savior of the world, You died for me. Today, I accept You. I ask You to come into my heart and be my Savior. In Jesus's name, amen." Bishop Hardy said, "Praise the Lord, praise the Lord, all of you who just accepted Jesus as your Savior. Let me congratulate you on your new life. You have just stepped from eternal darkness into eternal light."

After the service, Jake asked his parents how they enjoyed the service, and they said they learned a lot about the future. They wanted to tell the world about Jesus and how they could receive eternal life and know the future and not worry about it. The next day, Jake went to school and said, "David, guess what," and David said, "What?" Jake said that his parents have accepted Jesus Christ as their Savior. David said, "That's good, and how did you get in here? I thought you didn't go to school here." Jake said, "My parents put me in the school. I go here now." David said, "That's good." Jake said, "Yeah, it is. I'm happy that they have accepted Jesus as their Savior because either when they die or Jesus returns, they will go to heaven along with me."

During history class, Jake asked David if he could come over and spend the weekend at his house, then go to church with him on Sunday. David said he had to ask his parents, but they would probably say yes. After school, David called his mom and asked her if Jake could stay the weekend. David's mother said yes. Jake walked home with David. Once they reached David's house, they dropped their book bags in David's room and went outside.

While Jake and David were outside playing, David's mother came outside and told Jake and David to come into the house because there was something on the news that she wanted them to see. Jake and David ran into the house, and Jake's mother turned on the TV to Channel 28. The news anchor said, "Thank you for joining us tonight. We start with some breaking news. Russians have attacked Israel in a surprise air attack. Surprisingly, no one from Israel was injured or killed, but every Russian airplane was shot down, and the Israelis said that they never fired a shot in defense but that the airplanes were shot down by fire raining down from heaven."

David's mother turned off the TV, and Jake said, "Why were Israel and Jerusalem attacked?" David's mother said, "Jerusalem was attacked because it's all a part of Bible prophecy." David's mother went and grabbed her Bible off her bookcase and turned to **Ezekiel 38–39**, and she said, "Here reads the word of the living God. Son of man, set thy face against Gog the land of Magog, the chief prince of Meshech and Tubal, and prophesy against him." Jake said, "What do you mean?" and David's mother said, "This means Jesus Christ is coming back soon, and that means World War III is coming soon. Anytime, Jesus can come back, and the seven-year tribulation will begin. But first, there must be a falling away. People will defect from the faith, and they will turn their backs on Jesus. **Second Thessalonians 2:3** says, 'Let no man deceive you by any means, for that day shall not come except there comes a falling away first, and that man of sin be revealed the son of perdition." Jake asked, "What will this antichrist dude do when he comes to power?"

David's mother said, "First, he will come as a man of peace. He will unite the world in a false peace. Next, the antichrist will unite all businesses and commoners. The antichrist will then convince most of the world that the people who were raptured were taken by aliens. Next, the antichrist will exalt himself above God and everything that is called god. In **2 Thessalonians 2:4**, it reads, 'Who opposeth and exalteth himself above all that is called God or that is worshipped so that he as God sitteth in the temple of God showing himself that he is God.'" Jake's and David's mouths were wide open. David's mother said, "That's enough for today. I will tell you more later." David and Jake went back outside, and they started to play again, but they still couldn't get the events of what just happened out of their mind. They still had a lot on their mind.

CHAPTER

4

Cody Miller was born on December 5, 1997. His parents taught him that there was no god and that we evolved from monkeys. They also taught him that the big bang theory was the reason the earth was formed when two gases came in contact with each other. When Cody turned eight, he started telling people that there was no god and that we evolved from monkeys. Some people who heard him listened, but some people challenged him and told him that we were created by God, who created everything that is on this planet. One boy also said that the earth wasn't created by two gasses. Cody asked the boy what his name was, and he said, "My name is Justin, and I'm a servant of God, and His name is Jesus."

Cody said, "Science and evolution prove that we evolved and god doesn't exist." Justin pulled out a book, raised it in the air, and said, "This book says otherwise." Cody said, "What is that book called?" Justin said, "This book is called the Bible. The first scripture that proves that there is a God is **Genesis 1:1**. 'In the beginning, God created the heavens and the earth.' Also in **Genesis 1:26–27**, 'And God said, Let us make man in our own image and after our likeness, and let them have dominion over the fish of the sea and over the fowl of the air, and over all the earth, and over every creeping thing that creepeth upon the earth. So God created man in his own image, in the image of God he created them male and female.' I'm not going to keep quoting scriptures, but the other scriptures you can look up are **Mark 13:19**, **Romans 1:20**, and **Revelation 3:14**."

Justin walked away, and everybody who was listening to Cody left and went after Justin, asking him to tell them more about Jesus. Just as Cody was about to leave, some kids came to him and told him, "Don't lose your hope. They are being deceived." While Cody was talking to those kids, Justin was preaching, and hundreds of kids were giving their lives to Jesus. Justin finished preaching, and he was going to tell Cody that he was sorry for yelling at him. When he was about to turn the corner, he heard some people talking to Cody to join their club, and he said yes. Justin turned back around and prayed for Cody. Later on, Cody was walking when the same kids he had run into earlier came and told him about the meeting that they were having and that it was starting right now.

Cody followed the kids to the classroom where the other kids were meeting. Cody entered the room and found himself a seat. When everyone was seated, a teenager got out of his seat and said, "I'd like to welcome you to our little group we have every single week. We discuss how a lot of people put too much faith in religion and how they don't believe in themselves to do anything."

Around this same time, Justin was attending CROWN. When Justin got to CROWN, he was greeted by Daniel, and Daniel said, "Welcome to CROWN," and Justin said thank you. When everyone was seated, Daniel got out of his seat and welcomed everyone to CROWN. "Before we get started, I want to tell everyone what CROWN stands for. The initials stand for Christ Rules Our World Now. Today, we are discussing when Jesus returns to take everyone to heaven, which is called the rapture. No one knows when He will come. It says in **Matthew 25:13**, 'Watch, therefore; ye know neither the day nor the hour wherein the Son of man cometh. He will come as a thief in the night.' **Second Peter 3:10** says, 'But the day of the Lord will come as a thief in the night, in which the heavens shall pass away with a great noise, and the elements shall melt with fervent heat, the earth also, and the works that are therein shall be burned up." Daniel asked if anyone knew what would happen next, and everyone said yes, then Daniel said, "The tribulation will start, and it will be the worse seven years the world has ever seen. We will discuss this next week, but is there anyone who wants to give their life to Jesus?" Five people raised their hands, and Daniel said, "Praise the Lord." Then Daniel told them to repeat after him. "Lord Jesus, Savior of the world, You died for me. You shed Your blood to save me. I ask You to come into my heart and be my Savior. I pray this in Jesus's name. Amen." When the meeting was over, Justin left.

Cody sat at his meeting, thinking as he listened to everyone talk about what the other kids were talking about, how Christians and religion tell you to accept their god as god or you will go to hell or something bad will happen to you. Cody asked the boy that was talking what his name was, and he said his name was Arnold Brown. Arnold Brown was fourteen years old. He was once a Christian, but he stopped believing in Jesus after his mother died from cancer.

After the meeting, Cody was walking home when he saw a billboard saying, "Jesus is coming back soon. Are you ready?" and under that was a scripture: **1 Thessalonians 2:19–20**, "For what is our hope, or joy, or crown of rejoicing? Are not even ye in the presence of our Lord Jesus Christ at his coming? For ye are our glory and joy." Cody looked at the billboard with disgust and kept walking home. When Cody got home, he did his homework, took a shower, and lay down. He tried to go to sleep, but he couldn't stop thinking about what the scripture meant. The next day, he ran into Justin and asked him, "Are you a Christian?" Justin said, "Yes, I am." Then Cody said, "Yesterday, I saw a billboard, and the scripture on the billboard was **1 Thessalonians 2:19–20**." He told Justin what the scripture said and asked what the scripture meant. Justin said, "What the scripture meant is that Jesus is coming back, and when He comes back, it will be a joyful day for the people who are saved and a sad day for the people who are left behind because soon after the rapture happens, everyone who isn't saved will see the appearance of the antichrist.

"The antichrist will come as a man of peace but will destroy the world. **Daniel 8:25** says, 'And through his policy also he shall cause craft to prosper in his hands and he shall magnify himself in his heart and by peace he shall destroy many he shall also stand up against the prince of princes, but he shall be broken without hand.'

The antichrist will form a one world government and a one world currency and a one world religion. **Revelation 13:7** says, 'And it was given unto him to make war with the saints and to overcome them and power was given unto him over all kindreds and tongues and nations.' Also, **Revelation 13:8** says, 'And them that dwell upon the earth shall worship him whose names are not in the book of life slain from the foundation of the world.'" Cody said, "Where in the Bible does it talk about the one world currency?"

Justin said, "I was just getting to that. **Revelation 13:16–18** says, 'And he causeth both small and great, rich and poor, free and bond, to receive a mark in their right hand or in their foreheads and that no man might buy or sell save he that has the mark of or the name of the beast or the number of his name. Here is wisdom: let him that has understanding count the number of the beast, for it is the number of a man, and his number is six hundred threescore and six: 666.'"

Cody said, "When will all this stuff take place?" Justin said, "All this stuff will take place after the rapture. The rapture is when Jesus comes back and takes all who believe in Him to heaven."

"I don't believe in this. I was just wondering what you thought." Cody started to walk away when Justin said, "Cody, don't walk away from this. He is coming soon, and you won't know that He has come until after He has come." Cody stopped and said, "How can He come without anyone knowing?" Justin said, "**Second Peter 2:10** says, 'But the day of the Lord will come like a thief in the night in which the heavens shall pass away with a great noise and the elements shall melt with fervent heat the earth also, and the works that are therein shall be burned up. Also, in **Revelation 16:15**: 'Behold I come as a thief in the night blessed is he that watcheth and keepeth his garments lest he will walk naked and they see his shame.' This last scripture I'm not going to quote, but you can look it up. **Revelation 3:3**, which will tell you more." Cody said, "I can't because that will go against everything I know and believe in." Justin said, "Just read the Bible, Cody. What will it hurt?" Cody said, "Okay, I will try," then he left.

As Cody walked home, he had a lot on his mind. He stopped at a store and bought a Bible and put it in his bag. When he got home, he went to his room and opened up the Bible. He went to **John 5:24**, which said, "Verily, verily I say unto you he that heareth my word and believeth on him that has sent me has everlasting life and shall not come into condemnation but has passed away from death unto life." Cody put the Bible away. He turned on the TV and started to watch cartoons.

Later, Cody was changing the channel when he saw a guy talking, and the guy said that it doesn't matter what you have done in the past, the blood of Jesus Christ has the power to wipe away every sin you have ever done or will ever do. All you have to do is receive the gift of salvation. The preacher said, "It's easy. All you have to do is—" and Cody changed the channel. He started watching other TV shows. Later on, he ate dinner and went to sleep. Cody didn't see Justin at school for a few days, and one day, Cody asked one of Justin's friends where Justin was, and he told Cody that Justin was dead.

Cody asked Justin's friend, "How did Justin die?" and Justin's friend said he was downtown witnessing, telling people about Jesus, when a person started shooting, and Justin was caught in the crossfire. They rushed him to the hospital, but they couldn't stop the bleeding, and he died. Cody didn't really know Justin that well, but it was sad when anyone died. Justin's friend said, "His funeral is Saturday at the Truth Church if you want to come, by the way. My name is Paul." Paul said, "Justin died serving Jesus. He's in heaven now." Paul put his hand on Cody's shoulder, but Cody pulled his shoulder away.

Cody said, "I don't need your sympathy. The only person I considered to be my friend is gone, and you expect me to be fine." Paul sat next to Cody as he cried, and Paul said, "Justin was my friend too, and he had a good life, but now he's in heaven with Jesus. He's in a better place, and when you die, you can be there too. All you have to do is receive the free gift of salvation and accept Jesus Christ as your personal Lord and Savior, and you will be saved."

Cody said, "I will never accept a God that will have a person serve Him only to be shot and killed for no reason." Paul said, "Everything works together for them that love the Lord, as it says in **Romans 8:28**." Cody said, "I will come to the funeral, but I will never put my faith and trust in Jesus." Cody got up and left. Paul sighed and prayed, "Lord Jesus, please show Cody the light so that he will accept You as his personal Lord and Savior. In Jesus's name, amen."

Cody was sad the rest of the week. He didn't talk to anyone; he just woke up, went to school, came home, did his homework, then went to sleep. On the day of the funeral, Cody got up and put on his best dress clothes. He told his parents where he was going, and they said okay. When Cody got to the Truth Church, he saw Paul. Paul walked up to Cody and said, "Thank you for coming." Cody said, "I had to come. Justin is…was my friend." Paul said, "Let's get inside the sanctuary. Justin's parents both said that they missed him, but they would see him again in heaven when they die, or the rapture comes."

Cody asked them, "What's the rapture?" and Justin's parents both said, "The rapture is when Jesus comes back for all the people who have accepted Him, and He takes them to heaven. Even though Justin is dead now, he will rise again when Jesus comes back." Cody asked them what they were talking about. Justin's mother said, "I will tell you what we are talking about, and you can look the verses up for yourself. In **1 Corinthians 15:52–57**, it says, 'In a moment, in the twinkling of an eye, at the last trump: for the trumpet shall sound, and the dead shall be raised incorruptible, and we shall be changed. For this corruptible must put on incorruption, and this mortal must put on immortality. So when this corruptible shall have put on incorruption, and this mortal shall have put on immortality, and then shall be brought to pass the saying that is written, Death is swallowed up in victory. O death, where is thy sting? O grave, where is thy victory? The sting of death is sin; and the strength of sin is the law. But thanks be to God, which giveth us the victory through our Lord Jesus Christ.'"

Cody said, "I'm confused about what those scriptures mean." Justin's mother said, "The scripture means that if you have accepted Jesus Christ as your Savior and you die before He comes back, you will be resurrected and taken to heaven." Cody said, "Won't we see them being taken to heaven?" and Justin's father told Cody, "No, only the people who have received Jesus as their personal Lord and Savior." Cody looked at both of Justin's parents strangely and turned to leave. Justin's father said, "Cody, this could be your only chance to receive Jesus as your Savior. Once Jesus returns for His people, things will get a whole lot worse." Cody stopped and looked back at Justin's parents, then he turned and kept walking. Justin's mother prayed, "Lord Jesus, please let Cody find the truth that You are the only way and that if he will accept You as his personal Lord and Savior, You will forgive him for his sins and You will forget that he ever committed them. I pray this in Jesus's name, amen."

Cody walked home crying, and when he got home, he read Justin's obituary. The obituary said Justin loved the Lord. He told people about the goodness of Jesus Christ until he was accidentally killed. "Justin will be missed, and he will always be in our hearts, and we know he's in heaven with Jesus." The last thing the obituary said was that his dying wish was that his friend Cody would accept Jesus as his Savior. Cody broke down and started crying. He read the last three sentences in the obituary. "Cody Miller was Justin's friend, and Justin prayed for him up to the point of his death." After Cody read the obituary, he said, "Why couldn't that have been me who died instead of Justin? Justin was a good boy. He didn't deserve to die by getting shot for no reason. All he was doing was preaching what he believed in." Cody kept crying until he fell asleep. The next day, Cody went to the Truth Church and talked to Bishop Hardy. Michael Hardy was five foot seven and weighed a hundred fifty pounds. He had a white shirt on, a black tie, black shoes, black pants, and a black jacket.

Bishop Hardy saw Cody come in. He turned around and said, "May I help you?" Cody said yes. He introduced himself. "My name is Cody Miller, and I have a question for you." Bishop Hardy asked him what was his question, and Cody said, "Why would a so-called loving God allow someone who served with so much loyalty to die by a gunshot?" Bishop Hardy told Cody that Justin did love the Lord, and when he was killed, he received the crown of life from Jesus. He was able to get into heaven because he received Jesus Christ as his personal Lord and Savior and remained faithful to Jesus until the end. Cody asked Bishop Hardy, "How could anyone serve God? Look at all the evil in the world. People are killing each other. There are wars on every continent. There's destruction. Children are disrespecting their parents. School isn't safe because kids are coming to the school shooting. The world is out of control."

Bishop Hardy said, "The Bible foretold that this was going to happen in **Matthew 24:6**: 'And ye shall hear of wars and rumors of wars see that ye be not troubled for all of these things must come to pass but the end is not yet.' If you don't know what that means, it means that after Jesus comes back, the world will experience seven years of tribulation. During the tribulation, there will be forty-two months of peace after the antichrist signs a seven-year peace treaty with Israel. There will be a third World War. There will also be famines. The antichrist will rebuild the Jewish temple in Israel, and then he will desecrate the temple." Cody asked Bishop Hardy, "How will the antichrist get away with this?" Bishop Hardy told Cody, "The antichrist will bring a false peace to the world, and the world will accept him and follow him where he leads them. The antichrist will sacrifice an animal in the temple. Next, he will have an image of himself put in the temple and demand that the world worships him as the one true god. Daniel calls this the abomination of desolation in **Daniel 9:27**: 'And he shall make a strong covenant with many for one week, and for half of the week he shall put an end to sacrifice and offering. And on the wing of abominations shall come one who makes desolate, until the decreed end is poured out on the desolator.' Also in **Matthew 24:15**: 'When ye therefore shall see the abomination of desolation, spoken of by Daniel the prophet, stand in the holy place (whoso readeth, let him understand).' I won't tell you everything that will happen, but by the time the tribulation ends, two-thirds of the world will be dead, and all of those who survive the tribulation who accepted Jesus as their Savior will enter into the millennium kingdom. All those who have taken the mark of the beast and worshiped the image of the beast will be sentenced to the lake of fire, and all those who rejected Jesus as their Savior and didn't take the mark of the beast or worshipped the image of the beast will also find their places in the lake of fire."

Cody asked Bishop Hardy, "Why would a loving God send people to hell or to the lake of fire?" He said, "Jesus is a holy God, and He can't allow sin in His presence. Everyone has sinned, and that includes you, me, and Justin. Jesus came to die. **John 3:16–17** says, 'For God so ever loved the world that he gave his only begotten son that whosoever believeth in him shall not perish but have ever lasting life. For God did not send his son into the world to condemn the world but through him the world might be saved.' The Bible says that God is willing that no one shall perish but that everyone would come to the knowledge of Jesus Christ. He wants you, Cody, to come and let Him change your life and make your life better than it was before." Bishop Hardy said, "Cody, do you want to receive Jesus as your Lord and Savior?"

Cody said, "I can't and won't accept Him because based on what you have told me, this God you serve is a violent God that allows the world to be destroyed, but He tells the world that He's a loving God who has only the world's best interests at heart." Bishop Hardy said, "He's a loving God, but when people refuse to accept Jesus as their Savior, they are choosing to be sent to hell, and they choose to receive the wrath of God." Cody said, "I have to go." As he was turning to leave, Bishop Hardy said, "Cody, Jesus can come back at any time, and once He comes back and your name isn't in the Lamb's Book of Life, you will be left behind, and the world as you know it will never be the same."

Cody said, "You are scaring me. I can't keep listening to this." Cody turned and ran out of the Truth Church and ran home. He went up to his room and started crying. For the next few weeks, Cody didn't talk to anyone about how he missed Justin, and every time someone brought him up, he would change the subject. One day, Paul came up to him and asked him what his deal was. Cody said, "What are you talking about?" Paul said, "Every time someone brings up Justin's name or brings up something about him, you are quick to change the subject." Cody said, "I don't want to talk about it." Paul said, "Cody, if you want to heal from loss, you have to talk to someone about it."

Paul continued, "We all miss Justin, even though we know he's in a better place. We still miss the good times we had with him, but we know we will see him again." Cody said, "Don't start with that religion mess again. I keep telling you that I don't need your religion. I'm doing fine. I'm doing fine by myself." Paul said, "If you want to have that hole in your heart filled, you need to put your faith and trust in Jesus." Cody said, "Why should I?" and Paul said, "Because that was Justin's dying wish, and Justin would be happy knowing that you have received Jesus Christ as your personal Lord and Savior. That's how we are getting through the loss of Justin." Cody said, "Why do you people keep insisting that I receive Jesus as my Savior? If you are happy with your religion and your God, I'm happy for you, but don't keep trying to push your religion on me. I don't want Jesus, and I don't need Jesus. All I need in my life are my parents and myself, so quit trying to convert me, and leave me alone." After Cody finished, Paul turned and left. Cody felt like he had hurt Paul's feelings, but he felt that Paul and his friends kept badgering him and kept trying to force him to believe in something that he had no desire or interest in.

Cody thought to himself that he had to go to school and apologize to Paul and explain to him that he wasn't mocking his religion, but he wasn't in the mood to be preached to. He said all he wanted to do now was be alone. The next day, Cody ran into Paul and apologized for mocking his religion, that he was just expressing his religion in the wrong way, and asked Paul to forgive him. Paul told Cody that he forgave him, and afterward, Cody left. After they finished talking, Paul went into a corner and prayed for Cody. He prayed that Jesus would fix Cody's heart so that he would ask Him into his life in Jesus's name.

During the weeks leading up to Christmas, Cody and his atheist friends were exchanging gifts, and the friends of the late Justin were exchanging gifts and going out and feeding the homeless. A couple of days later, Paul asked Cody how his weekend was, and Cody said, "Not so good." Paul asked why, and Cody said that both his parents died. Paul said, "How?" Cody said that his father had a heart attack, and his mother was so stressed out that she had a stroke, and now they were both dead.

Paul asked Cody if his parents were Christians, and Cody said no. Paul turned his head, and Cody said, "What's wrong?" and Paul said, "Since your parents weren't saved, they are not in heaven." Cody asked him what he was talking about, and Paul said, "Anyone who doesn't receive Jesus Christ as their Savior before that person dies, they won't enter the kingdom of heaven." So Cody asked sarcastically, "What happens if a person doesn't receive Jesus as their Savior?" Paul said, "Anyone who doesn't receive Jesus as their personal Lord and Savior before they die will be sentenced to eternity in hell, and once you go to hell, you won't get out." Cody said, "If this God of yours is so loving, why does He send people to hell?" Paul explained, "Jesus doesn't send people to hell. People send themselves to hell because when you refuse to accept the free gift that Jesus gave when He died on the cross for your sins, you choose to reject eternal life that only faith in Jesus Christ can give you. You choose to die in your sins and go to hell.

"**Romans 3:23–24** says, 'For all have sinned and come short of the glory of God. Being justified freely by his grace through the redemption that is in Christ Jesus.' God doesn't send you to hell. You choose hell. Jesus has made a way for us to get to heaven through the blood of Jesus." Cody said, "Why would my parents be in hell? They were good people." Paul said, "They might have been good on earth in your eyes, but no one on earth is good enough to enter into heaven. The Lord desires perfection, and no one is perfect, and that's why Jesus had to die. Besides going to heaven, accepting Jesus will also give you peace that the world can never give you, but you have to accept Him as your Savior." Cody said, "No, and quit bugging me about it." Then Cody left and went to class.

CHAPTER

5

Jason Michaels was born on July 22, 1998, in Battle Creek, Michigan. His parents, Sara and Sam Michaels, were Christians, and Jason himself was a Christian. On Sunday, he went to church, and everyone thought he was a good Christian. While Jason was in school, he was a totally different person. He cussed, made jokes about Jesus, and would get mad anytime he heard someone telling someone about Jesus or that they needed Jesus to save them so they will be able to get into heaven. One day while they were at lunch, Jason went up to the girl and boy and asked them, "What is your deal?" The boy and the girl said, "What are you talking about?" Jason said, "Why are you going all over the school preaching so much?" The girl said, "We preach because this school, just like the world, needs Jesus." Jason said, "I'm a Christian too, but I don't go around preaching. I believe that everyone will find Jesus, but that doesn't mean you have to go out and tell everyone about Him."

The guy quoted **Romans 1:16–18**, "For I am not ashamed of the gospel of Christ, for it is the power of God unto salvation to everyone that believeth to the Jew first and also to the Greek. For therein is the righteousness of God revealed from faith to faith as it is written. The Just shall live by faith. For the wrath of God is revealed from heaven against all ungodliness and unrighteousness of men who hold the truth in unrighteousness. Also, in **1 Corinthians 1:18**, 'For the preaching of the cross is to them that perish foolishness; but unto us who are saved it is the power of God.' Since everyone has sinned, we all should perish, but Jesus died and was resurrected and sent out His gospel so that if anyone receives Jesus as their Savior, they can go to heaven." Jason said, "What about the Quran? The Quran says that if anyone accepts Allah as their Savior, they will go to heaven. And what about the other religions that said that their god was the only way?" The boy said, "They are false gods. Jesus is the only way, and by the way, my name is Chris. In **John 14:6**, Jesus said, 'I am the way, the truth, and the life. No man comes to the Father but by me.' The last verse I'm going to quote is **John 3:18**: 'He that believes in him is not condemned but he that does not believe in him is condemned already because they have not believed in the only begotten son of God, and his name is Jesus Christ.' I have to go. We will talk later." Then Chris left.

Later on in the hallway, Jason saw Chris reading, and Jason asked him what he was reading, and Chris said, "I'm reading the Bible. I'm trying to get stronger in the Lord." Jason said, "Why are you reading the Bible to get stronger?" Chris said, "I'm reading the Bible to get stronger because of temptation. The devil is looking for whom he may devour. **First Peter 5:8** says, 'Be sober, be vigilant, because your adversary the devil is a roaring lion walking about seeking whom he may devour.' What that means is that the devil is trying to kill anyone and everyone. The only way you can stand up against the devil is to put on the full armor of God. **Ephesians 6:13–17** says, 'Therefore take up the whole armor of God, that you may be able to withstand in the evil day, and having done all, to stand. Stand therefore, having girded your waist with truth, having put on the breastplate of righteousness, and having shod your feet with the preparation of the gospel of peace; above all, taking the shield of faith with which you will be able to quench all the fiery darts of the wicked one. And take the helmet of salvation, and the sword of the Spirit, which is the word of God.'" Jason said, "What does that mean?" Chris said, "If you want to defeat Satan, you need to accept Jesus Christ as your Savior. The only way you can defeat him is by Jesus."

Chris asked Jason if he wanted to accept Jesus Christ as his Savior, but Jason said, "No, I don't need Jesus. My life is great. I don't need God, and I don't need Jesus." As Jason walked away, Chris started praying for him, saying, "Lord Jesus, please show Jason the truth that he needs You and that he can't do anything without You, in Jesus's name, amen." Jason went home after school and did his homework, watched TV, ate, then went to sleep.

The next day, he went to school and was walking when he passed by a room and heard someone talking. He cracked the door open enough for him to see who was in the room, and the person he saw was Chris. Chris was talking to a group of people, saying, "I welcome you all to our Bible study. We are here to learn more about Jesus, our King of kings and Lord of lords. Our topic today is the rapture. A lot of people don't know what the rapture is. The rapture is when Jesus comes back for all those who have accepted Him as their Lord and Savior, but for the ones who haven't, they will be left behind, and they won't even know what has just taken place on the earth. **Second Thessalonians 2:3** says, 'Let no man deceive you by any means for that day shall not come except there come, a falling away first and that man of sin be revealed the son of perdition.' Also, in the last days, there shall be false messiahs, false Christs, and false prophets. **Matthew 24:4–5** says, 'And Jesus answered and said unto them take heed that no man deceive for many shall come in my name and say that I am Christ and deceive many.' Also, **Matthew 24:11** says, 'And many false prophets shall rise and shall deceive many.'"

Chris went on to say, "I know some of you may be wondering, will any of your family members hear the word of God and get a chance to receive Jesus as their Savior? This is the last scripture I'm going to quote from the book of Matthew. **Matthew 24:14** says, 'And this gospel of the kingdom shall be preached in the entire world for a witness unto all nations and then the end shall come.' Immediately after the rapture will be the appearance of the antichrist. The arrival of the antichrist will start the beginning of a seven-year period of darkness, which will be called the tribulation. Jason came into the room and sat in the back where no one could see him.

Chris asked if anyone has heard of the Four Horsemen of the apocalypse. Almost everybody raised their hands. Chris asked everyone who had a Bible to open it to **Revelation 6:1–2**, and he read it out loud: "And I saw when the Lamb open one of the seals and I heard as it were the noise of thunder one of the four beasts saying come and see. And I saw and beheld a white horse, and he that sat on him had a bow, and a crown was given unto him, and he went forth conquering and to conquer.'" Chris said, "For the people who have never heard of this scripture, the person John is talking about is the antichrist. If you are wondering if he will rule the world through force, then the answer is no, but he will rule in diplomacy through a false peace that will promise world unity. **Daniel 8.25** says, 'Through his cunning he shall cause deceit to prosper under his rule; and he shall exalt himself in his heart. He shall destroy many in their prosperity. He shall even rise against the Prince of princes; But he shall be broken without human means.' This passage of scripture means that the antichrist will make a seven-year peace treaty with Israel, guaranteeing them peace, but three and a half years into it, he breaks it, and all hell breaks loose. Jesus will defeat him and not any humans. **First Thessalonians 5:3** says, 'For when they say peace and safety then sudden destruction shall come upon them to travail upon a woman with child and they shall not escape.'"

Chris said, "I have one more point to make, then I will let you go. During the tribulation, there will not be a safe place on the planet for believers in the one true God Jesus Christ. **John 16:2–3** says, 'They shall put you out of the synagogues: yea, the time cometh, that whosoever killeth you will think that he doeth God service. And these things will they do unto you, because they have not known the Father, nor me.' The last scripture I will quote will be **Revelation 20:4**. 'And I saw thrones, and they sat upon them, and judgment was given unto them: and I saw the souls of them that were beheaded for the witness of Jesus, and for the word of God, and which had not worshipped the beast, neither his image, neither had received his mark upon their foreheads, or in their hands; and they lived and reigned with Christ a thousand years.'"

Chris said, "I'm done teaching the Word of God for the week. Is there anyone here who isn't saved who wants to receive Jesus Christ as their Savior?" A few people raised their hands, and Chris prayed with them, and they received Jesus Christ as their Savior. Chris dismissed everyone, and Jason quickly and quietly left the room and got ready for his next class. The whole time Jason was in class, all he could think about was what Chris had said during the meeting and how he said there won't be a safe place on the earth for the true believers in Jesus. After school, Jason went home and started watching TV. While he was going through the channels, he saw a guy talking, and the guy caught Jason's attention. The preacher was saying that in the last days, things will get so bad that if God didn't keep the tribulation to seven years, everyone would be dead. "**Matthew 24:22** says, 'And except those days be shortened no flesh would be saved, but for the elect's sake, those days shall be shortened.'" The pastor said, "What this means is that the world will get so bad that if Jesus didn't return seven years later, nobody would be left on the earth alive." The pastor continued talking. "For anyone watching who is wondering, does the Bible spell this out in great detail? The answer is yes. **Matthew 24:21** says, 'For then shall be great tribulation such as not since the beginning of the world to this time, nor ever shall be.' This means the way the world will be during the tribulation will be so bad that after the tribulation when Jesus returns, the world will never be like that again. If you want to escape this before it all happens, all you have to do is receive the forgiveness that only faith in Jesus Christ can give, then I will lead you through the prayer. Repeat after me. Lord Jesus, Savior of the world, You died for me. You were beaten for me. Today I ask You to come into my heart. Be my Savior. In Jesus's name, amen."

Jason thought about praying that prayer to receive Jesus as his Savior, but he decided against it and turned off the TV, went to his room, and went to bed. The next day at school, he was walking to class when he saw Chris and some of his friends telling some people about Jesus, praying with some other people. They were passing out Bibles to the remaining people. Jason was about to turn and leave when Chris called Jason over. Jason walked over to Chris, and they shook hands. Chris asked how Jason was doing. Jason said, "I'm fine," and asked Chris how he was doing. Chris said, "I'm living in grace, favor, and life." Jason said, "What does that mean?" Chris said, "What that means is that Jesus, the Savior of the world, will give you the desires of your heart as long as you remain loyal and faithful to Him." Jason said, "I have all the desires of my heart, and I don't serve Jesus Christ." Chris said, "You might have all your so-called desires of your heart, but are you truly happy?"

Jason said, "I'm truly happy, so I don't need your religion, your God, or your Jesus, and I'm sick and tired of hearing about your God. I'm going to the principal, and I'm going to have him put a stop to this. I came to the school to get an education, not to listen to a bunch of extreme fanatics preach about a God that doesn't exist, a place that doesn't exist, and a coming that will never happen." Chris said, "By you saying that He's not coming back, you are fulfilling **2 Peter 3:3–4**, which says, 'Knowing this first, that there shall come in the last days scoffers, walking after their own lusts, and saying, Where is the promise of his coming? for since the fathers fell asleep, all things continue as they were from the beginning of the creation.'" Jason screamed, "I don't care about fulfilling some old fairy tale from a history book. All I care about is my family, my friends, and myself, and I will make sure your religion isn't preached in this school again."

Jason marched to the principal's office and asked if he could see Principal Baker. The lady at the desk told him that he could see the principal. Jason walked into Principal Baker's office. Principal Baker was a six-foot-five, heavyset man with glasses. Principal Baker told Jason to sit down, and Jason sat down. Principal Baker asked him what the problem was that he could help him with. Jason said, "I'm sick and tired of hearing Chris and his band of religious fanatics preach about Jesus." Principal Baker said, "It's a free school and country. He can talk about whatever he wants as long as he's not doing any physical harm to you. There's nothing I can do." Jason got up and stomped out of the room, mad. As he walked to his next class, he said, "I will get this religious crap out of this school if it's the last thing I ever do."

Jason went home, went on the Internet, and looked for anti-Christian groups in his school. He found a group called No Light. He went to their website to see what they thought. They thought that school was for education, not preaching, and that the No Light group was going to make sure that any time religion came into the school, they would crush it. The next day at school, Jason went looking for the group to join them in their quest to get rid of religion in school once and for all. He went looking all over the school, and just when he thought he wasn't going to find them, he ran across a girl with a button that said "A Member of No Light" on her shirt. He asked the girl where the No Light group was at. The girl said, "Why do you want to know?" Jason said, "It's because I want to join the group and eradicate religion from our school once and for all."

The girl told him to follow her to room 306, and when they got there, a young girl was up talking. She was saying, "I'm sick and tired of hearing people talk about religion in school, and I'm sick and tired of hearing about how this one god is the only true god. We hear that Allah is god, we hear that Jesus is God. In my opinion, and I think I speak for everyone here when I say this, we must put an end to this religion stuff before it gets out of control and we lose our school to a bunch of these religious fanatics and their cultlike followers." The girl kept talking and said, "We must get more people to our side. What I need everyone in this club to do is find people who are open-minded and bring them here so they can hear the truth and find enlightenment. The more we get to our side, the less those religious fanatics will have." Jason left and was on his way to class when he heard Chris talking and he said, "**Matthew 24:9–10** says, 'Then shall they deliver you up to be afflicted, and shall kill you: and ye shall be hated of all nations for my name's sake. And then shall many be offended, and shall betray one another, and shall hate one another.' Chris continued, "But instead of hating them, we will do what the Bible says in **Matthew 5:43–44**, 'Ye have heard that it hath been said, Thou shalt love thy neighbour, and hate thine enemy. But I say unto you, Love your enemies, bless them that curse you, do good to them that hate you, and pray for them which despitefully use you, and persecute you.'"

Jason felt a little guilty about what he was about to do, but he figured it was too late to turn back now. Jason went around the school recruiting students to the No Light group. Within a few weeks, the size of the No Light group doubled. When Chris found out that the group called No Light was recruiting more people to their cause, Chris and the group CROWN started reaching out and bringing people who were undecided to Jesus. Soon, the school was divided. Some people were with the No Light group, some people were with CROWN, and the rest of the school was undecided. No Light and CROWN were both planning rallies for Friday after school at three. Jason told the girl that he would be there, and then Jason asked her what her name was. The girl said, "I will tell everyone my name at the rally." Jason said okay and left.

Jason went home and spent the next three days preparing for the rally. He made signs, wrote a speech, and even printed off some quotes from some famous non-Christians, and before he went to sleep, he thought, *Tomorrow's the big day. The No Light will finally get rid of religion from our school.* On the day of the rally, Jason got dressed and left for school. On his way to school, he ran into a boy wearing a T-shirt saying, "**Romans 14:11**: For it is written as I live said the Lord every knee shall bow to me and every tongue shall confess to God." Jason got mad and walked faster to school. When he got to school, he was getting his books out of his locker when some kids walked up to him. He looked at them and said hi. They said hi back to him, and he asked them what they wanted. They said that they wanted to talk to him, and he said, "What about?" One of the boys said, "We want to talk to you about why you want to get rid of the Bible and Christianity from the school." Jason said, "I hate religion. All religion does is cause wars and create problems and division."

The boy said, "Yes, religion does cause that, but the problem is that everyone thinks Christianity is a religion, but it isn't. Christianity is a relationship with Jesus." Jason got really mad and said, "You're a member of that group called CROWN. Well, I'm a member of No Light." The boy said, "We were members of No Light until Chris came to us and explained the gift of salvation. We received Jesus Christ as our Savior, and now we are leading a lot of people from No Light to CROWN, and we want you to join us. Will you join us in CROWN?" Jason said, "No, I'm a member of No Light, and I will be a member of No Light until I leave this school for good and until I die." The boy said, "You are making a big mistake, and fatal mistake." Jason said, "The only mistake I made was not joining this group sooner. I will get rid of religion in school if it's the last thing I will ever do."

The boy said, "You will never get rid of the truth no matter how hard you try. You shall know the truth, and the truth shall set you free." Jason said, "Before I respond to that, what is your name? You never told me your name." The boy said, "My name is Joe." Jason said, "Joe, I know the truth, and I'm free. I'm free to help the school from the bondage of religion." Joe said, "If you think that you will stop the news of Jesus from spreading across the school, then you are crazy. We'll see in the final outcome and at the rallies." Then Joe and his friends left.

After school, Jason, Joe, and Chris went to their respective rallies. Joe and Chris went to the CROWN rally, and Jason went to the No Light rally. When Jason got to the No Light rally, the crowd went wild and asked Jason to give a speech, so he did. He told the crowd, "I'm sick and tired of religion. All religion does is start wars and create problems." He asked the crowd, "If you want to get rid of religion, we must band together and get these religious fanatics out of school." He asked the crowd if they were with him, and they said yes.

After Jason finished talking, a girl walked up to the podium said, "Welcome, my brothers and sisters of No Light. I know many of you are wondering who I am. Well, today, I will tell everyone my name. My name is Julia, and I'm the leader of No Light." Julia continued, "Are you sick and tired of dealing with religion being shoved down your throat?" and the crowd said, "Yeah," then she said, "Are you ready to be free?" and the crowd said, "Yeah," and the last thing Julia said before she dismissed everyone was, "Soon, we will have the tools we need to stop them good." Then she dismissed everyone.

When Chris and Joe reached CROWN, they were welcomed with applause and cheering. Chris held up a hand to silence the crowd and said, "I welcome you here by the power and authority of our Lord and Savior Jesus Christ. Some of you may be wondering why we are not trying to stop No Light from trying to stop what we are doing here. It's simple. The battle isn't ours. It's the Lord's. **Romans 12:19** says, 'Dearly beloved, avenge not yourselves, but rather give place unto wrath: for it is written, Vengeance is mine; I will repay, saith the Lord.'" The crowd cheered, and Chris said, "In other words, we don't have to fight our battles. God will fight our battles for us. **Galatians 6:7** says, 'Be not deceived; God is not mocked: for whatsoever a man soweth, that shall he also reap.' When you do something good, God will bless you. When you do something bad, God will get you for it. If we have to fight them, we will not fight them with physical weapons. We will fight them with the Word of God. We are not fighting them. We are fighting the spirits in them. **Ephesians 6:12** says, 'For we wrestle not against flesh and blood, but against principalities, against powers, against the rulers of the darkness of this world, against spiritual wickedness in high places.' We as Christians have to put our faith and trust in Jesus because He is the solid rock, and with Him, we can't be defeated. **Matthew 16:18** says, 'And I say also unto thee, That thou art Peter, and upon this rock I will build my church; and the gates of hell shall not prevail against it.'"

As Chris was talking, some people who were listening to Julia came over and started listening to Chris talk. One of the kids who came over from the No Light rally raised their hands and asked Chris, "How can we receive Jesus Christ as our Savior?" Chris said, "If you want to receive Jesus as your Savior and you are at this rally, or if you're in the No Light rally and you hear the sound of my voice and want to receive Him, repeat this prayer, and you have to mean it." Chris repeated the prayer. "Lord Jesus, Savior of the world, You died for me, shedding Your precious blood to save me. Today I receive what You did on the cross for me. I ask You to come into my heart and be my Savior. I pray this in Jesus's name, amen." The people who came over from No Light prayed the prayer and received Jesus as their Savior. Other people from No Light came over to the

CROWN rally. After Chris prayed with the crowd to receive Jesus as their Savior, he introduced Joe, who came to the stage. Joe brought a band, and they started playing gospel music, and the crowd praised God until 8:00 p.m. Then Chris and Joe came back on stage. They said, "Thank you all for coming out to praise and worship the true and living God Jesus Christ." Chris started praying. He said, "Lord Jesus, thank You for bringing us here together to worship You, and I thank You for all the new people who have become a part of the family tonight." Joe took over the prayer. "Lord Jesus, we ask You for traveling mercy and that we will all reach our destination so we can come back to school on Monday and go to church on Sunday. We pray this in Jesus's name, amen."

When Jason saw more people at the CROWN rally than at the No Light rally, he was furious. He said, "We must figure out a way to stop them. They have too much influence." Julia said, "We will." After the CROWN and No Light rally, Chris went home crying at what the Lord had done. When Jason got home, he was still mad. He said, "What is it that more people are following Chris and the CROWN group but not following the No Light group?" Jason said, "We have to do something."

Monday at school, Jason went to Julia and told her that they needed to have a meeting today and that the meeting was going to be an emergency meeting. Julia said, "Okay." When Jason got to the meeting, he was surprised that the group had dramatically dwindled in three days. A lot of people had left No Light and joined CROWN. Julia said, "I don't know what we are going to do. We don't have enough people and resources to continue the fight. We have two options. Either someone can assume my leadership, or we disband the group."

Jason stood up and said, "I will assume control of No Light. We can't let these setbacks stop us from achieving our goals. We will eradicate religion from our schools. We will redouble our efforts and bring more people to No Light. As soon as we eradicate religion from this school our school will be a better place." Jason dismissed the No Light group then went home. The next day, Jason ran into No Light member and former leader Julia. Jason asked Julia how she was doing, and Julia said she was fine. She said she was better than she had been since she received Jesus Christ as her Savior. Jason screamed, "What? You have betrayed us and the cause? You founded the No Light group, then you turn your back on us. Take it back, Julia, take it back." Julia said, "I was wrong. Christianity isn't a religion. It's a relationship with Jesus." Jason said, "How did this happen?"

Julia said, "After the meeting, I was on my way home when Chris and two former No Light members, now CROWN members, came up to me, and they started talking to me. Chris asked me if I knew Jesus. I told them no, I didn't know Him, and I didn't want to know Him. Chris said, 'You might not want to know Him, but He knows you and loves you.' The boy to the left of Chris said, 'Yeah, He loves you. Over two thousand years ago, He proved that when He died on the cross. He laid down His life. **John 15:13** says, "Greater love hath no man than this, that a man lay down his life for his friends." Jesus showed that love when He died on the cross for our sins. He laid down his life so we wouldn't have to. Three days later, He was resurrected from the dead. He ascended into heaven, and, yes, He's coming back again.' The boy to the right of Chris said, 'He doesn't want you to be religious. All He wants you to do is put your faith and trust in Him. Will you receive Jesus Christ as your Savior today and gain eternal life?' I said yes and received Jesus as my Savior. That's my story, Jason."

Jason said, "You're pathetic," and he walked away. Julia sighed and said, "He will learn." Then she prayed for him and then went to class.

CHAPTER 6

I felt a little relaxed since William had found out that I was a Christian. I was able to hang out with Daniel more and go to church, and I started reading my Bible more. One day when I came home, my parents asked me where I had been lately. I replied, "I don't know what you mean." My mom said, "I mean that you have been leaving a lot lately." Before I could answer, William came downstairs and said, "Antowon has been hanging out with his friend Daniel, and he's been helping me with my project for science class." Our father said, "Who is this Daniel that you have been hanging out with?" I said, "He's a friend from school that I've been hanging out with." Mom said, "You should invite him over for dinner one day." I said okay, then asked William if I could talk to him in his room for a minute. He nodded his head, and I followed him to his room.

When we got to his room, I closed the door and asked him why he had covered for me with our parents. He said, "I told you that I would keep your secret, and I see that also involves me covering for you when you go do your Christian activities." I hugged him and said, "Thank you, bro. I pray for you every day that you will see the light and accept Jesus Christ as your Savior." William said, "I pray every day that you will see the error of your ways and return to where you belong and become a Muslim again." I said, "Bro, I can't turn my back on Jesus. I know the truth, and I've found unspeakable joy." William said, "But, bro, you have turned your back on everything that you have learned all your life." I said, "I know, bro, but everything that we were taught growing up was a lie. Then Daniel, Brittany, Jasmine, and everybody else taught me the truth." William said, "I can't accept that." I said, "Bro, I need you to do me a favor," and he said, "What is it?" I said, "I need you to cover for me tomorrow because I'm going to the hospital to visit Jasmine and Brittany, then I'm going to church later on that night."

William said, "I'm going with you to the hospital, but I'm not going with you to church," and I said, "That's fine." I left William's room, went to my room, did my homework, then went to bed. The next day, I was so ready for school to be over so that I could meet with Daniel and go see Jasmine and Brittany in the hospital. After class, William and I met with Daniel, and we went to the hospital. When Jasmine and Brittany saw us enter their room, their face lit up; they were so happy to see us. Jasmine said, "Antowon, we haven't seen you in a long time. How's life being a Muslim?" I said, "Jasmine, you don't have to pretend around my brother anymore. He knows that I'm a Christian." Jasmine said, "How did he find out that you are a Christian?" I told her that he found out when he saw me praying with Daniel. "That was when I found out that you and Brittany were in the hospital. He heard me praying to Jesus that night."

Jasmine said, "Oh, do your parents know that you're a Christian now?" I said, "No, only William knows, and he has promised me that he will keep my secret and cover for me when I need him to, like tonight, after I leave here and go with Daniel to church." Jasmine turned to William and asked him, "How do you feel about your brother becoming a Christian?" William said, "It hurts that my brother has turned against the religion of Islam to become a Christian, but there's nothing I can do but pray that he comes to his senses and returns to where he belongs." Jasmine said, "Okay, and I pray that you accept Jesus as your Savior and join us." I said, "We're all praying for that. We all want you with us." William said, "I will never join you. I'm staying faithful to Allah." I told Jasmine that we were about to go. "But before we do, let us pray." Jasmine said, "Okay."

Everyone but William grabbed hands, and I started the prayer. "Lord Jesus, thank You first of all for being God all by Yourself, and thank You for leading all of us to the truth. Also, we want to thank You for protecting Jasmine and Brittany in the car accident. We also pray that they will get out of the hospital." Daniel took over. "Lord, we pray that we can be the light of the world and bring unbelievers to You, and we pray that the group CROWN will be around for people to get saved, either before we die or the rapture comes, and help us to stay focused on our mission. In Jesus's name, we pray, and we thank You, Lord. Amen." After we prayed, Daniel, William, and I left the hospital, and I dropped William off at home. Then Daniel and I went to Bible study at the church.

When we got inside the church, everyone greeted us, then we had praise and worship. After praise and worship, Pastor Harold came to the podium and said, "Open your Bibles to **Revelation 13:7**, which says, 'And it was given unto him to make war with the saints, and to overcome them: and power was given him over all kindreds, and tongues, and nations.' Also, **Revelation 13:15–18** says, 'And he had power to give life unto the image of the beast, that the image of the beast should both speak, and cause that as many as would not worship the image of the beast should be killed and he causeth all, both small and great, rich and poor, free and bond, to receive a mark in their right hand, or in their foreheads: And that no man might buy or sell, save he that had the mark, or the name of the beast, or the number of his name. Here is wisdom. Let him that hath understanding count the number of the beast: for it is the number of a man; and his number is six hundred threescore and six 666.'"

Pastor Harold said, "I'm going to stop here for a minute. When the antichrist comes to power, he is going to control the entire world. The same thing that had brought Adolf Hitler to power in Germany is the same thing that will bring the antichrist to power over the world. Adolf Hitler came to power in Germany due to the collapse of the German economy. Hitler promised the German people peace, but he untimely led them straight to war. The antichrist is going to promise world peace, but he will bathe the world in blood. **Daniel 8:25** says, 'Through his cunning, he shall cause deceit to prosper under his rule; and he shall exalt himself in his heart. He shall destroy many in their prosperity. He shall even rise against the Prince of princes; but he shall be broken without human means.' This means that the antichrist is going to sign a seven-year peace treaty with Israel and the rest of the world, but from day one, he will not keep it. After he controls the world, the antichrist and his false prophet will force the entire planet to receive the mark of the beast, and whoever accepts the mark of the beast will be lost forever and will go to hell. **Revelation 14:9–11** says, 'And the third angel followed them, saying with a loud voice, If any man worship the beast and his image, and receive his mark in his forehead, or in his hand, the same shall drink of the wine of the wrath of God, which is poured out without mixture into the cup of his indignation; and he shall be tormented with fire and brimstone in the presence of the holy angels, and in the presence of the Lamb: And the smoke of their torment ascendeth up for ever and ever: and they have no rest day nor night, who worship the beast and his image, and whosoever receiveth the mark of his name.' **Revelation 16:2** says, 'And the first went, and poured out his vial upon the earth; and there fell noisome and grievous sores upon the men which had the mark of the beast, and upon them which worshipped his image.' There's a flip side to this. There will be people during the tribulation who will refuse the mark of the beast because they have accepted Jesus Christ as their Savior, and the antichrist is going to kill them by beheading them. **Revelation 20:4** says, 'And I saw thrones, and they sat upon them, and judgment was given unto them: and *I saw* the souls of them that were beheaded for the witness of Jesus, and for the word of God, and which had not worshipped the beast, neither his image, neither had received *his* mark upon their foreheads, or in their hands; and they lived and reigned with Christ a thousand years.'"

After service, Daniel went with me to my house to spend the night. We went up to my room, and we started praying that William would receive Jesus as his Savior and that if he does get left behind, he won't take the mark of the beast. "In Jesus's name we pray, and we thank You, Lord. Amen." After we finished praying, I told Daniel that I wanted him to meet my parents in the morning, and he said okay. Then we went to sleep.

* * * * *

Cierra and her mother had a very strenuous relationship ever since she became a Buddhist. They didn't talk a lot, and when they did, it usually ended in an argument about who was right. When Cierra went to school, she went to her guidance counselor and said, "I need to talk to you about a problem that I'm having at home." Her guidance counselor, Stephanie Lynn, said, "What's the problem?" Cierra said, "My problem is my mom. She's a Christian, and she's driving me crazy with her out-of-this-world beliefs, and I don't know what to do." Ms. Lynn said, "Have you tried talking to her?" Cierra said, "Yes, but every time we talk, it turns into an argument, and I'm tired of it." Ms. Lynn said, "Okay, what I would recommend is that you bring in a mediator who can calmly listen to both sides and render a decision." Cierra said, "Thank you so much." After school, Cierra went home and to her room, then she got on her computer and typed in "mediators for families with different religious views." Three hundred results popped up, and she clicked on the fourth one that said it was the "perfect way to bring peace between families with different religious views."

Cierra clicked the tab that said, "Contact Us." She put in her mother's name and her name, plus all the information that the website requested. The last thing she typed in was a note: "You can contact me at (513) 787-5923." Then she clicked submit. The screen said, "Thank you for submitting your information. Someone will contact you in four to eight business days." Cierra said, "I hope this works." She went into the kitchen and saw a note that said, "Gone to take care of your Aunt Suzie. Will be back in two weeks. Also, I left four hundred dollars for you to buy food and for emergencies. Love, your mom." Cierra said, "Looks like I have the entire house to myself for the next two weeks." Well, the first thing I'm going to do is throw the biggest party of the year."

Cierra went on the computer to her Funbook account and posted on her wall, "Party at my house for anybody in my neighborhood of Nashville, Tennessee, that wants to party. The party starts at 8:00 p.m. and ends at 4:00 a.m." The last thing she said was "Bring anything you want to the party because the party isn't going to stop." And then she posted the status. Two minutes later, she received over one hundred comments asking the address to her house. She replied, "My address is 1881 Adams Road. Zip code 24658." Cierra went out and bought fifty dollars' worth of food and drinks for the party. She got home and cleaned up, then she took a nap for a couple of hours, then she was awakened by a knock on the door. She got up and answered the door, and it was her former friend Jenny. Cierra asked her what she wanted. Jenny said, "I'm here for your party. I brought some of my friends. You invited everyone who lives in your neighborhood to come, and here we are an hour early to help you set up and have fun."

Cierra said, "Okay, come in and put anything that you brought for the party in the kitchen." Everyone went to the kitchen, put their stuff down, and helped Cierra cook the food and finish cleaning the house. Twenty minutes later, everyone else started showing up. While everyone was partying, Cierra was drinking a lot and acting weird. Jenny tried to stop her, but she wouldn't stop. It got to a point where she was slurring her words, and Jenny told Cierra that either she was going to stop drinking or she was going to leave. Cierra said, "No," and, "See ya, bye," and "Who needs you, fun crusher?" Jenny looked shocked at the way Cierra had talked to her and said, "Fine, I'm gone." Then Jenny and her friends left. Cierra said, "Who needs you?" and kept partying.

Later on, she started talking to a boy named Joe. They started kissing, then Joe said, "Let's go upstairs to your room," and she said okay. Twenty minutes later, she came downstairs crying. She went into the bathroom and called the police and gave them her address. Ten minutes later, everybody heard the sirens, and people were cleaning up and running out of the house in droves. One of Cierra's friends ran up to her and slapped her in the face. "Why did you call the police? Now we all could get in trouble for drinking at your party." Then the girl left.

When the police entered the house, there were only fifteen people left at the party, and they were all underage and drunk. The police arrested everyone but Cierra and put them in the police cars. One of the officers walked up to Cierra and said, "Are you the one who called us?" Cierra said, "Yes, I'm the one who called you." The officer said, "What's the problem here?" Cierra said, "I was assaulted tonight during my party, and I know who did it. His name is Joe. He didn't tell me his last name." The officer asked, "What happened?" She said, "I threw this party. Everyone but a few people were drinking, and after a while, those people left. I was talking to Joe, and he asked me to go upstairs to my room, and I said okay. Then we went to my room, and he assaulted me." The officer said, "Did you clean your bed or take a shower?" Cierra said, "No, why?" The officer replied, "We need the sheets and comforters as evidence. Also, we need to take you to the hospital to get examined, then we are going to take you downtown to officially get your statement." Cierra said, "Okay, but first I need to call my mother and let her know what's going on." He said, "Okay, but hurry. Every second we wait, the more evidence is lost."

Cierra left and called her mother. When her mother answered, it was 3:00 a.m. Her mother said, "Hello," and Cierra said, "Mom, I have something to tell you."

"What is it?"

Cierra said, "I was assaulted in my bedroom."

At that moment, Cierra's mother was fully awake. "What happened?"

Cierra said, "I threw a party, and everyone but Jenny and her friends was drinking. Then Jenny and I got into an argument, then she left. I was talking to a boy named Joe, and he asked me if I wanted to go upstairs to my room, and I said okay. When we got up to my room, he assaulted me, and I did say no."

Cierra's mother said, "First of all, you had no business throwing that party or drinking, but we will deal with that later. I'm on my way home. I will meet you at the hospital." Cierra said okay and hung up the phone. The police took her to the hospital and took her statement while the doctors examined her. Once the doctors were done, Cierra waited for her mother to come and pick her up.

While she was waiting, a chaplain came into the room and asked her if he could talk to her for a minute, and she said yes. He introduced himself and said, "My name is Chaplain Paul." He and Cierra shook hands. Paul continued talking. "I specialize in helping people cope with what happened to you this evening."

Cierra said, "I feel so depressed and stressed out that I don't know what to do."

Paul said, "What you need to do is cast your cares upon Jesus." Cierra said, "Why?" Paul said, "It's because what happened to you is a burden that no one should have to carry, and Jesus is the person that you need to give all your cares to. **Psalm 55:22** says, 'Cast your cares on the LORD, and he will sustain you; he will never let the righteous be shaken." Cierra said, "At this point, I'm desperate. I will pray to Him tomorrow once I get some sleep." Chaplain Paul said, "Can I pray for you before I leave?" and she said yes. Paul closed his eyes and said, "Lord Jesus, even though we don't always understand why things happen, we do understand that You're in charge of everything. Tonight I lift up Cierra because of what happened to her, and we pray that you give her the spirit of peace and comfort that when things happen, she can trust in You because You will never let her down. In Jesus's name, we pray. And we thank You, Lord, in advance for all that You have done in her life and everything You will do in her life. Amen."

Cierra said, "Amen." Then Paul gave her his card and told her that if she ever needed to talk, call him, and he will talk to her. Also, he told her that he had a group that dealt with these kinds of things and that she was welcome to come anytime she wanted. She said, "Okay." He left. Cierra started crying again and kept crying off and on until her mother showed up two hours later. She asked her how she was doing. Cierra said, "Fine, as much as to be expected." Her mother said, "I love you," and she said, "Me too." Then they went home.

* * * * *

Jake and David went to church on Sunday, and Bishop Hardy continued his six-week series on the signs of the times. Bishop Hardy said that during the tribulation, the sun is going to turn black, and the moon is going to turn into blood, then the great and mighty men were going to run to the hills and ask God to hide them from the wrath of the Lamb. This was going to be a terrible time to be on the earth. "**Revelation 6:12–17** says, 'I watched as he opened the sixth seal. There was a great earthquake. The sun turned black like sackcloth made of goat hair, the whole moon turned blood red, and the stars in the sky fell to earth, as figs drop from a fig tree when shaken by a strong wind. The heavens receded like a scroll being rolled up, and every mountain and island was removed from its place. Then the kings of the earth, the princes, the generals, the rich, the mighty, and everyone else, both slave and free, hid in caves and among the rocks of the mountains. They called to the mountains and the rocks, "Fall on us and hide us from the face of him who sits on the throne and from the wrath of the Lamb! For the great day of their wrath has come, and who can withstand it?" What the Bible is explaining with these scriptures is that things are going to get so bad that the most powerful men, the men who can get anything they want to be accomplished, are going to run to the mountains and ask the Lord to hide them from His wrath, but He won't.

"Some of you may be wondering why God will pour out His wrath on the world. The reason is a part of His redemption process to get the lost to respond to Jesus Christ and also to punish unbelieving Israel and the world. Even though all of this will be happening, there will still be people who reject Jesus Christ as their Savior, and they are going to curse God. **Revelation 16:10–11** says, 'The fifth angel poured out his bowl on the throne of the beast, and its kingdom was plunged into darkness. People gnawed their tongues in agony and cursed the God of heaven because of their pains and their sores but they refused to repent of what they had done.' I'm closing with this. Now is the time to give your life to Jesus, not wait until after the rapture, because you will have to deal with the deception of the antichrist, and you will be going through the worst period in human history. **Matthew 24:22** and **Mark 13:20** say that 'except that the Lord had shortened those days, no flesh should be saved: but for the elect's sake whom he has chosen he has shortened the days.'"

Bishop Hardy said, "Does anyone want to receive the gift of salvation and accept Jesus as their Savior? Come up here." Five people came up to receive Jesus Christ as their Savior. After service, Jake told David, "I would be scared to death if I had never received Jesus Christ as my Savior." David said, "Yep, that's why I told you to abandon Chrislam because it is not of God." Jake said, "I want everyone else to get saved, but I know it won't happen."

The next day, Jake and David were walking to school, talking about what they had learned on Sunday. Jake said, "I've learned a lot about what's going to happen in the future. How can anyone reject Jesus after everything that is going to happen during the tribulation?" David said, "Many people will come to know Jesus. **Revelation 7:9–10** says, 'After this I looked, and there before me was a great multitude that no one could count, from every nation, tribe, people and language, standing before the throne and before the Lamb. They were wearing white robes and were holding palm branches in their hands. And they cried out in a loud voice: "Salvation belongs to our God, who sits on the throne, and to the Lamb." Verses 13 and 14 of the same chapter says, 'Then one of the elders asked me, "These in white robes—who are they, and where did they come from?" I answered, "Sir, you know." And he said, "These are they who have come out of the great tribulation; they have washed their robes and made them white in the blood of the Lamb."' But for the people who give their lives to Jesus during the tribulation, a lot of them will pay for their faith with their lives."

Jake said, "Where in the Bible does it say Christians will pay for their faith with their lives?" David said, "**Revelation 13:7** says, 'It was given power to wage war against God's holy people and to conquer them. And it was given authority over every tribe, people, language and nation.' Also, **Revelation 6:9** says, 'When he opened the fifth seal, I saw under the altar the souls of those who had been slain because of the word of God and the testimony they had maintained.'" Jake said, "Wow." As they were finishing up their conversation, they arrived at school. When they got to school, they saw some people arguing. David and Jake went up to them and asked them, "What's going on?"

One of the kids said, "The other kids are saying that Jesus and Allah are both God, and they are saying merging Christianity and Islam into Chrislam is the right thing to do." David looked at Jake and said, "Do you want to take the lead with this?" Jake said, "Yeah," and he asked the name of one of the kids who said Chrislam was right. The boy said, "My name is Jack." Jake said, "Chrislam is wrong, and I know it's wrong because I used to believe in Chrislam before my friend David led me to the truth."

Jack said, "Who is David?" David stepped forward and said, "I'm David, and what Jake is telling you is the truth. Chrislam is wrong because you have two different religions with two different views. Christians know that Jesus is God and the Messiah, and Islam believes that Jesus was a prophet. Also, Christians believe that anyone who doesn't believe that Jesus Christ is God will go to hell. Islam believes that anyone who says that Jesus is the Christ will go to hell. The last thing that separates Christianity from Islam is that in the Bible when Jesus comes back after the tribulation, He comes back as the King of kings and the Lord of lords to stop the violence. The Jesus of Islam comes back to tell the world that He didn't die on the cross and that He faked and rigged it all, then He smashes all the crosses because He doesn't support Christianity. The merging of Christianity and Islam also plays into the coming one world religion."

Jack said, "What do you mean by a one world religion?" Jake said, "During the tribulation, there will be a one world religion that will force the world to worship the antichrist by his helper, the false prophet. **Revelation 13:11–15** says, 'Then I saw a second beast, coming out of the earth. It had two horns like a lamb, but it spoke like a dragon. It exercised all the authority of the first beast on its behalf, and made the earth and its inhabitants worship the first beast, whose fatal wound had been healed. And it performed great signs, even causing fire to come down from heaven to the earth in full view of the people. Because of the signs it was given power to perform on behalf of the first beast, it deceived the inhabitants of the earth. It ordered them to set up an image in honor of the beast that was wounded by the sword and yet lived. The second beast was given power to give breath to the image of the first beast, so that the image could speak and cause all who refused to worship the image to be killed.'"

The kids behind Jack were mumbling, and Jake continued, "The only way you can escape the tribulation is to receive the gift of salvation and accept Jesus as your Savior." One of the kids asked, "How can we accept Jesus Christ as our Savior?" Jake said, "Repeat this prayer after me and mean it. Lord Jesus, Savior of the world, thank You for dying for me, shedding Your blood to save me from my sins. I ask You to come into my heart and be my Savior in Jesus's name, amen." Everybody but Jack and one other kid accepted Jesus as their Savior. David said, "For those who have just received Jesus as your Savior, David and I welcome you to the kingdom of Jesus. Now you have crossed from the kingdom of darkness into the kingdom of light." They said thank you, and when Jake and David left, everyone who had accepted Jesus as their Savior left, and those who were arguing with Jack left too.

During lunch, David, Jake, and everyone who were with him earlier sat down at the table prayed and started eating. All those who had accepted Jesus earlier asked Jake, "What do we do now?" And he said, "Now you read the Bible and get into a church that teaches the Bible only and teaches that Jesus Christ is God alone." They said okay, and David said, "Now that you are saved, the devil is going to try everything in his power to discourage you and make you renounce Jesus Christ as your Savior, but don't do it. That will be the worst decision you could ever make." Everybody said, "No matter what, I would never turn on Jesus." After school, Jake told David, "I'm happy that those kids gave their lives to Jesus. I want to be a part of the harvest that brings more people to Jesus." David said, "So do I, because He's coming back soon," and Jake said, "Yes, He is."

Two weeks later, Cody ran into Paul, and when Paul saw him coming, he said hi. Cody said, "What's up? I have a favor to ask you," and Paul said, "What is it?" Cody said, "Ever since my parents died, I've had a hard time paying the rent, and I'm getting evicted in two weeks, so I want to know, can I stay with you and your parents?" He said, "I will have to call my parents and ask them, but most likely they will say yes. I will tell you what they said after school." Cody said, "Okay," and went to class. After school ended, Paul walked over to Cody and said, "I talked to my parents, and they said yes, you can stay with us as long as you want to." Cody said, "Thank you. I'm going to put most of my stuff in storage, and I will bring a few things over to your house," and Cody said, "Okay." Paul said, "Do you need any help packing up and putting your stuff in storage?" Cody said, "Yeah, I do." Paul said, "Okay, I will help you," and Cody said thank you. They walked to his apartment, which was about a mile away. When they got to his apartment, it was a mess, which was to be expected. They started cleaning up and packing up his stuff.

Paul called his mom and asked if she could rent a mover's truck for Cody because he had too much stuff to carry. Paul's mother said that she and his father would get the truck and bring their van; also they would help pack and put his stuff in storage, and Paul said, "Okay." When Paul's parents got there, they started putting his stuff in the truck while Cody and Paul continued packing up his stuff. Once they finished packing and cleaning his apartment, he closed and locked the door. Then he told Paul, "I'm coming back in the morning to make sure we got everything out of here, then I'm going to turn in the keys to the rent office." Paul said okay, and Cody locked the door. They got in the van and went to Paul's house. By the time they got to Paul's house, it was 8:00 p.m. It was too late to put his stuff in storage, so they parked the truck on the side street. When they got inside, Paul and Cody were surprised that there was food on the table. Paul said, "Mom, what's this?" She said, "I cooked this earlier when you asked me if Cody could come and stay with us." Paul said, "What all did you fix?" She said, "I fixed chicken, macaroni and cheese, greens, and rolls, and for dessert, I made a chocolate cake." Cody said, "I don't know what to say," and Paul's parents said,

"It's nothing to it. We just wanted to make you feel welcomed." Cody said, "You have, thank you."

Everyone sat down. Paul and his parents grabbed hands, then they looked at Cody. Cody grabbed Paul's hands, and Paul prayed, "Lord Jesus, thank You for this day. Thank You for this food we are about to receive. We pray that You bless it for the nourishment of our bodies, and thank You for allowing Cody to become a part of our family. In Your Son Jesus's name, we pray. And we thank You, Lord. Amen." Everyone said amen, then they started eating.

Paul's mother asked Cody, "How was school?" Cody said, "School was good, but I was bored because everything that they were teaching I already knew." She said, "That's good," then Paul's father asked him what he learned in school today. Paul said, "I learned about the atom and how the United States made the atomic bomb so they could drop it on Japan." He said, "They are going to drop the atomic bomb again." Cody said, "What do you mean they are going to drop the atomic bomb again?" Paul's father said, **"Zechariah 14:12** says, 'And the LORD will send a plague on all the nations that fought against Jerusalem. Their people will become like walking corpses, their flesh rotting away. Their eyes will rot in their sockets, and their tongues will rot in their mouths.' This scripture is the perfect description of a nuclear exchange."

Cody asked, "Why is this going to happen?" Paul's father said, "This is going to happen because God is going to let the nations of the world bring judgment on themselves. The world has been telling God that if He leaves us alone, we will make things better. So during the tribulation, God is going to let the world face Satan's wrath mixed with man's wrath that will face the wrath of God. God's wrath is going to be so bad that all who survive will know that Jesus Christ is Lord."

Cody said, "Why does God send us to hell?" Paul said, "God doesn't send us to hell. We send our own selves to hell. He doesn't want us to go to hell, but when we refuse to accept the payment for our sins that Jesus paid when He died on the cross, you choose to die in your sins and go to hell. **John 3:16–17** says, 'For God so loved the world that he gave his one and only Son, that whoever believes in him shall not perish but have eternal life. For God did not send his Son into the world to condemn the world, but to save the world through him.' **Second Peter 2:9** says, 'The Lord is not slow in keeping his promise, as some understand slowness. Instead he is patient with you, not wanting anyone to perish, but everyone to come to repentance.' The last scripture I'm going to quote is **John 11:25**. 'Jesus said to her, "I am the resurrection and the life. The one who believes in me will live, even though they die."' Jesus gives us a choice to either follow Him or the devil, and when we reject Jesus, then we choose the devil."

Paul said, "In the Bible, it says to choose this day whom you will serve. The choice you make will decide your eternal destiny. Cody, which side do you choose?" Cody said, "I'm not choosing Jesus. He's not god. There's no god. If there's a god, why is all this evil happening?" Paul's mother said, "It's because the United States, and the world, have turned their back on God, that's why. **Psalm 9:17** says, 'The wicked go down to the realm of the dead, all the nations that forget God.'"

Cody said, "Can I be excused?" Paul's mother said yes. Cody got up and asked Paul where he would be sleeping. Paul said, "My room. I have a spare bed in there." Cody said, "Thank you." He went to Paul's room and went to sleep. The next day, Cody went back to his apartment to make sure that he and Paul had gotten everything out. When he saw that he and Paul had cleaned out the apartment, he closed the door and locked it. He went to the rent office and turned the keys over to the manager. The manager asked him if he got all of his belongings out of the apartment, and he said, "Yeah." She said, "Okay, all I need you to do is sign these papers saying that you have gotten all of your belongings out of the apartment and that you are surrendering the keys." Cody signed the papers and gave her the keys, then he left and went back to Paul's house. He asked Paul's father if he could drive him to Don's Storage to put his stuff in storage. Paul's father said, "Yeah, I will drive you." Paul's father took Cody to Don's Storage and went inside with Cody to make sure everything went all right.

Once inside, Cody negotiated with Don, the manager, to rent a storage room for fifty bucks a month. Don agreed to it. Cody and Paul's father started putting his things in the storage room. It took them two hours to put all his stuff in storage. Then Cody closed the door and locked it. He got in the car, and they went back to the house. Cody said, "Thank you again for taking me to put my stuff in storage, and also thank you for all the kindness that you have shown me." Paul's father replied, "We are just doing what Jesus would do," and Cody said, "Yeah, I can tell," then he went to Paul's room.

Three months later, Cody's attitude changed dramatically. His grades dropped dramatically, and he even joined a gang and was terrorizing the streets. He was also selling drugs. One day, Paul walked up to Cody making a deal, and he said, "Cody, what are you doing?" Cody said, "I'm in the middle of making a deal." Paul turned to the man Cody was making a deal with and said the deal was off, and the man left. Paul said, "Cody, why are you doing this?" Cody replied, "I need some money. I'm tired of letting you and your family take care of me." Paul said, "You don't have to do this. Just get a normal job." Cody said, "I tried to get a job, but no one ever called me back to hire me." Paul said, "Accept and trust in Jesus, man, because He will provide for you. **Philippians 4:19–20** says, 'But my God shall supply all your needs according to his riches in glory by Christ Jesus. Now unto God and our Father be glory for ever and ever amen.'"

Cody then said, "I've done too much for Jesus to love me, especially because of what I'm doing now." Paul said, "**Romans 8:38–39** says, 'For I am persuaded that neither death nor life, nor angels, nor principalities, nor power, or things to come, nor height, nor depth, nor any other creatures shall be able to separate us from the love of God which is in Christ Jesus our Lord.'" Cody replied, "I can't talk about this right now. I have to work for two more hours. Can we talk about this later?" Paul said, "Yeah, but before you go to bed, we're going to talk. I don't care how tired you are." And Cody said, "Okay."

Cody came home at 2:30 a.m. When Cody saw Paul, he jumped. "Dang, Paul, you scared me half to death." Paul said, "Let's talk right now," and Cody said, "Okay." Paul said, "Cody, you have become like my brother, and as your brother, I can't stand by and watch you destroy your life, man. You need to stop selling drugs, and you need to quit that gang that you are in." Cody's eyes got big, and he said, "How did you know that I was in a gang?" Paul said, "The Lord revealed to me that you were in a gang. He even told me that you were selling drugs, and He even told me where you were selling the drugs." Cody said, "Have you told your parents that I'm selling drugs?" Paul said, "No, I haven't told them, and I'm not going to tell them if you stop this right now." Cody said, "I will think about it, but I have to think very hard about it." Paul said, "I'm giving you two weeks to make a decision, and if you don't make the right decision, I will tell my parents, and I will also go to the police and tell them too." Cody said, "Okay." Then Paul and Cody went upstairs to Paul's room. Paul prayed for Cody, then they both went to sleep.

* * * * *

Jason was mad. His No Light group was down to ten members, and he was even madder that Julia, the founder of the No Light group, had betrayed them by accepting Jesus as her Savior and joining CROWN. Jason was also mad because the funding to keep the No Light group afloat was basically nonexistent. Jason told the remaining ten members of No Light that he was going to form a council of six people including him to help govern and expand the No Light group. Jason continued, "If anybody wants to be a part of this council, send me an email, or if you can't email me, come talk to me sometime during the week. I will be making decisions in the next two weeks."

After the meeting, Jason went home and started making positions for people to fill once they started applying for them. Two days later, three people applied for the position of vice president of No Light: a boy named Tommy, a girl named Vickie, and a boy named Phil. Jason looked at the applicants and decided he would pick Tommy as vice president. Vickie would be the expansion manager, and he was going to make a position for Phil to fill. The next day, Jason ran into Julia. Julia said hi, and Jason coldly said hi back. Julia said, "What's your problem?"

Jason said, "You turned on us and gave it all up, for what? Nothing." Julia said, "I gave it all up so I could gain everything because I have Jesus Christ as my Savior." Julia continued. "In my short time as a Christian, I've learned a lot. For example, the first scripture I learned is **1 John 3:14–16**, which says, 'We know that we have passed from death to life, because we love each other. Anyone who does not love remains in death. Anyone who hates a brother or sister is a murderer, and you know that no murderer has eternal life residing in him. This is how we know what love is: Jesus Christ laid down his life for us. And we ought to lay down our lives for our brothers and sisters.' In other words, a person can say that they are a Christian, but if they hate their brothers, then the love of Jesus isn't in them."

Jason said, "It's good that you are learning about your new religion, but don't try to force that on me. I'm going to finish what you started but failed to finish. I'm going to eradicate Christianity from our school." Julia said, "I'm ashamed that I started that group. I was afraid of what I didn't understand, and if I knew then what I know now, I never would have started that group." Jason said, "I'm glad that you did start this group because out of the seed of your brain, a revolution will succeed. As we speak, I'm reforming the group and starting a council that will help me govern the group and expand to other schools." Julia said, "CROWN is already ahead of you. We are expanding to other schools to teach people the good news of Jesus." Jason was really mad and said, "I will stop you, all of you." Then he stomped away.

Two weeks later, Jason was on his way to a No Light meeting when a few kids walked up to him, and they said, "Are you Jason Michaels?" Jason said, "Who wants to know?" One of the kids stepped forward and said, "I do. My name is Rick. I'm the leader of a group called the Light. We are a group that believes that religion has no place in schools, and we want to eradicate religion, especially Christianity, out of school." Jason said, "What do you want with me?" Rick said, "We want to merge our group, the Light, with your group, No Light, to form a supergroup and complete our goals. If we combine our resources and our manpower, we can achieve our goals, then we can go our separate ways." Jason said, "What school do y'all go to?" Rick said, "We go to George Washington Middle and High School." Jason said, "Isn't that school just down the street from our school?" Rick said, "Yeah, but what is your answer to our business proposition?" Jason thought about it for a minute, then he said, "Yeah," and shook Rick's hand. Rick said, "You have made the right decision. Now that we have merged our groups, what shall we call ourselves?" Jason said, "How about we keep your name and call ourselves the Light?" and Rick said okay.

Jason said, "We are coleaders of the Light, and I have a person who's the vice president of my former group, No Light. I want him to be the vice president of our new merged group. Is that all right with you, Rick?" Rick said, "That's fine. We need to have a council that will help us govern and expand the group." Jason said, "It's weird that you said that. I was forming a council to govern and expand No Light, but who besides Vice President Tommy deserves to be a part of our council?" Rick said, "I don't know. I'm going to have to meet with my group and see who wants to be a part of the council. Also, we have to tell them about the merger of our groups." Jason said, "Okay. Well, I have to go or I'm going to be late for my meeting." Rick said, "Okay, keep in touch with us, brother."

Jason got to the school and ran to room 306 just as the meeting was getting started. Phil was up talking about how CROWN was taking over the school with all their spiritual talk, and very soon, the entire school would be lost to those religious fanatics. "Does anyone have any ideas on how we can defeat them?"

Jason said, "A dude named Rick walked up to me when I was on my way here, and he said that he ran a group that had the same goals as us. They want to eradicate religion, especially Christianity, from their school and ours. Rick and I have merged his group, the Light, and our group, No Light, to form the new Light group."

Vice President Tommy said, "How many people are in his group?"

Jason said, "I don't know, but I'm going over to his school tomorrow when class is over to meet with him and see how many members he has."

Tommy said, "Okay, who will be the vice president of the group?"

"You will still be the vice president. I told Rick I still wanted you to be the vice president, and he said okay."

Phil said, "Are you still going to start the council?"

Jason said, "Yes, we are still going to start a council to govern and expand the group. So far, the council consists of Rick and I as coleaders or copresidents, and Tommy will be vice president. Is there anyone else who wants to be a part of our council?" Three people raised their hands, and Jason said, "Okay, send me your information, and I will talk to Rick." Jason dismissed everyone, then he left and headed home. On his way home, he was thinking that he was close to achieving his goal when he saw a billboard with the scripture **Acts 9:3–5**. He saw a Bible on the ground, and he picked up the Bible and read **Acts 9:3–5**: "As he neared Damascus on his journey, suddenly a light from heaven flashed around him. He fell to the ground and heard a voice say to him, 'Saul, Saul, why do you persecute me?' "'Who are you, Lord?' Saul asked. 'I am Jesus, whom you are persecuting,' he replied." Jason closed the Bible, put it in his book bag, and kept walking to his house.

Once he got home, he was heading to his room when his parents called him, and they told him that they were about to go to church. Jason said, "I'm not going." Jason's mother said, "What's wrong, are you sick?" Jason said, "I'm not sick, but I don't believe in Jesus or God anymore. I'm an atheist now. There's no god. God is dead." Jason's father said, "You're wrong. God does exist. His name is Jesus Christ, and He created the world and everything in it." Jason said, "All religion does is create conflict and start wars." Jason's mom said, "Yes, religion does create conflict and start wars, but Christianity isn't a religion. It's a relationship with Jesus. Jesus died to save us from our sins. Adam brought sin into the world, and Jesus brought salvation. **First Corinthians 15:22** says, 'For as in Adam all die, so in Christ all will be made alive.' **Romans 5:12** says, 'Therefore, just as sin entered the world through one man, and death through sin, and in this way, death came to all people, because all sinned.'"

Jason said, "What does that all mean?" Jason's father said, "That means that Adam brought death into the world by sinning, so sin is in our nature. **First Corinthians 15:56–57** says, 'The sting of death is sin, and the power of sin is the law. But thanks be to God! He gives us the victory through our Lord Jesus Christ.'" Jason said, "I hate God and Jesus Christ." Then he left. Jason's mother and father both cried, and they prayed, "Lord Jesus, please show Jason that You are real and that You love him. In Jesus's name, we pray. And we thank You, Lord. Amen." Then Jason's parents left to go to church, and Jason went to bed.

7

Two years later, I was eighteen and a senior at Austin High School, and William was sixteen and a sophomore. I was still trying to convince William that Jesus is God, but William wouldn't listen. He kept saying that the Quran says that if anyone says that Jesus Christ is God, they will burn in hell forever. One day, while I was driving to school, I said, "Bro, do you remember you told me the Quran says that if anyone says that Jesus Christ is God, they will burn in hell because Allah had no kids?" He said, "Yeah," and I said, "I've memorized a lot of scriptures like **Hebrews 1:8**, which says, 'But of the Son he said, Thy throne, O God, is forever and ever, and the scepter of uprightness is the scepter of thy kingdom.' **Matthew 28:16–20** says, 'Then the eleven disciples went to Galilee, to the mountain where Jesus had told them to go. When they saw him, they worshiped him; but some doubted. Then Jesus came to them and said, "All authority in heaven and on earth has been given to me. Therefore go and make disciples of all nations, baptizing them in the name of the Father and of the Son and of the Holy Spirit, and teaching them to obey everything I have commanded you. And surely I am with you always, to the very end of the age."'

"The final scriptures I want to use are **John 3:16–18, John 3:36, Luke 4:8, John 8:24**, and **1 John 2:22–23. John 3:16–18** says, 'For God so loved the world that he gave his one and only

Son, that whoever believes in him shall not perish but have eternal life. For God did not send his Son into the world to condemn the world, but to save the world through him. Whoever believes in him is not condemned, but whoever does not believe stands condemned already because they have not believed in the name of God's one and only Son.' **John 3:36** says, 'Whoever believes in the Son has eternal life, but whoever rejects the Son will not see life, for God's wrath remains on them.' **Luke 4:8** says, 'And Jesus answered and said unto him, Get thee behind me, Satan: for it is written, Thou shalt worship the Lord thy God, and him only shalt thou serve.' **John 8:24** says, 'Therefore I said to you that you will die in your sins; for unless you believe that I am *He*, you will die in your sins.' **First John 2:22–23** says, 'Who is the liar? It is whoever denies that Jesus is the Christ. Such a person is the antichrist—denying the Father and the Son. No one who denies the Son has the Father; whoever acknowledges the Son has the Father also.'"

William sighed and said, "Okay, bro, tell you what I'm going to do. Tonight, come to my room and tell me everything you know about the Bible and Christianity, and I will listen to everything you have to say, and I won't interrupt you unless I have a question or unless I need some clarification." I said, "Okay, what's the catch?" He said, "If I sit down and listen to everything you have to say, then take a few days to take it all in and tell you what I think, will you promise me that you will tone down with me about this?" I said, "Yeah," and we shook hands. Then I parked the car, and we went to class. During lunch, I sat down with Jasmine, Brittany, and Daniel. Everyone said, "Hey, Antowon, what's up?" I said, "I have some good news."

"What's the good news?"

I said, "I talked to William on the way to school, and he told me that tonight, I can tell him everything I know about the Bible, and he will listen and think about it, then he will tell me what he thinks if I agree to lay off talking to him about Jesus a lot, and I said okay."

Daniel said, "What are you going to talk about?"

I said, "I'm going to talk about the tribulation, and what's going to happen in the future."

Brittany said, "That's great. He needs to know what's going to happen in case he gets left behind, or if he gets saved, he can tell more people so they can give their lives to Jesus and get saved," and Jasmine said, "Yep." Daniel said, "Can I come over tonight and talk to him?" I said, "Sure, that would be great." Then Jasmine and Brittany both said, "Can we come over too?" and I said, "Yeah, I will order pizza for us, and we can have Bible study," and everyone said, "Okay." After class, William met me at the car, and when he got in, I told him that Daniel, Brittany, and Jasmine want to come over and listen while we talk. "Is that all right with you?" He said, "I don't care." I said, "Okay, can you do me a favor?"

"What?"

"Can you call Liberty Pizza and order three pizzas? Two with pepperoni, and then you can order whatever kind of pizza you want."

William said, "Okay," and he called Liberty Pizza. The pizzas came to thirty dollars. After we got the pizzas, we stopped at the store, got some drinks and chips, then went home. Five minutes after we got home, Daniel, Brittany, and Jasmine came over. We got our food, then went up to William's room. Daniel, Brittany, Jasmine, and I held hands, and Brittany prayed, "Lord Jesus, thank You for this day, and thank You for this food that we are about to receive. We pray that You bless it for the nourishment of our bodies. In Jesus's name, we pray, and we thank You, Lord. Amen." Everyone started eating, and William said, "Whenever you're ready, bro, you can begin," and I said, "Okay, well, I'm not going to talk to you about Jesus being God, because I've already told you about that, so I'm going to tell you what's going to happen to all those who reject Jesus as their Savior, and I'm not talking about hell."

I continued. "Soon, millions of people will vanish off the face of the earth, and this is called the rapture." I opened the Bible and turned to **1 Thessalonians 4:16–18**. "'For the Lord himself will come down from heaven, with a loud command, with the voice of the archangel and with the trumpet call of God, and the dead in Christ will rise first. After that, we who are still alive and are left will be caught up together with them in the clouds to meet the Lord in the air. And so, we will be with the Lord forever. Therefore encourage one another with these words.' Also, **Revelation 3:10** says, 'Because thou hast kept the word of my patience, I also will keep thee from the hour of temptation, which shall come upon all the world, to try them that dwell upon the earth.' The last two scriptures I'm going to use for this part of what we call the end times is **Matthew 24:27** and **Mark 14:62**. **Matthew 24:27** says, 'For as lightning that comes from the east is visible even in the west, so will be the coming of the Son of Man.' In **Mark 14:62**, Jesus says, 'I am. And you will see the Son of Man sitting at the right hand of the Mighty One and coming on the clouds of heaven.'"

William said, "When will Jesus come back, and when will the rapture happen?" I said, "No one knows when it all happens. All those who have accepted Jesus as their Savior will disappear with their bodies gone, but the clothes will remain." Daniel took over. "After the rapture, the world will be in chaos because planes will be falling from the skies, ships will be sinking, cars will be crashing on the roads, and buildings will explode and catch fire because the occupants that were once there will be raptured. In the midst of all of this chaos, a world leader will come to power, and he will come as a man of peace, but he will bathe the world in blood, and he will be the antichrist. **Daniel 8:25** says, 'He will cause deceit to prosper, and he will consider himself superior. When they feel secure, he will destroy many and take his stand against the Prince of princes. Yet he will be destroyed, but not by human power.'"

William said, "Why would anyone follow a man that would destroy them?" Daniel replied, "The world is going to follow him because the world will believe that he has all the answers. Also, they will believe that he is the messiah because of his peace contract with Israel and the rest of the world, so they will worship the antichrist. **Daniel 9:27** says, 'He will confirm a covenant with many for one "seven." In the middle of the "seven" he will put an end to sacrifice and offering. And at the temple he will set up an abomination that causes desolation, until the end that is decreed is poured out on him.'"

Brittany took over and said, "That means that the antichrist shall sign a seven-year peace treaty with Israel guaranteeing them peace, but he breaks it three and a half years into it, and all hell breaks loose. **Revelation 13:6–8** says, 'Then he opened his mouth in blasphemy against God, to blaspheme His name, His tabernacle, and those who dwell in heaven. It was granted to him to make war with the saints and to overcome them. And authority was given him over every tribe, tongue, and nation. All who dwell on the earth will worship him, whose names have not been written in the Book of Life of the Lamb slain from the foundation of the world.'" Brittany continued. "Three and a half years into the tribulation, a Jew who finds out who the antichrist is and what he really is about shoots him in the head, and Satan will indwell inside the antichrist, and he will come back from the dead, emulating the death and resurrection of Jesus Christ. **Revelation 13:3–4** says, 'And I saw one of his heads as if it had been mortally wounded, and his deadly wound was healed. And all the world marveled and followed the beast. So they worshipped the dragon who gave authority to the beast; and they worshipped the beast, saying, "Who *is* like the beast? Who is able to make war with him?"'"

Jasmine took over. "After the antichrist comes back from the dead, he will declare himself god and set up his image to be worshipped, and then he will force the entire world to take his mark, which will be called the mark of the beast, on their right hand or their forehead. **Second Thessalonians 2:4** says, 'Who opposes and exalts himself above all that is called God or that is worshiped, so that he sits as God in the temple of God, showing himself that he is God.' **Matthew 24:15–16** says, 'Therefore when you see the 'abomination of desolation,' spoken of by Daniel the prophet, standing in the holy place (whoever reads, let him understand), then let those who are in Judea flee to the mountains.' **Revelation 13:15–18** says, 'He was granted power to give breath to the image of the beast, that the image of the beast should both speak and cause as many as would not worship the image of the beast to be killed. He causes all, both small and great, rich and poor, free and slave, to receive a mark on their right hand or on their foreheads, and that no one may buy or sell except one who has the mark or the name of the beast, or the number of his name. Here is wisdom. Let him who has understanding calculate the number of the beast, for it is the number of a man: His number *is* 666.'"

William said, "What will happen to those who refuse the mark of the beast, and what will happen to those who take the mark?" Jasmine grabbed the Bible and turned to **Revelation 20:4**. "'And I saw thrones, and they sat on them, and judgment was committed to them. Then *I saw* the souls of those who had been beheaded for their witness to Jesus and for the word of God, who had not worshiped the beast or his image, and had not received *his* mark on their foreheads or on their hands. And they lived and reigned with Christ for a thousand years.' **Revelation 14:9–11** says, 'Then a third angel followed them, saying with a loud voice, If anyone worships the beast and his image, and receives *his* mark on his forehead or on his hand, he himself shall also drink of the wine of the wrath of God, which is poured out full strength into the cup of His indignation. He shall be tormented with fire and brimstone in the presence of the holy angels and in the presence of the Lamb. And the smoke of their torment ascends forever and ever; and they have no rest day or night, who worship the beast and his image, and whoever receives the mark of his name.'"

I took over and said, "The tribulation will accommodate at Armageddon when all nations will attack Israel and Jesus will come back and put an end to the violence. **Revelation 16:16** says, 'And they gathered them together to the place called in Hebrew, Armageddon.' The last scripture I'm going to quote is **Revelation 11:15**, which says, 'Then the seventh angel sounded: And there were loud voices in heaven, saying, "The kingdoms of this world have become *the kingdoms* of our Lord and of His Christ, and He shall reign forever and ever!"' All of that was an outline of the tribulation. I will tell you the rest of it at another time, so what do you think?"

William said, "That's a lot to take in. I have to process all of this, then I will tell you what I think." Daniel said, "Okay, we're all going to crash in Antowon's room for the night." William said, "Okay," and everyone got up and went to sleep. William closed his eyes and went to sleep. When everyone got to his room, they grabbed hands, and prayed, "Lord Jesus, we come to You today asking You to open William's eyes so that he will give his life to You and that he will be able to tell others about You so that they can get saved. In Jesus's name, we pray. And we thank You, Lord." And everyone said, "Amen." Then we all went to sleep.

* * * * *

Two weeks after the incident, Cierra was still depressed. She spent the better part of two weeks crying and screaming. The next day, Cierra went into her mom's room and said, "Mom."

Her mother looked up and said, "What is it, honey?"

Cierra said, "I want to talk to you about what happened two weeks ago." Cierra continued talking; she said, "When you left, I wanted to have a party, so I posted an announcement on Funbook. I said that anybody who lived on the street could come to the party. Jenny and some of her Christian friends came to the party, and everybody but Jenny and her friends was drinking."

Cierra's mother said, "Why were you drinking? You are under the age of twenty-one. The police could have arrested you after you called them."

"Yes, I know, and I'm sorry about doing that. I won't do that again."

Cierra's mother said, "Okay, so what happened next?"

Cierra said, "Well, I was drunk. Jenny tried to stop me, but I wouldn't listen. I even told her to get out, so she left. Then the boy Joe started talking to me, and then we started kissing. Next, we went upstairs to my room, and in my room, he assaulted me. The rest you know."

Cierra's mother said, "Okay, I'm taking you to the police station. You can talk to a sketch artist so that they can find Joe and arrest him."

"Okay. Can I go see Jenny after so that I can apologize to her?"

Her mother said yes. An hour later, Cierra got dressed, and her mother drove her to the police station. The desk sergeant said, "May I help you?" Cierra said, "I need to speak to a sketch artist so that I can give a description of the person who attacked me two weeks ago." The desk sergeant told her to sit down. "The sketch artist will be with you in a minute."

About five minutes later, the desk sergeant opened the door and said, "The sketch artist will see you now." Cierra got up and followed the sketch artist. They went into a room and sat down, and Cierra told the sketch artist how Joe looked. Once Cierra was done, the sketch artist told her that he would give the description to every police officer in the city and the state. Cierra asked him, "How long will it take before you have him in custody?" The sketch artist said, "I don't know. It might take a few days, months, or years. It all depends on if we get any tips and how reliable and credible the tips are." Cierra said, "Okay," and she walked out. Her mother asked her if she was ready to go, and she said, "Yeah."

Cierra got into the car, and her mother drove her to Jenny's house. Cierra asked her mother to wait in the car, then went to the door and knocked. Jenny opened the door and said, "What do you want?" Cierra said, "May I please come in?" and Jenny said, "Yeah, sure." Once inside, Cierra said, "Jenny, I want to apologize for the way I was acting at my party. I should have treated you with more respect. I know that you were just trying to look out for me, and I should have listened to you. If I'd listened to you, I wouldn't have been assaulted."

Jenny said, "What? You were assaulted? When?"

"Right after you left. I went upstairs with a boy named Joe, and he assaulted me in my room."

"Okay, you need to go to the police to give them your statement, and also go to the hospital to get checked out."

Cierra said, "I already went to the hospital, and I went to the police station and gave them his description, and they said that they will be in touch when they find him."

Jenny said, "Okay, how are you holding up?"

"I'm holding up fine, but I feel violated, hurt, and betrayed."

Jenny then said, "I'm so sorry that this happened to you. If I could, I would trade places with you in a heartbeat." Cierra started crying. Jenny hugged her and said, "Cierra, everything will be all right. I will be here for you as someone to talk to, and I will always be here as a friend." Cierra kept crying as she said, "Okay."

Ten minutes later, Cierra got in the car and left with her mother. Her mother asked her, "How did everything go with Jenny?"

"I told her what happened. I also apologized to her for getting angry and kicking her out of the house."

"What did she say?"

"She said that she accepted my apology. I cried, and we hugged."

"Okay, that's good."

When Cierra got home, she ate some food, went into her room, and went to bed. Two days later, Cierra called Jenny and asked her if she felt like going to the park, and Jenny said, "Yeah." Cierra said, "Okay, I will pack us a lunch, and I will meet you at your house in half an hour, then we will walk to Fire Woods Park." Jenny said, "Okay, see you in thirty minutes." Cierra prepared four ham and cheese sandwiches, some chips, two bowls of chicken noodle soup, and four cans of pop. Thirty minutes later, Cierra knocked on the door, and Jenny opened it. Cierra said, "Are you ready to go?" Jenny said, "Yeah," and closed and locked the door. They walked for about two or three miles to the park. When they got to the park, they walked around for a little while, and while they were walking, Jenny said, "Look at the trees and waterfall. This place is amazing. It's a shame that we don't appreciate the beauty of nature that we see every day."

Cierra said, "That's true. We are so busy with our lives that we don't have a chance to enjoy nature."

Jenny said, "That's the problem. We need to make time for the most important things in our lives so that our lives can be better."

"Like what?"

"Like getting to know our Creator. We spend so much time with our lives that we don't give God a second thought."

Cierra said, "A lot of people are happy the way their lives are going."

"I know, but I have this joy, and I want to tell people what they are missing." Jenny continued. "I'm going to tell you something that hardly anybody knows about me. I used to be an atheist."

Cierra's eyes got big, and she said, "You used to be an atheist? What happened? How did you become a Christian?"

Jenny said, "I was in the eighth grade. I was happy, or at least I thought I was happy. I didn't have a care in the world. When my uncle Joe died of a heart attack, I was at home when the phone rang. I picked it up. It was my grandmother calling to let us know that my uncle Joe had collapsed in the bathroom and that the paramedics were on the way.

"My mom and I got dressed real quick, and we went over to my grandmother's house, but by the time we got there, he was already gone. I cried very hard, and I even yelled at God. I told Him, 'I don't ever want to believe in You if this is how You treat the ones that follow You.' Well, a few months later, I was so stressed out from losing my uncle that an ulcer opened up in my stomach, which caused me excruciating pain. I had to spend ten hours at the hospital. At this point, I started becoming angrier at God, even though being an atheist meant that I believe that there was no god. In the back of my mind, something was telling me that I was wrong, and that God existed, and that He loved me. As time went on, I went from being angry to being deeply depressed that I thought that I would never get out of. Then in 2010, I lost my dog Tango, whom I'd grown up with and had since he was a puppy. At this point, I was so depressed that I was ready to commit suicide."

Cierra said, "What stopped you?"

"The next day, I was going to commit suicide. I was writing a letter to my parents explaining to them why I was ready to die. Then there was a knock on my window. It was my friend Dave, and he said, 'Let's go for a walk,' and I said, 'Okay.' And as we were walking, Dave started telling me that I was going to commit suicide, and I was surprised because I had just decided to do it that day. I asked him how he knew that I was going to commit suicide. Dave said, 'Jesus told me that you were going to commit suicide, and He also wanted me to tell you He wants you and that He will never leave you or forsake you, and He wants you to trust Him and put your faith in Him and let Him guide your life.' Dave continued. He said, 'Will you accept Jesus Christ as your Savior and let Him guide your life?' I thought about the decision for a few minutes, and I said yes, I want to accept Jesus Christ as my Savior, and I want Him to guide my life. Dave led me through the sinner's prayer, and I received Jesus Christ as my Savior."

Cierra said, "So the change came instantly?"

Jenny said, "No, I was still doing what I wanted. The change came slowly. As days turned into weeks, weeks turned into months, and months turned into years, I started to change what I was doing. I started reading the Bible and praying. My mom and dad started seeing the change in me, and they even asked me about the change in my life. I told them that the change came after I accepted Jesus as my Savior. My dad said, 'What are you talking about?' I told him that a few years ago, after Tango died, I was walking in the park with Dave; and he was talking to me about the beauty. Also, he was talking about how we don't spend a lot of time getting to know our Creator. I said a lot of people are happy with the way their lives are going. Dave also told me that he knew I was thinking about committing suicide. My mother's eyes got big and she said, 'You wanted to commit suicide? Why?' I said I wanted to commit suicide because I was deeply depressed after the deaths of Uncle Joe and Tango. I was ready to end my life because I believed that there was nothing that could help me cope with my depression.

"I had just thought about it and decided to do it that day. Also, the crazy part is that I didn't tell anyone what I was going to do, but I did write a letter to my mom, and dad explaining why I was going to kill myself. When Dave told me everything that I had thought, I asked him how he knew what I was thinking and was planning on doing. He told me that Jesus told him everything. He also told Dave that I was planning on committing suicide that night, so He told him to come talk to me today because talking to me would save my life. Later on that day, he asked me if I wanted Jesus Christ as my personal Lord and Savior."

Cierra asked, "What happened after you told your parents that you had become a Christian?"

"My mom was sad, and my dad was mad and hurt. He told me to take it back. I told him that I'm not taking it back. I'm happier now than I've ever been in my life. Then he told me to take it back or I had to get out because Jesus isn't god, also there will be no religions, especially Christianity, in this house. I said okay, and I left."

Cierra said, "Where are you at now?"

"I'm back home," Jenny said. "I will tell you the rest of the story later." They ate lunch, then went to Cierra's house.

* * * * *

A month later, Jake spent the night at David's house. They were watching TV and clicking through the channels when they saw on the news that riots were breaking out in the city of Buffalo, New York. The news anchor said that buildings had been set ablaze along with vehicles. Also, stores had been looted and vandalized in which could be described as the worst riot in history, even worse than the riots in California during the 1960s. Thirty police officers had been critically injured or killed; four hundred people had been arrested, with three hundred sixty-six of them being adults and thirty-four of them being juveniles. Governor Austin had issued a state of emergency and declared martial law for the city and the entire state.

Also, Mayor Evans had declared a city-wide curfew starting the next day from 11:00 p.m. to 6:00 a.m. for the next two weeks or for as long as was needed to settle civil unrest in the city. David muted the TV and went to tell his mom what had happened. She said, "This is a sign that Jesus is coming back soon." Jake asked, "Is this a major sign?" David's mother said yes, then she grabbed her Bible, turned to **Matthew 24:6–8**, and read, "'And ye shall hear of wars and rumors of wars: see that your heart not be troubled: for all these things must come to pass, but the end is not yet. For nation shall rise against nation and kingdom against kingdom: and there shall be famines, and pestilences, and earthquakes in diverse places all these are the beginning of sorrows.' Our government and the governments of the world are losing trust in their people, and the people have lost faith in the police and other law enforcement officials." David's mother continued, "This is a crucial end-time prophecy. The people of the world are going to get so sick and tired of their elective officials letting them down that when the antichrist arrives after the rapture, they will follow him. When the antichrist arrives, he will speak to everyone as a friend. Also, he will tell the world that all those who were raptured when Jesus comes back were taken by UFOs or some other lie to cover up for the rapture. Next, he will gain control of the world through a false peace that promises world unity. When this happens, it's the beginning of the great tribulation."

Jake looked at David's mom and said, "Will the whole world follow the antichrist?"

She said, "Most of the world will follow the antichrist, but some people will know that he's the antichrist and will resist him. The antichrist will make it right and politically correct that anyone who will not follow him should be killed because they are being narrow-minded and are enemies of the state. During the tribulation, people will give their lives to Jesus, but most will be killed. That's why it's important for people to give their lives to Jesus now, not then."

Jake said, "How can a person become a Christian during the tribulation if all the Christians are raptured?"

David's mother said, "A person can become a Christian during the tribulation because of the 144,000 witnesses, and they will be responsible for bringing a multitude of people to Jesus during this time of great tribulation. As soon as these people accept Jesus as their Savior, the antichrist is going to kill most of them by cutting their heads off. Another thing I want to tell you is that after the rapture, everything that concerns the rapture and Jesus coming back will be hidden. The people of the world will also be told that evolution has happened and taken the people who have been raptured, and people will believe it, but it will be up to the Christians who get saved after the rapture to convince the world that Jesus has come back for those who have accepted Him as their personal Lord and Savior. Also, they will have to convince them that the man who comes to power after the rapture isn't the Savior of the world but the antichrist, the devil incarnate. After the antichrist comes to power and signs the seven-year peace treaty with Israel, he's going to have his officials attack different parts of the world, then he's going to blame it on the Christians and anybody who is against his regime."

David interrupted and said, "Wow, it's going to be the worst time in the history of mankind."

Jake said, "That's why it's important to tell people about Jesus now before it's too late and the rapture comes and a lot of people are left behind." Jake continued. "I want to start a website that will explain what salvation is, how to receive it, and why it's important to accept Jesus Christ as your Savior."

David said, "That's a great idea. We can reach the world without having to travel all over the world. Okay, let's eat, and over the next few days, we can figure out the format, the name, and ways we can link with other websites and other people to make our website stronger."

Jake said, "Okay," and asked David's mother, "What are we having for dinner?" She said, "We're having tacos." Jake and David helped her fix the tacos and then sat down and started eating. David said, "What do you want to call the website?"

Jake said, "I want to use a scripture for a name, and I want to use a scripture that's rarely known so that when people ask us what the scripture says, we can use it as a witness opportunity."

David said, "I don't know what scripture we can use as a name that most people don't know the meaning of. Mom, do you know what scripture we can use?"

She said, "I don't know right now, but I'm going to look through the Bible tonight, and I will have one for you tomorrow." After dinner, David and Jake went up to his room and started playing video games, talking about what kind of activities they were going to put on the website.

Jake suggested that they put trivia on the website so that people who had never heard of the Bible or anyone who's never read specific books in the Bible could learn. The website could also be a place for Christians to learn more or even ask for prayer. David said, "Everything you are suggesting is a good suggestion. Maybe Sunday we can ask Bishop Hardy if he has any suggestions for the website." They kept playing video games until about ten, then they went to bed. In the morning, they woke up and went downstairs to eat, and while they were eating, David's mother came down and said, "I prayed last night and asked the Lord for a scripture for you to use that will help bring more people to Jesus, and He came to me in a dream and said tell them to use **John 18:36**, which reads, 'Jesus answered, My kingdom is not of this world; if my kingdom were of this world, then would my servants fight, that I should not be delivered to the Jews; but now is my kingdom not from hence.'"

Jake said, "That's good. When someone asks us what the scripture means when we get the website up and running, we can tell them that it means Jesus's kingdom is not of this world but of heaven, and the only way a person can enter into heaven is to accept Jesus Christ as their Savior. I want to tell people who follow Chrislam that they are following a lie, and if they repent and accept Jesus Christ as their Savior, He will forgive them and forget that they ever committed the sins."

David said, "That's one of the things we can put on the website, how you accepted Jesus as your Savior." Jake said, "I didn't think about that. It will make our website more credible since we are making the website." David also said, "We can upload videos from people all over the world showing how God is moving all over the world." Jake said, "Yeah, we can do that, but also when we talk to Bishop Hardy, we can ask him if there is anything else missing or if there is anything he can add to make the website better." They finished their breakfast, then went outside to play.

Jake stayed over at David's house until Sunday, then went to church with David. Bishop Hardy was preaching about what was going to happen to people who take the mark of the beast and worship him, and what's going to happen to those who refuse the mark and refuse to worship the image of the beast. "When the antichrist forces the world to take the mark of the beast as prophesied in **Revelation 13:16–18**, millions all over the world will take the mark and worship the image of the beast." He continued, "A lot of people won't realize that taking the mark and worshipping the image of the antichrist will seal their fate. **Revelation 14:9–11** says, 'And the third angel followed them, saying with a loud voice, If any man worship the beast and his image, and receive the mark in his forehead or in his hand, The same shall drink of the wine of the wrath of God, which is poured out without mixture into the cup of his indignation; and shall be tormented with fire and brimstone in the presence of the holy angels, and in the presence of the Lamb. And the smoke of their torment ascendth up forever and ever and they have no rest day or night, who worship the beast and his image, and whosoever receiveth the mark of his name.' Also, the last seven of the twenty-one judgments and the first of the last twenty-one judgments will fall on everyone who has taken the mark and worshipped the image of the beast. **Revelation 16:1–2** says, 'And I heard a great voice out of the temple saying to the seven angels, Go your ways, and pour out the vials of the wrath of God upon the earth. And the first went and poured out his vial upon the earth, and there fell a noisome and grievous sores upon the men which had the mark of the beast, and upon them which worshipped his image.'

"Now that I've talked about what's going to happen to those who take the mark, I want to talk about those who refuse the mark. During the tribulation, there will be people who accept Jesus Christ as their Savior and refuse to follow the antichrist because they know that following him will mean complete damnation. Most of the people who become Christians during the tribulation will be killed by the antichrist. **Revelation 13:7** reads, 'And it was given to unto him to make war with the saints, and to overcome them: and power was given him over all kindreds, and tongues, and nations.' **Revelation 7:13–14** says, 'And one of the elders answered, saying unto me, What are these which are arrayed in robes? And whence came they? And I said unto him, Sir, thou knowest. And he said to me, these are they which came out of the great tribulation and have washed their robes, and made them white in the blood of the Lamb.' The last scripture I'm going to use is **Revelation 20:4**, which says, 'And I saw thrones, and they that sat upon them and judgment was given unto them: and I saw the souls of them that were beheaded for the witness of Jesus, and for the word of God, and which had not worshipped the beast, neither his image neither had received his mark upon their foreheads, or in their hands; and they lived and reigned with Christ for a thousand years.' The choice is yours to choose for Jesus Christ or the antichrist," Bishop Hardy said as he ended the service.

* * * * *

Even though Cody had promised to leave the gang life and to stop selling drugs, he kept selling drugs and stayed with the gang. The only difference was that now, he was sneakier with his activities. On June 30, he snuck out of Paul's house at 2:00 a.m. to meet with his gang. When Cody got to the meeting place, which was at an abandoned warehouse, the gang leader, Drake, walked up to Cody and gave him the drugs and a gun, then told him to go sell the drugs and bring him back the money tomorrow night at the same spot. Cody went to the corner of Cedar and started selling the drugs. Two hours later, some members of the rival gang, the Destiny Dragons, came to him, and they asked him, "What are you doing on our turf?" He said, "Your turf? This is our turf, and I'm not going anywhere until I'm done with my job."

One of the Destiny Dragons said, "No, you're leaving now," and the boy pulled out a gun. Cody pulled out his gun and said, "I'm not leaving." As both of them held their guns at each other, Paul came out of nowhere and said, "Stop it right now." Cody said, "Paul, what are you doing here, and how did you know where I would be?" Paul said, "I saw you leave the house, and I followed you to the warehouse, then I followed you here." Paul continued. "Now you have a choice. Put the gun down and come back home, or you can keep doing this. Choose now." Paul walked up to Cody, and as he got in front of Cody to take the gun away from him, the other two members of the Destiny Dragons started racing toward Cody. They tried to pull the gun away from him. The gun fired, and the bullet hit Paul in the chest. Paul grabbed his chest as he fell to the ground. Cody dropped his gun and put his hands on the wound to add pressure. He screamed, "Someone call 911! My brother has been shot! Someone help me."

A man was driving his car down the street when he saw Cody next to Paul. He stopped the car and said, "Hey, need some help?"

Cody said, "Yes, my brother has been shot." The man got out of his car and helped put Paul in the back seat. Cody got in the back as well as the man drove to the hospital. The man was driving sixty miles an hour trying to get Paul to St. Joel Memorial Hospital. When they arrived, Cody ran into the hospital and said, "I need a doctor right now. My brother has been shot in the chest. He needs help right now." The receptionist ran to the back and called out a doctor and nurses to come out ASAP. "We have a shooting victim in the lobby."

Two nurses ran out with a stretcher to get Paul. Another nurse walked up to Cody and asked what had happened and how he had gotten shot. Cody told her that he was selling drugs when three members from a rival gang came up to him and ordered him to leave. "And when I refused, one of them pulled a gun out on me, and I pulled my gun out on him. Paul followed me and was telling me to put the gun down. I was about to when the other two members jumped me. They were trying to get the gun away from me, and the gun went off, and Paul was shot in the chest."

The nurse said, "Okay, I'm going to go check on Paul. I will come out and update you on his condition." He asked the nurse if there was a phone he could use to call their parents. The nurse pulled her phone out and said, "Make it quick. I have to go check on Paul," and he said, "Okay." He called Paul's parents and told them that Paul had been shot in the chest. Paul's mother said, "How?" He said, "I can't tell you on the phone, but I will tell both of you when you get here." Paul's mother woke up her husband and told him what had happened. He asked her what hospital they were at, and she asked Cody. Cody told her that they were at St. Joel Memorial Hospital. She told Paul's father, and he told her to tell Cody that they were on their way.

Cody was nervous, stressed out, and hurt all at the same time. He was stressed out because he didn't know if Paul would die, and whether he would be going to jail. He was also worried whether Paul's parents would forgive him or not and whether his parents would put him out of their house. He was also hurt because he was trying to do better, and it blew up in his face. As he was thinking about all of this, Paul's parents came into the emergency room, and they said,

"Cody, what happened to Paul? How was he shot?" As Cody was about to answer, the nurse came up to them and said, "Paul has lost a lot of blood, so we had to transfuse him. Also, the pain was so severe that he's slipped into a coma after we did the surgery to remove the bullet." Paul's mother started crying as the father asked the nurse, "How long will he be in the coma?" She said, "I don't know, there's no timetable on how long he will be in the coma." Paul's mother stopped crying and said, "Can we see him?" She said yes, and Cody said, "Can I see him too?" and she said yes.

Paul's parents and Cody followed the nurse to Paul's room. He was in room 116. When they entered the room, Paul was lying in the bed, not moving. His mother started crying again, and seeing the tears coming from her eyes made Cody start crying. He said, "It's all my fault that he's in a coma." Paul's mother said, "What are you talking about?" He said, "Paul was shot because he was trying to talk some sense into me. A while after I moved in with you, I got tired of you taking care of me. I started selling drugs to make money so I wouldn't have to rely on you to provide for me. I also joined a gang so that I could have protection just in case someone tried to rob me or threatened to kill me. Paul was shot because I snuck out of the house around 2:00 a.m., and Paul followed me. Three people from a rival gang called Destiny Dragons appeared and surrounded me. One of the gang members told me to leave, and I told them that I wasn't going to leave until I was done. Then he pulled a gun on me, and I pulled my gun on him. Paul saw me holding my gun, ready to shoot, and he walked over to me and told me to put the gun down and come home. Also, he wasn't going to tell you what I was doing. He got right in front of me and began to lower my gun when the other two members of the rival gang rushed me. We were fighting over the gun, and it went off and shot him. Also, this isn't the first time he's busted me selling drugs. A few weeks ago, he told me that Jesus had told him that I was selling drugs and where I was selling the drugs. He also told me that Jesus told him that I was in a gang. I told him that I was going to stop, but I started being even sneakier with it."

Paul's mother said, "We let you come into our home, and we treat you like family, and this is how you treat us." She continued.

"Because of you, we might lose our son." As they were talking, the police came into the room and said, "Are you Cody Miller?" Cody said, "Yes, I'm him." Then the police said, "Put your hands behind your back. You are under arrest for the shooting of Paul Brown." The cop continued. "You have the right to remain silent. Anything you say can and will be used against you in a court of law. If you can't afford an attorney, one will be appointed to you by the state. Do you understand these rights as I have read them to you?" Cody said, "Yeah."

As they were taking him away, Paul's mother and father both said, "You can't take him. We have decided not to press charges against him." The cop said, "Okay," and left the room. Cody looked confused. He looked at Paul's parents and said, "Why didn't you let them arrest me?"

Paul's father said, "We believe in second chances. Plus, we forgive you for shooting Paul, just like Jesus forgives us for our sins. Also, we wanted to show you the love that only faith in Jesus Christ can give you." Cody started to cry, and he said, "I don't know what to say. I don't deserve your love and forgiveness, especially because I might have cost you your son's life." Paul's mother joined in, saying, "Can I pray for you?" He said yes, and she started praying. "Lord Jesus, we thank You for bringing Cody into our lives. We thank You for our son, Paul, and the years that You have blessed us with him. Lord, we pray that You bring Paul out of this coma, but if it's Your will that our son is to be called home, then we accept this as Your will." Paul's father took over. "Lord, we pray that Cody will forgive himself for what he's done, and we pray that he will accept You as his personal Lord and Savior. We pray that he will change his life around and serve You. Also, we pray that if it's Your will that Paul lives, please let this be a miracle so great that the doctors and nurses will give their lives to you, in Jesus's name, amen."

Cody was overwhelmed by emotion. He walked outside into the hall and thought to himself, *How can they forgive me after I shot, and possibly killed, their son? Plus, they are showing me tremendous love.* And he thought, *I know now what I must do.* He walked back into Paul's room and said, "How's he doing?" Paul's mother said he was still in a coma. Cody sat down and said, "I have something to tell you." Both Paul's parents said, "What?" Cody said, "Whether Paul recovers or not, I'm leaving." The mother said, "Why?" He said, "I've caused you too much pain and heartache, and I don't deserve your love and forgiveness, so I'm leaving." The father said, "If he doesn't make it, we want you to stay with us, and if he does make it, we want you to stay with us. You are a part of the family now. You're his brother." Cody said, "Well, if I'm his brother, I'm a bad brother. My stupidity has put my brother in the hospital."

"Everything will be all right. We don't have to worry because everything is in God's hands." The doctor came in and said, "Has there been any movement since the last time I came in?" The mother said no, and the doctor said, "I want you to know that we are doing everything in our power to see that he comes out of this coma." The mother said, "Okay," and started praying again, saying, "Lord Jesus, even though we believe that everything is in Your control, we ask that You do a miracle, and our son comes out of this coma with no problems, in Jesus's name, amen." Cody said, "Jesus, please bring him out of this coma. If You do, I will serve You. In Jesus's name, amen."

* * * * *

The war between CROWN and the Ultimate Light continued. The Ultimate Light gained ground in schools around the city thanks to the merger of the two groups, the Light and No Light. Even though Jason and Rick were the overall leaders of the Ultimate Light group, they appointed subleaders to run the groups at the other schools. The Ultimate Light took majority control of two schools, which made Jason very happy. He said, "At this rate, we will have more schools under our control in no time." Chris and his CROWN group were expanding too. He was also appointing subleaders to run and expand the CROWN group. A few days later, the subleader of the George Washington Middle/High School group reported to Chris that the majority of the school had fallen to the Ultimate Light group. Chris said, "We must redouble our efforts to bring more people to Jesus." The subleader said, "What will you have us do, sir?" Chris said, "I don't know yet. First, I have to pray and ask the Lord what to do, and whatever He tells me to do, I will do it."

The subleader said, "Okay." Chris asked him what his name was, and he said, "My name is Zack." Chris said, "Zack, I thank you for stepping up and taking charge of the CROWN group at the George Washington Middle/High School," and Zack said, "It's my pleasure. Also, it's my pleasure to serve our Lord and Savior Jesus Christ because He is the King of kings and the Lord of lords." Chris said, "Yes, amen." Chris went home and started praying. He said, "Lord Jesus, we want to bring more people to You. We are doing everything in our power to bring more people to You, but this atheist group is trying to permanently rid the school of You. Please tell us what to do. In Jesus's name, amen." The same night, Chris had a dream in which the Lord Jesus gave him the answer to his prayer.

Monday, Chris called for a meeting after school in room 408. After class, all the members of CROWN attended the meeting. When everyone was in the room, Chris came up to the podium and said, "Welcome to CROWN. For those who are here for the first time or those who have been here but don't know what CROWN stands for, it stands for Christ Rules Our World Now. Yesterday, I found out that the Ultimate Light have taken majority control of a bunch of schools around the city. The only school where CROWN has majority control is Jackie Robinson Middle/High School. I prayed last night and asked the Lord what to do to bring more people to Him. When I went to sleep, the Lord came to me in a dream, and He told me, 'I've given you everything that you need to bring more people to Me. All you have to do is use what I've given you.'"

Chris continued. "What we are going to do is have a convention and some workshops in order to bring more people to Jesus and show people the love of Jesus. The workshops will be for people who are saved and who want to learn how to bring more people to Jesus. The convention will be a three-day convention. People who have never heard of Jesus will be able to know about Him, even people who have heard about Him or have backslidden."

Zack said, "That sounds like a good idea," and he asked the other members of CROWN what they thought. Everyone agreed that it was a good idea. Zack said, "Let's plan it for two months from today. Today is June 22. We will have the convention on August 22. Before we dismiss, let's pray. Lord Jesus, thank You for allowing us to come together to praise Your name. Thank You for helping us to come up with a plan to bring more people to You. In Jesus's name, we pray. And we thank You, Lord. Amen."

Jason went to Rick's house. They were coming up with plans to finally crush Christianity and CROWN for good. One thing he suggested was sending a spy into CROWN. "Once the spy gets into CROWN, the person will gain their trust and rise up in the ranks. Then that person will send us their plans and secrets in order for us to crush them." Rick said, "Okay, I will do it." Jason said, "No, you can't do that. They know you are loyal to the Ultimate Light and that neither you nor I will ever desert the group. Let's send in the vice president to infatuate their group. We will destroy them from the inside." Jason called Tommy and asked him to come over. When Tommy got there, Jason said, "We want you to infatuate CROWN and bring them down from the inside." Tommy said, "No, I don't want anything to do with that group, and I don't want to become corrupt, like Julia did, and betray you."

Rick said, "Who is Julia?" Jason responded, "Julia was my predecessor as leader and founder of the No Light group. She turned on No Light to join CROWN, and now she's the third highest-ranked member of that group." Jason said, "As long as you stay loyal to the Ultimate Light, you won't be corrupted. What do you say?" He put out his hand. Tommy thought about it for a second, then shook Jason's hand. Rick said, "You have made the right choice by doing this. Also, to keep this legit in front of everybody else, we're going to strip you of your vice president status, but you will still be vice president behind the scenes. Another thing is that in order to convince them that you are one of them, you will have to start going to church, reading the Bible, and praying in front of them. Lastly, we are going to figure out a way to exile you from the group publicly, so that they will believe that you are one of them."

Tommy said, "How will I be able to prove to them that I'm on their side?" Jason pulled out the Bible that he had found on the ground out of his book bag, and he said, "Here, take this." He handed the Bible to Tommy. Tommy took the Bible and asked him where he got it. Jason said, "I found it on the ground when I was on my way home. I kept it in case I ever needed it for something, and now I have a reason to use it. We're going to destroy CROWN and Christianity with their own Bible." Tommy said, "Okay, and what I am going to do is I'm going to come into the school reading the Bible, and you are going to see me reading, and you will confront me and take the Bible out of my hand and ask me what I am doing. I'm going to tell you, then you will get so furious that you will say, 'You are hereby stripped of your position as vice president, and you're kicked out of the Ultimate Light.'" Jason said, "Lastly, you're going to say, 'I don't care because I found the truth, and the truth is that Jesus is God, and He's the only way to heaven.' Then you are going to find Cody, Chris, and Julia, and ask them where the meeting place is at. Go join them. Lastly, you're not going to meet with us for at least a month."

Tommy said, "Why can't I meet with you for at least a month?" Rick said, "You can't meet with us because if one of them follows you to one of our homes, they will know that you are faking." Tommy said, "Okay," and left. Jason said, "Now begins the fall of CROWN and the fall of Christianity." He and Rick got some pop, and they said, "All we have to do now is wait until our plans manifest and succeed." Then they went to Rick's room and went to bed. Jason stayed at Rick's house until Monday, and when he woke up, he said, "It's time to execute the plan."

When he got to school, he saw Tommy reading the Bible that he had given him, and he said, "What are you doing?" and Tommy said, "I'm reading the Bible. I'm a Christian now." Jason said, "What? You are the vice president of the Ultimate Light. You can't turn your back on us." Tommy said, "Well, I have, and now I'm going to join Chris's group CROWN."

Jason said, "Tommy, you are hereby stripped of your rank of vice president, and you are hereby exiled from the Ultimate Light." Tommy said, "I don't care about being stripped of my rank and exiled. I'd rather be in CROWN and know the truth than to be in the Ultimate Light, be the vice president, and be in a group that's a lie." Jason said, "Tommy, you will regret turning on the group," and Tommy said, "I will regret nothing." Then he left.

Tommy went looking for Chris all over the school. He found him outside reading, and he said, "Chris, I've been looking for you everywhere," and Chris said, "Why, what's up?" Tommy said, "I've defected from the Ultimate Light, and now I want to join your group, CROWN. I want to fight alongside you to help preach the gospel of Jesus Christ, and I want to learn more about being a Christian. Can I join your group?" Chris said, "Yeah, come to room 308 after school is over." As Tommy left, he said, "The plan is working. Soon the Ultimate Light will destroy the CROWN group, and we will destroy Christianity, then the schools and the city will be a better place."

After class, Tommy went to room 308. He saw Chris and said, "Hey, Chris." Chris said, "Hey, Tommy, are you ready to go inside?" and he said, "Yeah." Chris opened the door, and Tommy went inside and sat down. Chris got in front of the room and said, "I would like to welcome everyone to CROWN, and I especially would like to welcome the newest member of CROWN, Tommy, a former member of the Ultimate Light." Then Chris said, "Tommy, what did you do in that group?"

He said, "I was the vice president of the Ultimate Light."

Chris said, "How did you find Jesus?"

"Well, I had heard you saying that Jesus is God and that He was the only way to heaven, but I thought it was propaganda, and that you, and every other Christian, wanted to brainwash me into believing whatever you all believed. Well, a few days ago, I asked the Lord to show Himself to me. I said, 'Jesus, if You are real, please show Yourself to me. Also, if You do, I will follow You for the rest of my life.' Two days later, I had just woken up when there was a big bright light, and the light was so bright that I had to cover my eyes. The next thing I heard was 'Tommy, Tommy,' and I answered, 'Who's there?' The voice said, 'I am Jesus, the maker of heaven and earth. I am He who was, is, and is to come. I am the first and the last.' At that moment, I got down on my knees, and I said, 'Lord, what must I do to be saved?' He said, 'Believe in Me, and you will be saved.' Then

He disappeared. After He disappeared, I cried out for Jesus to save me, and He did."

Chris walked over to him and hugged him, and he said, "I'm happy that you have found the light and accepted Jesus Christ as your personal Lord and Savior." Tommy said, "I am too." Chris said, "I have an announcement. In two months, Cody and I will be having a convention and a workshop. The workshop will be for the people who are saved and want to know how to bring more people to Jesus, and the convention is designed to bring more people to Jesus. It will be a three-day convention." Tommy said, "Perfect. This will work out perfectly."

CHAPTER

8

I was in my room reading the Bible. I was reading **1 Corinthians 2:9**, which says, "But as it is written, Eye hath not seen, nor ears heard, neither have it entered into the heart of man the things which God hath prepared for them that love him." When I finished reading that, I went to **Galatians 2:20**, which read, "I am crucified with Christ: nevertheless, I live, yet not I, but Christ lives in me: and the life which I now live in the flesh I live by the faith of the son of God, who loved me, and gave himself for me." I closed my Bible and got on my knees and said, "Lord Jesus, I thank You for dying for me. I'm sorry that I've sinned against You, and I thank You for saving me. Also, Lord, I ask You to save my brother and my family. I want them to go with me to heaven. In Jesus's name, I pray, amen."

When I was done praying, I turned on the TV. My parents walked into my bedroom and asked me what I was doing. I said, "I'm watching TV, then I'm going to bed." They said okay, and as they were closing the door, William came into the room and said, "Daniel is on the phone for you." I went downstairs to get the phone. When I said hello, Daniel said, "Hey, Antowon, how are you doing?" I replied, "I'm doing good. What about you, Daniel?" And Daniel said, "I'm doing good. I was calling to let you know that we have a meeting tomorrow, but it will take place at my house instead of school." I said okay, then I said, "Daniel, pray for my brother and my parents that they see the light and accept Jesus as their Savior."

Daniel said, "I will. And now I have to go. I will talk to you later. Bye." I went back to my room and saw that William was watching TV, and he said, "What did Daniel want?" I said, "He wanted to let me know that we have a meeting tomorrow at his house instead of at school." William said, "What time is the meeting?" I said, "I don't know. I'll ask him tomorrow, and I will drop you off here before I go." William said, "No, I want to go with you." I said, "I'm happy that you want to go with me, but why do you want to?" He said, "You might have turned against our religion, and you might be hiding it from our parents, but beyond all of that, at the end of the day, you are still my brother, and I'm going to stick by you no matter what." Then William hugged me. I said, "Okay, well, I'm going to sleep, but you can watch TV until you are ready to go to bed or you can crash in here if you fall asleep," and he said okay. As I went to sleep, I prayed that William would get saved and that these meetings he was going to would change his heart for the better. Then I closed my eyes and went to sleep.

The next day at school, I met up with Daniel, and he asked me how my weekend was, and I said it was good. I asked, "What's this meeting at your house going to be about?" Daniel said, "My church is planning a retreat for next week, and we want you to come." I replied, "What will we be doing at the retreat? Also, how much is the retreat going to cost?" Daniel said, "The retreat is free. Our church has raised the money for forty people to go, and so far, including me, Jasmine, Brittany, and Eric, we have thirty-eight people attending the retreat. We have room for only two more, and I told my pastor about you. And he told me to ask if you and William wanted to go, and if you said no, he was going to ask two other teenagers to go. So are you in or out?" I said, "Yeah, I'm in. After school and before the meeting, I'm going to ask William if he wants to go." Daniel said, "Okay, and to answer the second part of your question about what we will be doing at the retreat, one of the things that I know we will be doing is having Bible study. Also, we will be staying in lodges, so

I guess we will be going swimming and eating s'mores, among other things."

I said, "Okay, I will see you at the meeting." The only thing I could think about was the retreat and how being among thirty-eight believers would be a small taste compared to the billions of believers that I would see once I was in heaven.

When my final class was over, I went all over the school looking for William, and when I found him, I asked if he was ready to go to the meeting, and he said, "Yeah." Once we were in the car, I started talking and asking him how his last class was, and he said, "Good," then asked me how my last class was, and I said it was good. I continued. "I saw Daniel, and he told me a little about what the meeting is going to be about. He told me that his church is having a retreat next week, and he asked me if I wanted to go." William said, "What did you tell him?"

"I told him yes, I'm going, and he asked me to ask you if you want to come too." William said, "I will think about it, but I'm not making any promises," and I said, "Fair enough, but let me know by Thursday, so I can let Daniel know," and he said, "Okay." I continued, "I can't wait to go. Being around thirty-eight believers will be a small taste compared to the billions or trillions of people praising the name of Jesus in heaven." William said, "Bro, I have a question to ask you." I said, "What's the question?" He said, "What made you become a follower of Jesus Christ?" I said, "As a Muslim, I was never happy. I always felt like something was missing. I always felt empty, and when I heard Daniel, Eric, Brittany, and Jasmine talking about the love of Jesus, and how He died for me, and that He was willing and wanted to forgive me for my sins, I realized that I had finally found what I was missing, and now I have peace. It's a peace that I can't explain. What do you say, bro? Will you accept Jesus Christ as your Savior and embrace unconditional love and peace?" He said, "I don't know, bro. Give me time to think about it," and I said, "Okay." When we reached Daniel's house, we got out of the car and saw that Daniel, Eric, Brittany, and Jasmine were waiting for us. When they saw us, they embraced us. They asked us how we were doing, and we told them that we were doing well. Then Daniel said, "Let's go inside the house so we can have this meeting." And everybody walked into his house and into Daniel's room.

Once everybody had sat down, Daniel prayed, "Lord Jesus, first of all, we thank You for being God. Also, we thank You for the opportunity to bring more people to You, and we also thank You for allowing Antowon and William the opportunity to be in your presence, and for them to learn more about You. Lastly, we pray that William will give his life to You and serve You. In Jesus's name, we pray. And we thank You, Lord. Amen." Eric turned to William and asked if he would be going to the retreat, and William said, "Yes, I will go, because I promised Antowon that I would have his back until the end, and I intend to keep my promise." Jasmine said, "How you are going to get permission to go on the retreat since it's a Christian event?" William said, "I'm going to tell our parents that we are going to spend the weekend with Daniel and his parents, then we will go on the retreat. Our parents don't know that any of you are Christians, which is a good thing, because if they found out that Antowon has been hanging out with Christians, and he's a Christian now, they would probably kill him or disown him or arrange to have him killed."

They all looked at each other and agreed they wouldn't let anything happen to Antowon. Brittany chimed in and said, "Also bring your Bibles and any games that you have, board games or cards or anything like that, but don't bring your video games because we don't want anything to happen to them." And everyone shook their heads.

I raised my hand and said, "Is the meeting over?" Daniel said, "It will be in a minute. Jasmine is about to close us out in prayer. Why?" I said, "I'm hungry, and if all of you are up to it, we can hop into my car and go out to eat, and I will pay for it." Everyone said okay, and Jasmine said, "Everyone please bow your head," and she prayed, "Lord Jesus, thank You for everything that You have done in our lives in the past. We are eagerly anticipating a great move from You this weekend. I pray that we all get to where we are going to eat and get home safely and that we will be ready to see what You are going to do this weekend. In Jesus's name, amen."

After we prayed, everybody got into the car, and we went to the Grill to eat. We sat down, and the waiter came and took our orders. I got a triple cheeseburger with french fries, cheese sauce, and a milkshake. William ordered a veggie burger and some fries, Daniel ordered a double cheeseburger and some fries, Eric ordered a cheeseburger and some fries, Brittany ordered some chicken tenders with barbecue sauce and honey mustard, and Jasmine ordered a hamburger with only mustard. While we were waiting for our food, Jasmine said, "While we wait for our food, how about we have some Bible study?" and everyone said okay. She turned to William and said, "Do you know how we know that Jesus is coming back soon?" and he said no. She opened her Bible to **2 Timothy 2:3** and read, "'People will be lovers of themselves, lovers of money, boastful, proud, abusive, disobedient to their parents, ungrateful, and unholy.' Also, there are other signs that He's coming back. There's violence on every continent, famines, pestilences, and earthquakes everywhere, and there have been a lot of revolutions against governments, and also people are going to turn against God. Another sign is that people are going to get so sick and tired of their government officials lying to them and letting them down that they are going to turn to the antichrist, and he's going to be the biggest deceiver of them all.

"After the rapture, the entire world will be in chaos, and the world will be looking for a leader that can unite a shattered world politically, military, and economically, and he will appear to be a savior, but he will be the evilest person in the history of mankind." Jasmine continued, "He will unite the world under a one world government, one world currency, and a one world religion, and he will make a seven-year peace treaty with Israel, but he will break it in three and a half years, and this treaty will begin the tribulation. In the first three and a half years, he will solve world problems, and the world will follow him, and the Jews will call him the messiah. Most of the world will follow the antichrist, but some people will know that following will mean that they will lose their soul."

William said, "What will happen next?"

"After the first three and a half years, a Jew is going to find out who the antichrist is and what he's really about, and he will shoot him in the head and kill him. After three days, Satan will indwell inside of him, and he will rise from the dead." As Jasmine was talking, the food came, and before we ate, we prayed. Then we smashed the food, and I took everyone home. When we got home, I went to my room and turned on the TV, and as I was going through the channels, I saw on the news that a tsunami had hit China and that over a million people had been killed, and millions more were injured and homeless. I went on the Internet and searched for scriptures on natural disasters, and **Luke 21:25–26** popped up on the screen. I clicked on the link and read, "And there shall be signs in the sun, and in the moon, and in the stars; and upon the earth distress of nations, with perplexity; the seas and the waves roaring. Men's hearts failing them for fear, and looking after those things which are coming on the earth: for the powers of heaven shall be shaken."

I sat back and said, "Wow, we are very close to the return of Jesus." I closed the window on my computer and called William to the room, and when William came, I told him, "Look at what's happened in China." The man on the news repeated what I had heard thirty minutes ago. "A major tsunami has just rocked China, and over a million people are dead. Also, millions of people are injured and are left homeless." He continued, "We will give you more information on the aftermath of this disaster as we receive them. This is Ben Hagee with CCN, the Christian Channel Network." I turned the TV off and asked William what he thought about this. He said, "I think that it's tied to your Bible and one of the signs that Jesus is coming back, according to what you have told me." I said, "It's true. Things are going to get worse. That's why I've been telling you to accept Jesus as your Savior." William said, "I'm still struggling between what you have told me and what's in the Quran." I said, "Bro, I'm not going to force you to accept Jesus as your Savior, and neither is He. I'm going to let you decide, but let's change topics to what we are going to do this weekend at the retreat. I'm planning on making new friends and getting stronger in the Lord. What about you, bro?"

He said, "I'm going into unfamiliar territory. I know a little about the Bible from what you and your friends have told me." I went and grabbed my Bible, gave it to William, and said, "Take it. I will get another one from Daniel, or I will buy another one." William hesitated, and he said, "Bro, this feels like I'm betraying everything I know," and I said, "Just take it. You don't have to read it. I just want you to have it as a gift from your brother, as a gesture of good faith." William took the Bible and put it in his room. When he came back, I hugged him, and he said, "Why are you hugging me?" I said, "I'm hugging you because you are my brother, and I want the best for you and our parents. I found the truth, and I want everyone to know the truth." William said, "I appreciate that, bro. I will think about it." I said, "Okay," and we started playing video games.

* * * * *

When the girls got to Cierra's house, they went to Cierra's room. In her room, Cierra asked Jenny how she got back to her parent's house. She said, "After my dad kicked me out, I went to stay with Dave and his parents, and they welcomed me with open arms, and I was happy. Two months later, my mom called me, and she said that she wanted to talk to me. I said okay, let's meet in the park. When we got to the park, my mother said, 'I talked to your father, and he said that you can come back. But you have to renounce this myth about Jesus being God and renounce your Christianity.' I said, 'No, I'm not going to renounce my Christian faith, and I'm not going to renounce Jesus Christ as Savior.' Mom said, 'Why won't you renounce your faith?' I said, 'After everything that's happened with me being depressed and about to commit suicide, Jesus saved my life, and He gave me something that I never really had—happiness.' I continued and said, 'Mom, I want you to do something for me. I want you to go home tonight and pray, and I want you to call out to Jesus, and say, If You are God, show Yourself to me, and prove to me that You are the only true God, and He will do it. Mom said okay, then I said, 'Meet me here in a few days or in a week to tell me what happened,' and I left."

Cierra said, "What happened next?"

"After I talked to my mom, I went back to Dave's house, and I was praying. I cried out, 'Lord Jesus, I want my parents to give their lives to You, and I want to be able to go home again, and I want to be able to sleep in my bed again. In Jesus's name I pray, and I thank You, Lord. Amen.' Well, a month had passed, and I still hadn't heard anything from my mom. I started to lose hope that I was going to hear from her and that maybe I pushed her too hard when my cell phone rang, and it was my mom. She told me to meet her at the park ASAP. I got my clothes on and went to the park. When I got there, my mom was already there waiting for me. When she saw me, she ran up to me and hugged me. I said, 'You seem very happy,' and she said, 'I have done something that I thought I would never do. I've given my life to Jesus and have accepted Him as my personal Lord and Savior.' I said, 'What happened?' She said, 'Once I got home, I thought about doing what you asked me, and I didn't, but I couldn't shake the feeling. I tried everything to get rid of the feeling, but I couldn't. Well, two weeks later, I got down on my knees, and I said, "Jesus, if You are the Savior of the world, and You are the one true God, send me a sign and prove to me that I need You, and I will follow You." Three weeks passed, and I didn't see any signs, and I thought that my prayer was going unanswered when something happened. A bright light shone in my room, and the light was so bright that I had to close my eyes, and I said, "Who are you?" A voice said, "I'm the Alpha and the Omega, the Beginning and the End, the First and the Last. I am Jesus Christ, the Savior of the world." Terrified, I said, "What do You want from me?" Jesus replied, "I died for you, and I want you to put your faith in Me. I want to forgive your sins. Will you put your trust in Me?" I said, "Yes, I will put my faith and trust in You, and I accept You as my personal Lord and Savior." He replied, "Today, you have become My daughter, and as of today, you will be with Me in paradise," then He disappeared.'

"I said, 'Your testimony is amazing. What did Dad say when he found out that you're a Christian?' She said, 'He was furious. He told me that I've become weak and that he didn't want to see me become weak. I said it's not weak to follow Jesus. It's weak to see that He's God and ignore it, but it takes strength to embrace Jesus as God, and now that I've found happiness, I wouldn't trade it for anything in the world.' She continued, 'He told me that I can stay a Christian, but I better not try to force anything on him, and I said I won't, but I said I was going to pray for him, and I hoped he gives his life to Jesus. He said, "You can keep your prayers to yourself. I will never give in to weakness and accept your religion. I'm doing fine on my own. I'm a self-made man." I said, "I'm still going to pray for you," and he said, "If that's going to make you feel better, then do it." I also told him that you are coming back home and that I didn't care about what he said, and he said okay."

"I started crying, and Mom asked me what was wrong, and I said, 'I was praying, asking the Lord to make a way for me to get back into the house because I wanted to sleep in my bed again. Also, I asked Him to save both of my parents, and He saved you. He answered my prayers again.' Mom said, 'When are you coming home?' I said, 'I will be home in two weeks. I want to spend two more weeks with Dave and his family because I've grown a lot as a Christian. Plus, we have plans for the next two weeks including going out of town for a retreat. We are going to Washington for a week, then were going to Philadelphia because Dave and his family always go on a trip once a year, and they want me to go, and I told them that I would go.' Mom said, 'Okay, well, I will see you once you return.' Once I got back to Dave's house, I told him and his parents the good news about going home. Dave's parents were happy for me, but Dave wasn't happy. He left and went to his room."

Cierra said, "All of this happened to you? What happened between you and Dave when he left?"

She said, "I saw him leave, and I followed him. When I got to the door, I heard him crying, saying, 'I don't want her to leave. I've fallen in love with her since she became a Christian, and my love for her has intensified when she moved in with us.' I knocked on the door, and Dave turned on the TV and said, 'Come in.' I went in and asked him what he was doing. He said, 'I'm watching football.' I sat down on his bed and said, 'How do you feel about me going back home?' He said, 'That's good. I know you have been missing your family for a long time, and I'm happy that your mother gave her life to Jesus. Also, I hope your father gives his life to Jesus because we all need Him.' I said, 'I hope so too.' After about ten minutes of watching TV, I went into my room and started crying."

Cierra said, "Why didn't you tell him that you heard him say that he loved you?"

She said, "I want him to tell me when he's ready. Plus, I don't want to rush him into telling me, I turn him off, and he will resent me for it. A few days later, we went to Washington, and that was the most exciting time I ever had. While we were in Washington, we decided to walk around the city and see how nice the city was, and while we were walking, we heard screaming and gunshots, and we saw people running, but we didn't run. Instead of running, we walked up to where the shooting was taking place. Some people were grabbing us, telling us to stay away, but we kept walking, and when we finally got to where the shooting was taking place, the man had just stopped shooting.

"Dave asked the man why he was shooting people, and he said that he was shooting people because he was tired of people disrespecting him and making fun of him, then he told us to leave or he would kill us. I continued, 'You don't have to do this. You have so much more that you can do than this. Do you know Jesus?' He said, 'No, I don't, and this is your last chance to leave or I'm going to kill you, and I'm serious.' I said, 'What's your name?' and he said, 'My name is Sam. What's yours?' I said, 'My name is Jenny, and this is my brother, Dave. Now back to my question. Do you know Jesus?' Sam said, 'No, I don't know anything about him.' Dave said, 'He died on the cross for your sins, and He wants you to put your faith and trust in Him, and He wants to be your personal Lord and Savior. Will you accept Him as your personal Lord and Savior?'

"Sam said, 'Give me a few minutes to think about it.' We waited for about ten minutes, then he said, 'I want to give my life to Jesus. I want to make Him my personal Lord and Savior.' Dave and I were happy, then we grabbed each other's hand. Sam put his gun down and grabbed my hand, and I said, 'Repeat after me. Lord Jesus, Savior of the world, You died for me, You were beaten for me. I ask You to come into my heart and be my Savior. Forgive me of all my sins. I pray this in Jesus's name, amen.'"

Cierra said, "What happened after that?"

Jenny said, "As soon as we finished praying, the police came flying as fast as they could to where the shooting had taken place. They came out of their cars drawing their guns, and they told all of us to freeze, then one of the officers said, 'Who's the person that was shooting?' Everybody looked at each other, then Dave said, 'It was me. I was the one shooting.' Then Sam said, 'No, it wasn't him. It was me. I was the one shooting, but these teenagers talked me into putting my gun down, then they led me to Jesus Christ.' Another officer said, 'It's good that you have come to know Jesus as your Savior. I'm a Christian myself, but we still have to arrest you for disturbing the peace and shooting a weapon in public.'

"I stepped in front of Sam and said, 'No, don't arrest him. He didn't kill anyone. Yeah, he was shooting, but no one was injured.' Sam moved me out of the way and said, 'It's alright. I have to pay for what I did, but when I get out, everything will be different, and I have you and Dave to thank for it. You two have truly changed my life for the better, and I thank you for it.' I said, 'You're welcome. I expect great things from you,' and he said, 'I will make you proud of me.' Dave said, 'I know you will,' then the police took him away."

Cierra said, "How did that make you feel about Sam being taken away?"

"I was hurt seeing him being taken away, but I was happy that Sam gave his life to Jesus, and that once he was released from jail, he would turn his life around. After we left Washington, we went to Philadelphia for the rest of our trip, and we went to this restaurant that sold Philly cheesesteak sandwiches. That was the best sandwich I've ever had. I even brought some of them home." Jenny continued. "I'm still praying for you, that you will accept Jesus Christ as your personal Lord and Savior."

Cierra said, "I'm doing just fine, but I'm happy that you are praying for me. I really appreciate it." Jenny said, "You're welcome. I have to go home now. I will see you tomorrow." Cierra said, "Okay," then she left. Cierra was still thinking about everything Jenny had said. Jenny had gone up against a gunman, and the gunman didn't kill them or even try to shoot them.

* * * * *

Jake and David finished their website, and they were proud of the hard work they had done. They even went to church and showed their pastor, and he approved and said that he was going to make an announcement on Sunday to the congregation. Also, he was going to talk to the youth pastor, and he was going to tell him to make an announcement too. David said, "Thank you, Bishop Hardy," and he said, "You're welcome. Also if you need any assistance now or in the future, please let me know."

They went to David's house and to David's room, and they started praying. Jake started the prayer. "Lord Jesus, first, we acknowledge and thank You for being God. We are praying and asking You to do what You want to do with our website." David started praying. "Lord, we know that You will use the website for Your glory, and we know that people's lives will be changed. Also, we know that people will give their lives to You through this site. We pray this in Jesus's name, and we thank You, amen." Once they finished praying, they went on the Internet. They went to channel28news.com, and it said, "Breaking news: Egypt and Germany are officially in a civil war." David clicked on the link, and the article read, "What started off as peaceful protest in both countries have turned violent when military groups fired at Egyptian and German civilians, which prompted Egypt and Germans to return fire, killing eight militant soldiers and injuring three. Four soldiers and two civilians were killed. In Germany, ten militant soldiers were killed, and five were injured. Also, seven militant soldiers were injured and one was killed, and five civilians were killed. As I'm writing this, I'm getting word that more militant and military forces are clashing. Tune into Channel 28 News for the most updated coverage."

Jake said, "We're one step closer to World War III," and David said, "Yes, we are." Then he copied the link and posted it on their website. The next day at school, Jake and David were walking to class, talking about their website, when one of their friends walked up to them and asked how the website was going. Jake said, "Good. We are going to try to put a feature on there after we debut the site on Monday, and we are going to change the name to Christbook. It's going to be a site where Christians and non-Christians can upload videos and pictures, talk to one another, and just have a good experience. Also, we are going to upload articles and videos of breaking news and current events, so even if a person is busy or not at home, they can be up to date. And lastly, we are going to illustrate how current events have been predicted in the Bible." Jake asked the boy what he thought, and the boy said, "That sounds like a good idea." Jake said, "Thank you," then he and David went to class.

While they were in class, one of the students pulled out their cell phone and said, "A school in Nevada is being shot up right now." The teacher turned the TV on and put it on NNN, the National News Network. The reporter said that at exactly twelve o'clock eastern time, three o'clock central time, three gunmen entered Barack Obama High School and started opening fire inside the school. The police have surrounded the school, and dozens of students have been evacuated, but there are hundreds of students still inside the school."

The reporter continued. "As I'm talking, you can hear gunshots coming from the school. Also, there are rumors that at least a dozen people are dead and a few dozen are injured. We will keep everyone updated on this developing story as more information becomes available. Be sure to check NNN.com and the NNN app for the most up-to-date information." The reporter said, "One more thing I want to say: this is the worst school shooting in U.S. history. This is Rachel reporting from Barack Obama High School in Nevada. Now back to you, Carlos."

The teacher turned off the TV and said, "This is truly a sad day for America. It's sad that we are living in a time where people are so full of hate that they will kill innocent people instead of living in peace." David looked at Jake and said, "We are debuting the site tonight. After class, we're going to tell everyone about our site so we can start reaching more people for Jesus and warn people about what's about to happen so they can either accept Jesus as their Savior, or they can get prepared for the arrival of the antichrist, his false prophet, and his new world order." Toward the end of class, Jake and David tore pieces of paper, and they wrote, "If you want up-to-date information on current events and if you want to know how these events affect your life, go to Christbook.com." Then they put the papers in a bag and waited until class ended. Once it ended, they gave everyone the papers. When they got to Jake's house, they went to NNN.com and found the article about the shooting in Nevada. They uploaded the article to the site, then looked at how many people had made accounts for their site. Twenty out of the thirty people that had given flyers had made accounts on Christbook. Jake looked at David and said, "Not bad for our pre-debut, but we need more accounts. I want everyone to know what's going to happen in the future."

David said, "That's good, but we need to make a mission statement to let people know what we are about. How about this for a mission statement. 'At Christbook, we are determined to give you a pleasant experience and allow you to connect with people all over the city. Also, we want to update our site's current events and show how current events affect your lives. We want to show you how these events are connected to Bible prophecy. Signed Jake and David, co-owners of Christbook.'" Jake said, "I like that mission statement. Let's upload it to the site." David created a link called "About us" and typed in the mission statement on Christbook. David also said, "Let's put a link for suggestions on how to make the site better. Also, once we have the site down packed and working well, we can develop the Christbook app." Jake said, "Lastly, we can enable an option where people won't get notifications when we put articles on the site and on the app if they don't want it, and it won't appear on their page." Once David updated the site, he said, "That's enough for today. We can do more updates and promote our site tomorrow."

Jake turned the TV on and started going through the channels. He saw an update on the shooting in Nevada, and another reporter named Tommy from NNN was saying, "We can confirm that twenty-eight people have been killed, including twenty students and eight staff members. We also confirm that twenty-two people are injured in what is considered the greatest mass school shooting in U.S. history." Tommy continued, "From all of us here at NNN, we would like to give everyone our deepest sympathies during this time of mourning, and to let everyone know that we will be praying for you." Jake turned the TV off and said, "Let's pray. Lord Jesus, we know that You are still in control, and even though we don't understand why this happened, we still know that You are in control." David started praying, "Lord Jesus, we ask that You bring peace in this time of mourning and show them that You are still with them and that You will comfort them. We pray this in Jesus's name, amen."

The rest of the day, Jake and David played video games and watched movies. David's mom made tacos, and they ate, laughed, and had a good time. After dinner, David went home and went to bed. The next day, Jake checked Christbook and saw that ten more people had made accounts and were talking about the current events. Jake made a status on their official Christbook. The status read, "In the last days before Jesus returns, the whole world will be filled with violence, and no one will be safe. Also in the last days, things are going to get so bad that it's going to pave the way for the rise of the antichrist." Then he hit the publish button and got ready for school. When Jake got to school, he met with David, and David told him, "Some people are talking about our site, and they are telling their friends to make accounts on our site too." One of their classmates walked up to them and said, "I like that every time something major happens, you upload the events to the site so even if people aren't home, they can get the up-to-date news." David said, "Thank you. We do the best that we can, but we can always use more help if you would like to help and become an admin." He said, "Yeah," then Jake said, "When you get home, message me, and once we verify that it's you, we will put a check mark next to your name, and you will become an admin." The boy said, "Okay," and left.

Later at lunch, Jake and David were talking about ways to improve their site, and while they were talking, the same boy came and sat down, and he said, "I have two questions to ask you," and David said, "What are the questions?" The boy said, "Is there a way for people to post events as they actually happen? And also, is there a way for the site to automatically upload scriptures to encourage people, or when something happens in the world, can the site automatically upload to show how the current events prove that Jesus is coming and what's going to happen after the rapture?" David said, "No, but you just gave us some ideas that we can initiate to make our site better." David said, "You never told us your name." He said, "My name is Jack. I already sent you my Christbook account information so that when you get a chance, you can verify my account, I can become an admin, and we can expand the site." Jack continued, "I also think it's great that you are trying to warn people and reach people for Jesus." David said, "Thank you. We try our best. Our pastor is going to make an announcement on Sunday to our congregation to officially announce the debut of our site, but can you do us a favor?" Jack said, "Yeah, what is it?" David said, "Can you help spread the word about the site so more accounts will be made?" Jack said, "Yeah, no problem. I want more people to give their lives to Jesus, so I want as many people to come to this site as possible."

Jake said, "Thank you so much," and Jack said, "You're welcome." Jack, Jake, and David finished their lunch, then they went back to class. When they got to their history class, they studied the American Civil War and how the country was divided. Also how they were saying one thing but were doing the opposite. The teacher started talking. "The Civil War started because the North and the South were divided over the issue of slavery. The North believed that slavery was wrong, but the South believed slavery was right, and they believed that slavery was their only way to survive." She continued. "When Abraham Lincoln became President of the United States, the South seceded from the United States, which at the time was called the Union, to form the Confederate States of America. The Confederacy went to war with the Union from 1861 until 1865, when the Confederacy surrendered. The point I'm making is that the same division that existed during the Civil War exists today. As long as there are people on the planet, there will always be division."

As the teacher continued to talk, Jake turned to David and said, "If this country would turn to Jesus, then all of this division and hatred would be gone, because Jesus is the one person who can't disappoint." David said, "You're right, but this country doesn't want to follow Him. They want to do what they want, and that's the reason this country is in the shape it's in." After class, Jake went home, and David went home, and when Jake got home, he verified Jack's account, and Jack became a verified admin of Christbook. Later, he watched a little TV then went to bed.

That Sunday, Bishop Hardy talked about the shooting in Nevada and how in the last days, the whole world would be filled with violence. "**Matthew 24:37–39** says, 'But as in the days of Noah were; so shall also the coming of the Son of man be; For as in the days that were before the flood they were eating, and drinking, marrying and giving in marriage until the day Noah entered into the ark.'" As Pastor Hardy finished, he said, "I have an announcement. Jake and David have a website called Christbook. The site uploads videos and words of encouragement and also helps keep people up to date with the news, so check them out at Christbook.com." Jake and David looked at each other, proud of what they had accomplished. They prayed that this site would bring more people to Jesus, and they believed that it would.

* * * * *

A few weeks had passed, and Paul was still in a coma. The doctors had lost all hope that he was going to recover, but Cody and Paul's parents were praying and trusting Jesus was going to bring him out of the coma. The doctor came into Paul's room and talked to Paul's parents. "There's very little chance that Paul will come out of the coma, and even if he did, he would never make a full recovery, so it's in my expert opinion that you start making arrangements for him." The father said, "We appreciate everything that you have done, but we have faith that Jesus will bring him out of this, and even if He doesn't, we know that we will see him again in paradise." The doctor said, "It's good that you have this kind of faith. I wish all my patients had the kind of faith that both of you have." Paul's mother started talking. "We didn't get this faith overnight. We went through a lot of heartache and pain to get to this point, and we've seen God do miracles. I remember when I was very sick, and the doctor didn't know what was causing me to be sick. I was on the verge of dying, and I didn't think that I was going to be healed, but my husband believed, and he kept praying, and God healed me."

The doctor said, "Did anybody ever figure out what was making you sick?"

She said, "No, the doctor never figured out why I was sick, but that didn't matter. If God healed me when I was on death's doorstep, then He can bring my son out of this coma." As they were talking, the monitors started beeping, and everyone turned around. Paul opened his eyes. Paul's parents started crying, and they said, "We knew God was going to bring you out of this coma. All we had to do was pray and believe that He was going to do it."

As they were talking, Cody got up from his chair and started walking out of the room. Paul said, "Where are you going?" He said, "I'm leaving. I told your parents that whether you recovered or not, I was leaving because I caused you and your family too much grief, and after everything you've done for me, I don't deserve your love or forgiveness." Then Cody turned to leave. Paul got out of the hospital bed, walked over to Cody, and hugged him; he said, "I forgive you for shooting me. I know it was an accident. You were trying to put the gun down when those boys came rushing us, and the gun went off." Paul continued, "It would be an honor if you continued to stay with us, brother." Then he hugged Cody again. "I forgive you, just like Jesus forgives us of our sins, no matter if we do it intentionally or not. That's why my parents and I believe in Jesus. No matter how many times we mess up or fall short, Jesus still forgives us just like I forgive you."

Cody backed Paul up and said, "I don't know what to say. I shot you, and you almost died. I should be in jail for what I did to you." Paul screamed in pain and said, "It's all right. I'm going to live. The hardest part about forgiveness isn't God forgiving us. The hardest part is us forgiving ourselves." Paul's father started talking. "The reason it's hard for us to forgive ourselves is that we remember what we have done wrong, but Jesus casts all of our sins into the sea of forgetfulness, and He will remember our sins no more. **Micah 7:19** says, 'He will again have compassion on us: he will subdue and tread underfoot our wickedness (destroying sin's power); yes, you will cast all of our sins into the depths of the sea.'" Cody helped Paul to his hospital bed, and he said, "Okay, I'll stay, but what happened to you will never happen again. I will give my life to Jesus."

Paul said, "Praise the Lord. I've been praying that you would give your life to Jesus. I want to see you in heaven, either when we die or when the rapture comes." Cody said, "How do I accept Jesus as my Savior?" Paul said, "Admit that you're a sinner and that you need Jesus for salvation. Also, believe that Jesus died for you, and after three days, He was resurrected, He ascended, and He's coming back again." Cody said, "Yes," and Paul said, "Repeat after me. Lord Jesus, Savior of the world, You died for me, shedding Your blood to save me. Today I ask You to come into my heart and be my Savior. In Jesus's name, amen." Cody repeated the prayer, and Paul said, "Welcome to the family, brother."

A few weeks after Paul got out of the hospital, Cody stopped selling drugs. He left the gang life, and he started going to church with Paul and his family. Cody still felt bad for all the pain that he put Paul through. One day, Cody was sitting on his bed, depressed, when Paul walked into his room and asked, "Cody, what's wrong?" He said, "I still feel bad because of what I did. You were shot and almost killed, and I will never be able to forgive myself." Paul sat down on Cody's bed and put his hand on Cody's shoulder. "I forgive you just like God forgives you. The hardest part about forgiveness is forgiving ourselves because we remember every mistake and every sin that we do. That's the human trait in us, but God doesn't remember our sins when we give our life to Jesus. His forgiveness is as far as the east is from the west." Paul continued, "Since you have given your life to Jesus, all of your sins have been forgiven, and they are no longer held against you. Also, you will not be sent to hell. All you have to do is forgive yourself." Cody said, "Thank you. I needed to hear that. I was depressed about what I did because I was still blaming myself for what happened to you, but if God, you, and your family can forgive me, then I can forgive myself. God sent you into this room to help me to get out of this self-pity."

"Another way to not get depressed is to read the Word of God. God knows that people were going to get depressed since life will do that to you. Another thing I suggest that you do is pray. Even though God knows everything, He likes it when we talk to Him. That's how you build a relationship with anyone, even with God." Cody said, "I'm going to start doing that. Another thing, I feel different ever since I gave my life to Jesus. I feel better, but sometimes, I feel like I used to feel before I got saved." Paul said, "That's natural. We will never get rid of the side of us that did things our way and not God's way, but that's not going away until we die and see Jesus in heaven, but that doesn't give us a license to sin. We must strive to be like Jesus. Also, we must make Him number one in our lives." Cody hugged Paul and said, "Thank you for helping me and staying by my side through the good and the bad." Paul said, "You're welcome. That's what brothers are for. I will always have your back, no matter what." Cody said, "Thank you." Then Paul got up and left.

As Paul went back to his room, he started praying. "Lord Jesus, I thank You for answering my prayers and leading Cody to the truth that You are God. Also thank You for saving me and allowing me to live after I was shot. In Jesus's name, I pray and thank You, Lord. Amen."

A few days later, Paul and Cody were walking to the store when some members of Cody's former gang stopped them. They told Cody that Robert had been looking for him; he had a job for him to do. Cody told them, "I'm not in the gang anymore. I almost lost my brother being in the gang life, and I'm not about to lose him again." The gang members said, "That's too bad," and both of the gang members pulled out their guns and pointed them at Paul and Cody. Cody said, "You two don't want to do this. You both can walk away and say that you never saw me." The other gang member said, "No, we can't. We told you that once you joined the gang, the only way that you leave the gang is in a body bag, and that's a promise that we're going to make you keep. So you can do this the easy way or the hard way. You can either come with us peacefully, or we can shoot you and kill both of you right now. So what will it be?"

Cody said, "All right, I'll come with you. Just let my brother go." The second gang member said, "Who said that we were going to let him go? He's coming with us." Cody said, "Let him go. He has nothing to do with this. I was in the gang, not him." And the first gang member said, "Consider him collateral damage."

Paul said, "I'm not going anywhere, and neither is he." Paul went for the first gang member's gun, but the second gang member shot Paul in his left leg, bringing him to the ground. Cody said, "Paul, are you okay?" and Paul screamed in pain, but he said, "I'll be alright." The second gang member pulled Paul off the ground and took Cody and Paul to their car, then they shoved them into the car. Paul hit his left leg against the door, and he screamed again in pain, and Cody said, "I'm so sorry that you were shot again. This is all my fault. All I do is cause you trouble. I should have left after you got out of the hospital. I'm a curse to you and to your family since I came into your life." Paul said, "Cody, you had no idea that this was going to happen. We all make mistakes, but the question is not why we make mistakes but whether we learn from our mistakes." Paul kept talking. "If we learn from our mistakes, that means we're growing. If you don't learn, that means that you're not growing." Cody said, "I did learn from my mistakes. I left that life behind. I'm never going back to that lifestyle. That lifestyle is toxic, and I would be crazy as heck to go back to that toxic lifestyle."

As the two gang members were driving, they were hitting every pothole in the street, and that gave Paul a lot of pain. He took off one of his shirts and wrapped it around his leg wound. Cody asked Paul if he was okay, and Paul said, "Yeah, I'm just in a lot of pain. I haven't fully recovered from the last time I was shot, and now I've been shot in my leg. Even though this is my second time being shot, I still trust God because He knows how this will end, and He knows when it will end." Cody said, "I might be a young believer in Jesus, but I already know He's going to get us out of this situation." The two gang members stopped in front of a warehouse. They got out of the car, and they got Paul and Cody out of the car and took them to a room and threw them inside. Paul fell on his bad leg, and he screamed out in pain. Cody screamed, "Someone get some help. My brother has been shot, and he needs some medical treatment before his legs get an infection." He waited ten minutes, but no one came, so Cody started praying. He said, "Lord Jesus, I'm humbly asking You for help, not for me but for my brother, Paul. I'm asking that You heal his leg or let someone find us so that he can get medical treatment before infection gets into his leg. In Jesus's name, I pray, and I thank You, Lord. Amen." Besides hearing people moving around in the warehouse, no one came to talk to them or bring them anything.

Sometime later, the door to the room opened, and one of the gang members that took them walked into the room and pulled Cody to his feet. "Robert wants to see you." Cody said, "What about my brother?" and the guy said, "He doesn't want to see him. He wants to see you." Then he pushed Cody out of the room and said, "Move." The guy led Cody to Robert's office, and once they reached Robert's office, the guy pushed Cody inside, and Robert turned around in his chair and told the guy to leave him. Once the guy was gone, Robert said, "Cody, why did you do this to me? I gave you the world. I made you a made boy. You were climbing up the ranks in my organization quicker than anyone, and you threw it all away for nothing." Then Robert punched Cody in his stomach very hard, and he hit the ground. Robert started kicking him in the stomach and said, "I told you when you joined that the only way out was in a body bag. That's the only way you're leaving this gang." Then he kicked him again and he called for his guard to take him back to the room, and the guard took him back to the room.

* * * * *

When the Light found out that CROWN was having a retreat to recruit more people, they decided to do a counter retreat to try and disrupt what CROWN was trying to do. Jason told Rick, "Once Tommy tells us when the retreat is going to take place and we plan our retreat, we're going to make sure CROWN will die, and that they will never rise from the ashes again."

Chris met with Julia, and they started to discuss the retreat. Julia started the conservation. "Let's have the retreat at a lake. That way, we can have Bible study and enjoy the beauty of nature that God has created." Julia continued, "What we can do is that the ones who can drive can bring the ones who can't drive up to the lake." Chris said, "How about instead of going to the lake and possibly spending some money, we have a rally outside the school on the football field so we can still cover all our objectives?" and Julia said, "Okay." Chris then said, "We need a vice president of CROWN," and Julia said, "How about Tommy? He's the former vice president of No Light before becoming a Christian. He knows the Ultimate Light better than any of us. I believe he would be a great asset." Chris said, "I think Tommy would make a great vice president, but I've decided to make you the vice president of CROWN." Julia looked stunned and said, "I don't know what to say." Chris said, "You don't have to give me your answer now. Take some time to think about it and give me your answer in a few days," and Julia said, "Okay."

While Chris and Julia were planning the CROWN rally, Jason was meeting with his vice president turned informant. Tommy told Jason that CROWN changed where they were going to have their rally. Instead of having it at the lake like they originally planned, they were going to have it outside the school on the football field.

Jason said, "Good job, Tommy. How did you know where they are going to have the rally at?" Tommy told him that he heard Chris and Julia talking. "And I also heard that Chris offered Julia the position of vice president of CROWN." Jason turned red, and he said, "*What?* Julia was offered the position of vice president of CROWN? Did she take the position?" Tommy said, "No, she didn't. He told her to take a few days and think about it." Jason started again. "Tommy, you have to become the vice president of CROWN. This could be our only chance to get a position inside the government of CROWN. We need you to talk to Chris about becoming the new vice president. With this position, we can finally destroy CROWN and Christianity once and for all." Tommy said, "Okay, I'll talk to Chris about the position on Monday when I see him." Rick said, "Tommy, no matter what happens, even if you do become vice president of CROWN, you must stay the course and help us eliminate CROWN and Christianity from our schools."

Monday at school, Tommy saw Chris walking in the hallway. He walked up to him and said, "Hi, Chris, how are you doing?" He said, "I'm doing good. I slept well last night. What about you?" He said, "I slept well." Tommy continued. "I have a question to ask you," and Chris said, "What's the question?"

He said, "Friday when I was leaving school, I walked past a room, and I heard you and Julia talking about appointing a vice president for CROWN?" Chris said, "Yes, I'm appointing a vice president for CROWN." Tommy said, "I want to be the vice president for CROWN." Chris said, "What makes you qualified to be vice president of CROWN?" Tommy said, "I used to be vice president of No Light before I saw the light and became a Christian. The same passion that I brought to No Light as an atheist I believe I can bring to CROWN as vice president standing next to you as president." Chris said, "I was going to appoint Julia as vice president, but since you also want to be vice president, what I'm going to do is announce an election in November where you and Julia will have a chance to become vice president. Also at the rally, both of you will have the chance to convince the entire group why you or Julia should be vice president. We were going to have the retreat on August 22, but I've decided to move the date back until September 18 to give both of you time to come up with a speech that could possibly give you or her the vice presidency."

Tommy said, "Thank you, I promise I won't let you down." Tommy left, and as he was walking down the hall, he said, "Everything is going according to plan. Soon CROWN will go down in flames." He went to use the bathroom and ran into Jason. Jason said, "How did your talk with Chris go?" Tommy said, "I talked to him about becoming vice president, and he told me that he was going to appoint Julia as vice president, but since I also want to be vice president, he's going to have an election to determine who gets the position." Jason said, "Okay, this is a minor setback. Rick and I will help you with your speech so that you will crush Julia in this election, then we will crush CROWN for eternity." Tommy said, "Sounds like a plan."

After class, Tommy went to Jason's house, and Jason helped him write his speech. Jason said, "When you finish reading this speech, everyone in CROWN will vote for you to become vice president." Tommy said, "Eventually, I'm going to try to become president of CROWN, and once I become president, I will be in the perfect position to bring down CROWN for good." Jason said, "Baby steps, baby steps first. You will have to become vice president before you can become president. You will have to gain their trust to the point that they will never see it coming. Also, even though I helped you write a great speech, I know Julia. It won't be easy to defeat her. She's persistent. She won't go down easily, but you will take her down." Tommy said, "Okay, I will trust you."

Julia went to see Chris and asked him to help her write a speech that would persuade the members of CROWN to vote for her as vice president. Chris said, "Okay," and they started writing drafts of her speech. An hour into writing the drafts, she still didn't like what they had written. Julia said, "Chris, what can I say to beat Tommy? He has experience in being a vice president. I don't." Chris said, "He might have experience being vice president, but remember, you were the president of No Light before you gave your life to Jesus Christ, so if anyone has the experience, it's you, not him." Chris continued. "The best way to win is for you to be yourself. Tell them why you love CROWN and how you came to accept Jesus as your Savior and what God has done for you since you've given your life to Jesus." Julia said, "You're right. Instead of writing a speech, I'm going to shoot from the heart and tell them how I feel about CROWN, what I've done through Jesus for CROWN, and what I plan to do for CROWN once I become vice president." Chris said, "That's all you can do, and pray that you win. I will be rooting for you all the way until you become vice president of CROWN." Julia said, "Thank you. I appreciate your support and your trust." Chris said, "You're welcome. Before you leave let's pray." She said, "Okay," and he started praying, "Lord Jesus, we thank You for being God and saving us. We are coming to ask You that the members of CROWN pick the right person to become vice president, whether it's Julia or Tommy. Let the person who can do the job the best get the job, in Jesus's name, amen."

Julia said, "Amen," then she left. On her way home, she said, "Lord, if it's Your will, let me become vice president, but if it's not

Your plan, then let me lose this election to Tommy. I put this in Your hands, amen." The next day at school, Chris ran into Tommy and told him that he was going to announce that he and Julia were going to run for the office of vice president of CROWN at their meeting today. Tommy said, "Okay. If I see Julia, I'll tell her what you said." Tommy ran into Julia and told her that they had a meeting today after school and that Chris was going to announce them as candidates for the office of vice president, and Julia said, "Okay."

After school, CROWN met in their usual room. Chris prayed first, then he started the meeting. "Welcome to CROWN. I hope you all had a good day. I have some news to tell you today." He continued. "I was in the process of appointing Julia as vice president, but Tommy approached me and said he wants to be vice president, so I decided to have an election to determine who will become the first vice president of CROWN. Both candidates will have the opportunity to deliver their respective speeches and convince you why they should be vice president at the rally we're having. Lastly, a week after the rally, you will vote on whom you want to be vice president. It was going to be in November, but I changed my mind."

Everyone said okay, then he said, "Now that we have gotten the political stuff out of the way, let's have some Bible study. If you have your Bible, please turn to **Revelation 5:2–8** and follow me. 'And I saw, and behold a white horse: and he that sat on him had a bow; and a crown was given unto him: and he went forth conquering, and to conquer. And when he had opened the second seal, I heard the second beast say, Come and see. And there went out another horse that was red: and power was given to him that sat thereon to take peace from the earth, and that they should kill one another: and there was given unto him a great sword. And when he had opened the third seal, I heard the third beast say, Come and see. And I beheld, and lo a black horse; and he that sat on him had a pair of balances in his hand. And I heard a voice in the midst of the four beasts say, A measure of wheat for a penny, and three measures of barley for a penny; and see thou hurt not the oil and the wine. And when he had opened the fourth seal, I heard the voice of the fourth beast say, Come and see. And I looked, and behold a pale horse: and his name that sat on him was Death, and Hell followed with him. And power was given unto them over the fourth part of the earth, to kill with sword, and with hunger, and with death, and with the beasts of the earth.'

"The first beast is the antichrist, and he will rule the world, not by force but by a false peace that promises world unity. The second beast will take peace from the earth, and one-third of the population left behind will be killed in seven years. The third beast or horseman will cause worldwide famine, and when the Bible says a measure of wheat for a penny and three measures of barley for a penny, it means that a loaf of bread will cost a day's wages, which means a loaf of bread will be very expensive. The last beast or horseman will bring death and hell and will kill many more people. This is why I formed CROWN, to tell people the truth, to warn them, and give them a chance to accept Jesus as their Savior. As we close, is there anybody who wants to give their life to Jesus today?" Two people raised their hands, and Chris led them through the sinner's prayer, then he said, "Welcome the two newest members of the family," and everyone started clapping and saying, "Thank You, Jesus."

After the meeting was over, Tommy went home. He called Jason and gave him an update on what happened in the meeting, and Jason told him, "You better win this election and become vice president. We need you to infiltrate every part of CROWN until they are wiped off the face of the earth, and soon I will be sending more people to help you take them down from the inside." Tommy said, "Is there anything that you need from me?" Jason said, "No, all I need from you is to become vice president of CROWN." After he got off the phone, Tommy lay down and went to sleep.

The following week, CROWN and Ultimate Light had their rally on the same football field. Chris got up on the stage and said, "Welcome, everybody, to the rally. I also welcome you in the name of our Lord and Savior Jesus Christ." He continued talking. "Like I said at the meeting, Julia and Tommy will be running for vice president. Julia will deliver her speech first."

Julia came up on stage. She began, "I don't have a speech written, so I'm just going to shoot from the heart. My name is Julia, and I was the leader of No Light before I accepted Jesus as my Savior, and the same passion that I brought to that group I know I can bring to CROWN as vice president. Working with Chris and by the blessing of our Savior, Jesus Christ, we can take CROWN to places that it's never been before. This is the reason I'm asking for your vote to become vice president. Thank you."

After Julia was done, Tommy came to the podium, and he was like, "Thank you, Julia, for that wonderful speech. I don't know if I can top it, but I'll try. My name is Tommy, and I want to be your vice president because I want to bring change to CROWN. Ultimate Light has gotten way too powerful, and they have taken control of the school, but with Chris and I working together, we can stop them." The crowd cheered, and Tommy continued. "They want to get rid of Christianity because they believe that Jesus doesn't belong in school, but I say Jesus belongs in school, and I want to keep it this way." The crowd cheered again.

Chris came back to the podium and said, "That concludes the speeches. We have free food, so go and have fun. Also, we have a band that will be playing for us tonight. Please welcome the band Jesus Saves." The crowd cheered, and Jesus Saves started playing.

While CROWN was having their rally, No Light was having their rally. Jason came to the stage and said, "Welcome to our rally. I'm here to tell you that we have taken control of every school in the district but one. We have to keep control of these schools, so I'm asking all of you to keep pushing forward. Soon, we will have control of the last school, and CROWN and Christianity will soon be gone." The crowd cheered, and he said, "Let's jam and turn this place up," and everyone cheered.

CHAPTER

9

On Friday, I went to my parents and asked them if I and William could spend the weekend with Daniel and his family, and they said yes. I said, "Thank you," then went to William's room. Once there, I told him that our parents said we can spend the weekend with Daniel and his parents, and William said, "Okay." I continued, "I can't wait until this retreat. I want to keep growing in Jesus, and I want to surround myself with believers to help me when I'm weak." William said, "I understand, but I pray that you come back to our religion and become a Muslim again." I said, "If I wasn't happy, and if Jesus wasn't God, then I would, but since I know that Jesus is God, and I know that He died on the cross for my sins, there's no way I'm turning my back on Jesus. I also pray every day that you would give your life to Jesus so that you can experience the same happiness that I'm experiencing." William said, "While I appreciate you praying for me, I'm not turning my back on Allah. He's been too good to me for me to turn against him." I said, "I understand, li'l bro. I will let Daniel know about us going to the retreat when we see him at school," and he said, "Okay." Then I left and went back to my room.

In my room, I started praying. "Lord Jesus, I ask You to show my brother that You are the only true and living God because I don't want him to go to hell or be left behind to go through the tribulation. I pray this in Jesus's name, amen." When William and I got to school, I went looking for Daniel. When I found him, I told him that William and I were going to the retreat. Daniel said, "That's great. Praise the Lord. I've been praying that both of you would be able to attend the retreat. Also, I've been praying that William will give his life to Jesus, and I've been praying that you will get stronger in the Lord." He continued, "Satan isn't happy about you following Jesus, so he will try everything in his power to get you to recant Jesus and go back to serving a false god."

I said, "I will never turn my back on Jesus. I found the truth, and I want everyone else to find the truth too." Daniel said, "Amen, and before I forget, we are having a club meeting after school. It's going to be the last meeting before the retreat." During my third class, I was thinking about the retreat; that was all I could think about, and I thought, *I can't wait until the retreat. I'm going to have a lot of fun. Also, I'm going to make a lot of Christian friends. This is going to be one of the best things to happen to me.* After class, I met up with William and told him about the meeting after school. He said, "Okay, I'm going with you, then after the meeting is over with, can we go get some ice cream?" and I said, "Yeah, we can." After school, William and I went to the meeting.

Brittany was talking. "I'm going to give you an outline of things we're going to do. We are going to be shooting archery, shooting fireworks, hiking, and having Bible study, among other things. Another thing, while people from our school will be there, I heard that people from all over the state will be there too. Lastly, there will be two concerts—one to start off the retreat, and another one to end the retreat."

As Brittany was talking, I looked at William and said, "Sounds like we're going to have a lot of fun at the retreat," but William didn't say anything, and I said, "Bro, what's wrong?" William said, "I feel like I'm betraying everything I know, and I feel like I'm going to be disowned or, even worse, killed." I said, "You don't have to go if you don't feel up to it, and you don't have to support me through this. I don't want to put you in a position that makes you feel uncomfortable, and I don't want you to have to choose between me and your religion. I can handle what happens to me." William said, "As much as I appreciate that, I'm not abandoning you, big bro, no matter how uncomfortable I feel. I'm with you to the end of the line, and if our parents find out, and they try to kill you, they will have to go through me first." Antowon said, "Bro, I didn't know you felt like that." William said, "Even though my loyalty is to Islam and our parents, my ultimate loyalty is to you, bro."

I hugged William and said, "Thank you so much, bro. I appreciate the loyalty," and he said, "You're welcome." After the meeting, I went to talk to Brittany and told her about William's situation. She said, "I'll pray for him. What about you?" I said, "I'm fine. I just worry about him. He's so conflicted. On the one hand, he's loyal to our parents and to Islam, but on the other hand, he's loyal to me, and he's with me to the end. But I don't want him to be in a position where he has to choose between being loyal to me and being loyal to them." Brittany put her hand on my shoulder and said, "Don't let this burden get you down. Cast all your cares and burdens on Jesus, and let Him carry it. You do your part and pray, and you let Jesus do His part." I said, "Okay, I'll see you at the retreat."

William asked me what Brittany was talking about, and I said, "We were talking about the retreat, and what we're going to do after the retreat," and he said, "Okay." I felt bad that I had lied to William, but I didn't want to burden him more than he was already. We headed to the car. On the way to get ice cream, I kept thinking about how much pressure William was under; he was trying to stay loyal to Islam but was also being a good brother to me by keeping this from our parents, and I thought, *I don't know how to unburden him. I just don't know how.* I started praying, "Lord Jesus, I pray that You give my brother peace and that You help him to not be conflicted. Also, Lord, help me to become stronger in You. In Jesus's name, I pray, amen."

When William and I got to the ice cream parlor, I ordered cookies and cream ice cream, and William ordered chocolate, and after we got our ice cream, we sat down. While we were eating, William noticed the look on my face, and he said, "What's the matter, bro?" and I said, "Nothing's the matter." William said, "I know something's wrong. I can see it in your face."

I sighed and said, "I should know that I can't hide anything from you. It's just what you said to me earlier, how you're conflicted, and I feel like it's my fault. I should have never asked you to keep my secret. I wish you had never found out my secret." William said, "I'm happy that I found out because it has made us closer, and it might make me conflicted, but I would rather be conflicted and know your secret than not know your secret and be fine. Also, you have someone you can be honest with, someone whom you don't have to keep secrets from." I said, "Thank you, bro, this means a lot to me," and he said, "You're welcome."

When we got home, I went to my room and said, "Lord Jesus, I'm doing my part by coming to You and casting all my burdens and cares on You, and I'm trusting You, Lord, to do the rest because You're greater than my circumstances. In Jesus's name, I pray, and I thank You, Lord. Amen." After I prayed, I felt a huge weight being lifted off my shoulders. Then I went to bed.

When the weekend came, I was so excited for the retreat that I could barely contain myself. I went downstairs and fixed my food, got in the shower, and got dressed as fast as I could. After I was done, I went to William's room. When I got to his door, I saw that it was cracked open, and I saw William reading the Bible that I had given him. I almost cried with joy. As I was watching William read the Bible, I heard our parents walking up the steps. I ran into William's room and shut the door and locked it. William jumped and said, "Bro, what's wrong?" I said, "Our parents are coming up the steps, and they are headed for your room. You have to hide the Bible before they come in." William looked at me and said, "Right." He hid the Bible under his bed, then I unlocked the door and opened it just as our parents were about to knock on the door. Mother said, "What are you two doing?" William replied, "We were just talking about going to the movies and going out to eat with Daniel's family over the weekend. Also, we might go to the mall and pick out some video games to play."

Mother said, "Okay, we'll see you later," and they closed the door. I said, "That was a close call," and William said, "Yes, it was." After our parents left, I went back to my room and turned on my game system. I started playing a game called *Combat*, and while I was playing the game, William came in and said, "Bro, what are you doing?" I said, "I'm playing a game called *Combat*. It's a game where I have to save the world," and he said, "Can I play?" I said, "Sure," and we played the game for the rest of the day.

When Saturday came, I woke up early and got dressed, then I went downstairs and ate breakfast. After that, I went back upstairs and grabbed my bags and put them in my car. Then I went back upstairs to wake William up. When I got to William's room, I saw that William was still asleep. I said to myself, *I'll let him sleep for ten more minutes, then I'll wake him up so he can get ready.* While I was waiting on William to wake up, I started praying, "Lord Jesus, I come to You today to ask You to use this retreat to bring my brother, William, to You because You said it is Your will that none should perish but that all would come to repentance. In Jesus's name I pray, and I thank You, Lord. Amen." Once I had finished praying, I went back to William's room and woke him up. I said, "Bro, it's time to get up. We have to be at Daniel's in an hour," and William said, "Okay, I'm getting up. Go eat breakfast while I'm getting dressed." I said, "I've already eaten, and I've already taken my bags to the car." William said, "Can you take my bags to the car while I eat and get dressed?" I said, "Okay, I'll take your bags to the car."

After I put William's stuff in the car, I went back into the house, brushed my teeth, and went back to William's room to get his Bible from under his bed, but when I looked under his bed, I saw that his Bible was gone. I went looking for William to see if he had put the Bible in his bag, and I found William eating some cereal. I said, "Bro, did you know what happened to the Bible I gave you?" William said, "I put it in my bag last night while our parents were asleep so they wouldn't see me with it."

I sighed in relief. "I'm so happy that you told me that. I thought Mom and Dad had found it while you were asleep or while we were gone, but I feel so much better knowing that you put it away for safe-keeping." William shook his head while eating, and I kept talking. "When you are ready to go, meet me in the car." William nodded his head. About twenty minutes after I went to the car, our parents came out, and Mom said, "Be safe, and we will see you on Tuesday. And before I forget, let me give you this," and she handed William the Quran. Then she said, "Try to convert Daniel and his family to the truth while you are over there," and William said, "Okay," then he got in the car. I started the car, then we left. When we got far enough from the house, I stopped the car, and William said, "What's wrong?" I said, "I wanted to pray before we go to the retreat, but I didn't want Mom and Dad seeing me praying," and William said, "Okay." I started praying, "Lord Jesus, I thank You for being God, and I'm asking You for traveling mercies to the retreat, at the retreat, and coming back from the retreat. In Jesus's name I pray, and I thank You, Lord. Amen." After that, we started driving toward the campsite for the retreat. As we were driving, I said, "Bro, how are you feeling about going to a Christian retreat?" He said, "I'm nervous and scared. I'm scared because besides the people from school, I don't know anyone, and I'm scared because I don't want the wrath of Allah on me because I'm entertaining another religion."

I stopped the car and turned to William and said, "Bro, the wrath of Allah won't come to you, I promise." He said, "How do you know?" I said, "I know because once I gave my life to Jesus, I was also afraid that the wrath of Allah was going to come for me, but then I realized that the wrath of Allah was never going to come for me because I'm covered in the blood of Jesus, and since you are with me right now, you're covered, so don't worry. Nothing bad is going to happen to you, I promise," and William said, "Okay."

When we reached the campsite, we got out of the car and went looking for Daniel. We saw thousands of kids and teenagers around the site, and William said, "Bro, are all of these people Christians?" I said, "Some are, and some are just like you. They aren't believers, but people who are believers invited them to come, and they accepted the invitation." William said, "That's good. At least I know I'm not alone. That makes me feel a little better." William and I kept walking around the campsite until we found Daniel, and when Daniel saw me and William coming, he ran to us and hugged us. He said, "It's good to see both of you, especially you, William. I've been praying for you because I see the joy your brother has, and I want you to have the same joy as him." William said, "I appreciate it, I really do, but I'm just here to support Antowon. I'm not going to convert." Daniel said, "It's all right. A lot of people here are not Christians either. They are here to support a person who's a Christian, or they are curious about what we believe in, or they just wanted to get away from the city, but before any of you got here, Brittany, the pastor, and I arrived and prayed for everyone who was coming, that their lives might be changed and that they might give their lives to Jesus, and I know that Jesus is a prayer-answering God." I said, "Amen. He sure is."

While we were talking, we heard someone say from a bullhorn, "I welcome everyone to the first-ever revival retreat. Before all of you got here, some of us came up here and prayed that not only will people's lives be changed and people will give their lives to Jesus but that everyone will enjoy themselves and have a good time. The first thing we're going to do is break everyone into small groups so that everyone can get to know each other, then we're going to let you go swimming and do archery, among other things. And lastly, we're going to have a concert to kick off the first day of the retreat tonight at 8:00 p.m., and to close out the three-day retreat, we're going to have another concert. How does that sound?" People started screaming with joy. The pastor kept talking. "We're going to divide you up by grades." As the pastor was breaking people into groups, William turned to me and said, "I want to stay with you," and Daniel said, "That's fine for today, but tomorrow, you will have to hang with people in your own grade," and William said, "Okay."

Daniel kept talking. "We're already in a group. It's going to be me, you, William, Brittany, Eric, and Jasmine. I asked that we all stay together doing the retreat because we're all in the same grade with the exception of William." I said, "That was a smart thing to do," and Daniel said, "Thank you." We went to the picnic table, and the youth pastor came over and said, "Welcome, everyone, to the first day of the revival. I bet everyone knows each other. Daniel has told me about all of you and your group CROWN, so we're going to bypass getting to know everyone and jump into Bible study. I want to discuss the tribulation with you." He continued. "The Bible says when the time is right, a powerful leader will arise, and he will come as a man of peace, but he will bathe the world in blood. **Daniel 8:25** says, 'By his cunning he shall make deceit prosper under his hand, and in his own mind he shall become great. Without warning he shall destroy many. And he shall even rise up against the Prince of princes, and he shall be broken, but by no human hand.' The antichrist's reign will be so brutal that if God didn't stop it in seven years, everyone would be dead. **Matthew 24.22** says, 'And if those days had not been cut short no human being would be saved. But for the sake of the elect those days will be cut short.' For anyone who is wondering what this means, it means that after the rapture, things are going to get a whole lot worse, and all those who are left behind who accept Jesus as their Savior will know that they are living in the last days.

"The first thing the antichrist is going to do is come as a man of peace, and he's going to unite the world under a one world government. **Daniel 7:23** says, 'Thus he said as for the fourth beast there shall be a fourth kingdom on the earth which shall be different from all other kingdoms, and it shall devour the whole world, and trample it down, and break it to pieces.' Eventually, the antichrist comes to power, and he signs a seven-year peace treaty with Israel, guaranteeing them peace, but in the middle of the seven years, he's going to break it. Also, he's going to rebuild the temple in Israel, then he's going to desecrate it. Turn to **Daniel 9:27**, and here reads the Word of the living God. **Daniel 9:27** says, 'Then for one seven, he will forge many and strong alliances, but halfway through the seven he will banish worship and prayers. At the place of worship, a desecrating obscenity will be set up and remain until finally the desecrator himself is decisively destroyed.' During the middle of the tribulation, the antichrist will be shot in the head, and the world will mourn his death, but three days later, Satan will possess him, and he will rise from the dead, emulating the death and resurrection of Jesus Christ. **Revelation 13:3–4** says, 'One of the Beast's heads looked as if it had been struck a deathblow, and then healed. The whole earth was agog, gaping at the Beast. They worshiped the Dragon who gave the Beast authority, and they worshiped the Beast, exclaiming, There's never been anything like the Beast! No one would dare go to war with the Beast!'"

As the youth pastor was talking, William turned to me and said, "This antichrist character seems scary," and I said, "That's why I tell you to give your life to Jesus Christ, because you don't want to be here after the rapture," and William shook his head.

* * * * *

For the next few days, Cierra thought about what Jenny had told her about the gunman Sam, and how when she and Dave had confronted him, not only did he not shoot them but he gave his life to Jesus. *Even though I believe what Jenny said, I'm not giving up my freedom I've earned to follow some made-up God*, she thought. *I'm going to stick to what I believe in. It's never let me down before.* One night, while she was asleep, she had a terrible nightmare, and she woke up in a cold sweat. *What in the world did I just dream about?* She kept thinking. *Later on today, I'm going to tell Jenny about my dream.* Then she went back to sleep.

Later on that day, Cierra ran into Jenny and said, "Jenny, I need to talk to you. I had a nightmare." Jenny said, "Let's go sit down and talk." After they sat down, Jenny said, "What happened?" Cierra said, "Well, it happened like this. I was at school, and I was talking to a few students, and there was a building that wasn't there before, but it had the school logo on the building. Three of our classmates went into the building. One of the kids that I was with, Steven, said, 'Let's go inside too,' and everyone agreed. So we went into the building, and all we saw was darkness. We saw the three kids who went inside talking to three short people in robes, but we couldn't hear what they were saying, so we got closer to hear what they were saying, but they couldn't see us. One of the guys in the robes was talking to them, and he was saying, 'If you follow our master, you will be rewarded with power that you couldn't possibly dream of.' At that moment, we all got up from where we were hiding, and Steven said, 'You are on the wrong side if you choose them. Choose Jesus Christ. He's the only way you can truly have peace.'

"The three guys in the robes came toward us, and Steven said, 'Stop in the name of Jesus.' They stopped, and they looked at each other, then they started coming toward us again, and again Steven said, 'Stop in the name of Jesus.' This time they stopped and didn't move again. Steven saw that they were demons, and he turned to the other kids and said, 'These demons' master is Satan. He and his demons have already been defeated by the Lord Jesus Christ, and if you choose them, then you have chosen the wrong side.' The demons started laughing, and Steven said, 'What's so funny?' and they pointed to a window and said, 'Look.' We all went to the window, and we saw a man burning in hell, and he was screaming, 'Get me out of here. I'm burning. I didn't think it would be this bad.' And at that point, I woke up in a cold sweat."

Jenny said, "Wow, that was deep. I believe that this is the Lord telling you to give your life to Jesus before it's too late." Cierra said, "It might be because I watched too many scary movies in the past few weeks." Jenny protested. "How do you explain everything that happened in your dream?" Cierra said, "It isn't Jesus trying to warn me. It might be my subconscious overreacting." Jenny said, "I pray for you every day that you will see the truth as I have and accept Jesus as your Savior." Cierra said, "After what happened to me, I know there's no god. The only person that I can trust is me. You can pray for me until you are blue in the face, but it won't change anything." Jenny said, "It will. I just pray that it won't be too late for you." Then Jenny left to go be with her mom. After Jenny left, Cierra said, "After what happened to me, I'm an atheist. I know that there's no god. My mind was playing tricks on me. Maybe I need to go see a doctor and get on some medication so I can sleep better."

When she got home, she made an appointment with the family doctor for that Thursday at 10:00 a.m. Next, she went and told her mother about the dream, and her mother said the same thing that Jenny said. Cierra said, "Did you talk to Jenny about this before I told you?" and she said, "No, I didn't even know about the dream until you just told me." Her mother kept talking. "If Jenny and I are telling you the same thing, and neither one of us knew about it, then it must be coming from the Lord." Cierra said, "Answer me this. If God is love, why did He let me go through what I've gone through when Joe did what he did to me?" Cierra's mother said, "Sometimes the Lord uses our situation to bring us closer to Him. God can use this situation as a testimony. You could say, yes, I did go through this, but look at what God has brought me through."

Cierra said, "There's no god, and nothing you say or do will change that," and she left to go to her room. Her mother shook her head and started praying. "Lord Jesus, please soften my daughter's hard heart, and if her getting saved means that she has to go through the seven-year tribulation, then let her go through the tribulation, in Jesus's name I pray, amen." After Cierra's mother finished praying, she felt like a big weight had been lifted off her shoulders. She went into the kitchen to make a sandwich. When Cierra reached her room, she turned on the television, and on the news, she saw that some pipes owned by DX had busted, and over three point eight billion gallons of oil had spilled into the ocean.

The news anchor continued. "Emergency crews are working around the clock to contain this situation. We will keep you up to date as this situation develops. This is Jane from the National News Network." Cierra said, "What is going on in this world? Pipes burst, and the ocean is being filled with this toxicity. I feel bad for all those animals that are suffering. If God really did exist, He wouldn't allow this to happen to all of those innocent animals. If He did exist, He would put a stop to this. All this is showing me is that God is dead." She turned the TV off and went to bed.

Thursday morning, she got up at 8:30 a.m. to get ready to go to the doctor. As she was leaving, she got a bad headache and took some ibuprofen, but that didn't help her. When she got to the doctor, she told her about her headache and about her nightmare. Her doctor said, "I can't do anything about the dreams except recommend a therapist, but as far as your headaches are concerned, I can give you some oxycodone, which is a strong pain medicine, but it should do the trick." Cierra said, "Okay, thank you. Also, can I have the number and name of the therapist?" Her doctor said, "Sure. Her name is Stacy, and her number is (513)555-6477. Her business hours are Monday to Friday, 9:00 a.m. to 5:00 p.m. Call her when you get a chance, and she should be able to help you." Cierra said, "Thank you so much, doctor. I will call Ms. Stacy as soon as I get out of here."

When she got in the car, she called Ms. Stacy. "Hi, Ms. Stacy, how are you doing? I was referred to you by my doctor Jane. I've been having some bad dreams, and I need to talk to a therapist, and I heard that you are the best." Ms. Stacy said, "Yes, I am the best, and I'm willing to meet with you. Whenever you need me to see you, I'm available. My first meeting is free for an hour. After that, it's twenty dollars an hour." Cierra said, "Okay, can I come Monday?" Ms. Stacy said, "Yes, you can come Monday." Cierra said, "Thank you so much. I'll see you on Monday." Cierra thought to herself, *I will get to the bottom of this, and I'll figure out how to get rid of these bad dreams.* Then she went home and lay down.

The next few days were good days. She didn't have any bad dreams, but the day before she went to the therapist, she had a very intense dream. She woke up in another cold sweat and thought, *These nightmares have to stop. As soon as I get to see Ms. Stacy, I can go back to having a normal life.* Then she lay back down and went back to sleep. On Monday, she met with Ms. Stacy and told her about her first dream. Ms. Stacy asked her if she had any more dreams after the first one, and Cierra said no. Then she asked Ms. Stacy if she knew what her dream meant. Ms. Stacy said, "Right now, I don't know, but I promise you that I will find out." When Cierra was done seeing Ms. Stacy, she didn't feel any better, and she still didn't have the answers that she was looking for. She decided to go to Jenny's and talk to her. When she got there, she knocked on the door, and Jenny's mother answered the door. She said, "Hi, Cierra, how are you doing?" Cierra said, "I'm good. I was coming to see if Jenny was home." Her mother said, "Yeah, she's in her room. Go on up," and Cierra said, "Okay."

Cierra knocked on the door, and Jenny said, "Come in." When Cierra opened the door, Jenny was lying down watching TV. Cierra sat down on the bed and said, "I went to see my therapist, and she told me that she doesn't know what my dreams are telling me either." Jenny said, "I believe that God is trying to tell you something, but you refuse to listen. I asked the Lord what your dream meant, and He told me that the dream meant that He's trying to let you know that the demons are real, and that hell is real, and that He doesn't want you to go to hell. That's why He sent you this dream. Also, I knew your therapist wouldn't be able to answer your question because only God can answer your question. Do you think your dream can still be answered by a therapist?" Cierra said, "If Ms. Stacy can't answer my questions, then I might believe God is trying to tell me something." That night while she slept, she had another dream. She dreamt that her mother, Jenny, and other people vanished off the face of the earth with no explanation. She tried to get help from people, but every time she tried to get help, she would only find clothes where the person had been. She kept dreaming, and she was like, "Let me check the news to see what's going on." She turned on the television. Every station carried the same message. "Breaking news: Millions of people have vanished off the face of the planet with no explanation." And at that very moment, she woke up, and thought, *I have to talk to Jenny in the morning.*

* * * * *

In the morning, she called Jenny and asked her to come over to the house, and Jenny said, "Okay." When Jenny got to Cierra's house, Cierra took her up to her room and told her about her latest dream. Jenny said, "I know what this dream is about, and God didn't tell me. I know what your dream is about because it's in the Bible. **First Thessalonians 4:16–18** says, 'For the Lord himself shall descend from heaven with a shout, with the voice of the archangel, and with the trump of God: and the dead in Christ shall rise first: Then we which are alive and remain shall be caught up together with them in the clouds, to meet the Lord in the air: and so shall we ever be with the Lord. Wherefore comfort one another with these words.' I think God is showing you that Jesus is coming back soon and that you need to get your life right with Jesus now before you die, or the rapture comes."

Cierra said, "I don't care about the rapture or hell because it's all fairy tales anyway. You are real, this room we're standing in is real, but God isn't real." She continued. "I'm happy that you helped me figure out what my dream meant, but that's all I need." Jenny said, "What is it going to take for you to believe that what God is telling you is for real?" Cierra said, "When I see you and my mother vanish into thin air, that's the day I will believe what I'm seeing in these dreams and not a day sooner." Jenny said okay and left. After Jenny left, Cierra felt a little depressed and a little mad. She still harbored some resentment because Jenny didn't stop what happened to her, and she was a little depressed because she asked Jenny to come over so she could find out what her dream meant, and she bit Jenny's head off. She had a hard time going to bed that night. She tossed and turned all night, and about six o'clock in the morning, she said, "I'm going to call Jenny and ask her to meet me so I can say I'm sorry, and I'm going to ask for her forgiveness."

She finally went to sleep. When she woke up, she called Jenny and told her to meet her in the park and promised that she wasn't going to go off on her, and Jenny said, "Okay." When they met in the park, they sat down on the bench, and Cierra said, "First thing is I'm sorry that I went off on you. I asked for your help, and when you did come to help, I bit your head off." Cierra continued, "I need you to forgive me for doing that." She was crying. Jenny looked at Cierra and said, "I already forgave you, just like Jesus forgave the people who nailed Him to a cross. **Luke 23:34** says, 'Jesus prayed, "Father, forgive them; they don't know what they're doing." Dividing up his clothes, they threw dice for them. The people stood there staring at Jesus, and the ringleaders made faces, taunting, "He saved others. Let's see him save himself! The Messiah of God—ha! The Chosen—ha!"' If Jesus can forgive those people who laughed and mocked Him, the same people whom He came to save, then I can forgive you of your sins against me."

Cierra, with tears still in her eyes, hugged her, and she said, "Thank you so much for forgiving me." Jenny said, "You're welcome." After they talked, they went to a local restaurant to eat. They kept talking about different things, and eventually, Jenny said, "I have to go. I have to pick up my mom from work."

Cierra went home. She opened the door and called out, "Mom, I have good news for you," but her mom was nowhere to be found. Cierra kept looking when she noticed a red blinking light on the phone. She listened and heard the person on the voice mail saying,

"This is Dr. Bruce. I'm the doctor at St. Mark Hospital, and I'm calling to inform you that your mother has had a heart attack. We need you to come to St. Mark Hospital as soon as possible." Cierra dropped the phone and ran out of the house to hop in the car. She drove as fast as she could to the hospital. When she arrived, she parked, then ran into the hospital. She asked for Dr. Bruce, and the lady at the desk went to get him. He arrived, and Cierra asked him how her mother was doing.

He said, "She's in some pain, but she will recover in a few days," and she said, "Okay, can I see her now please?" Dr. Bruce said, "Yes, you can. I'll take you to see her." Dr. Bruce took her to see her mother, but when they entered the room, they saw that she was sleeping, and Dr. Bruce said, "I'll leave you two alone. If you need anything, please don't hesitate to call me." Cierra said, "Okay. Thank you, doctor." He left and closed the door. Cierra's mother heard the door close; she turned and said, "Cierra, when did you get here?" She said, "I just came in. The doctor brought me to your room." Cierra's mother said, "That was nice of him." Cierra said, "Enough about me. How are you feeling?"

"I'm in a little pain, but I'm fine. I'll be out in a few days, but I thank God that I was able to call for an ambulance and that they were able to get me here as fast as they did."

Cierra said, "You had a heart attack, and you still thank God for this? How can you still thank God for this?"

"I'm thanking Him because I could have died, but I didn't. **Romans 8:28** says, 'And we know that all things work together for good to them that love God, to them who are the called according to his purpose.'"

Cierra said, "Well, I'm just happy that you're still alive," and her mother said, "So am I." Cierra said, "You should get some rest. We'll talk later." While her mother was sleep, Cierra decided to take a nap herself to calm her mind. Cierra slept for a good six hours, and when she woke up, her mother asked her, "How did you sleep?" She said, "I slept well. I haven't slept this well in a long time. I needed this rest. This could help me recover quicker." Cierra said, "I have to go to work. I'll see you later." Her mother said, "Okay," and on the way out the door, she said, "Thank You, Jesus, my mother is still alive."

* * * * *

David, Jake, and Jack worked around the clock to make Christbook better. They took the ideas that Jack had given them at lunch. David said, "I have an idea that I want to run past both of you. How about we create a new feature where users can upload articles to our page? Once it's verified by one of us, it will automatically upload to our page for everyone to see unless they opt out." Jack said, "That's a smart idea. Let's add that, and while we're at it, is there anything else we should add?" Jake said, "That should be all for now. Let's not do too much that we crash our site. And speaking of, as soon as I hit this button, our site will officially launch. Who would like to do the honors?" David said, "How about we all hit the button at the same time since we all worked hard to make this site?" Everyone nodded in agreement. They clicked on the button, and the computer screen lit up with the message, "Welcome to Christbook, where we want you to make Christ a part of your everyday lives."

They looked at each other and said, "Let's pray. Lord Jesus, we come to You today in your precious name. We are coming to You today to ask You to use Christbook for Your glory. We pray that people will come to know You by what we do on this site and soon-to-be Christbook app. In Jesus's name, we pray. And thank You, Lord. Amen."

The next day, Jake and Jack were discussing ways to reach more people, and Jake said, "What we can do is we can put up flyers, and we can also try to witness to a few people and tell them about the goodness of Jesus." Jake said, "Okay, we need to tell David, and maybe if we tell a few more people and post it on Christbook, and we hit more than one neighborhood, we can reach as many people as possible." Jack said, "Okay." When Jack left, Jake said, "Lord, let this work, please. We want to reach as many people as possible for Your kingdom, but if we reach one person, we believe that it's worth it. In Jesus's name, I pray. And I thank You, Lord. Amen."

After Jake prayed, he went to get some food from a restaurant, and he saw a homeless man with a sign that said, "The End Is Near. Jesus Is Coming Back Soon," and Jake said, "Yes, He is coming back soon." Jake took five dollars from his pocket and gave it to the homeless man, and the man said, "Thank you." Jake went into the restaurant, sat down, and ordered a Philly cheesesteak sandwich and some mozzarella sticks, and while he was waiting on his food, he was reading his Bible. He turned to **Revelation 14:9–11**, which read, "A third angel followed them and said in a loud voice: 'If anyone worships the beast and its image and receives its mark on their forehead or on their hand, they, too, will drink the wine of God's fury, which has been poured full strength into the cup of his wrath. They will be tormented with burning sulfur in the presence of the holy angels and of the Lamb. And the smoke of their torment will rise for ever and ever. There will be no rest day or night for those who worship the beast and its image, or for anyone who receives the mark of its name.'"

Jake said, "Wow, I do not want to be here after the rapture. I don't want to be here to deal with the antichrist or the mark of the beast." He continued, "Lord, I pray that You keep me in Your hands, and keep me on the right path in Jesus's name, I pray, amen." After he finished praying, his server brought him his food, and he said, "Thank you." David came into the restaurant and saw Jake. He sat down next to him and said, "Hey, Jake, how are you doing?" Jake said, "Fine, I'm eating my food and just got done reading the Bible. I was reading about what will happen to those who take the mark of the beast." He continued, "I feel bad for those who take the mark of the beast because there's no way for people to not know about it in advance with all the technology that's available, and they still fall for it anyway."

David said, "That's true, but a lot of people know in advance. They choose to ignore it. That's why the Lord will send them a strong delusion that they will believe the antichrist over Jesus Christ. **Second Thessalonians 2:10–12** says, 'And with all deceivableness of unrighteousness in them that perish; because they received not the love of the truth, that they might be saved. And for this cause

God shall send them strong delusion, that they should believe a lie: That they all might be damned who believed not the truth, but had pleasure in unrighteousness.'" David continued. "God is going to allow people to listen to the antichrist and believe him because they have refused the truth and the light of Jesus Christ. Also, **Revelation 16:10–11** says, 'And the fifth angel poured out his vial upon the seat of the beast; and his kingdom was full of darkness; and they gnawed their tongues for pain, and blasphemed the God of heaven because of their pains and their sores, and repented not of their deeds.'" David kept talking. "The whole point of the tribulation is to bring judgment on unbelieving Israel and the world, but it's also designed to bring people to repentance during those times of great tribulation. There will be a multitude of people who will receive Jesus as their Savior, and a lot of those people will be killed by the antichrist. That's why it's important for people to give their lives to Jesus today while it won't cost them their lives."

Jake took out his laptop, typed down the entire conservation they had, and posted it on Christbook. Jake started talking. "It's going to be a terrible and awesome time to be alive, but I want to see all this happening from heaven, not on the earth. That's the reason my name is in the Book of Life," and David said, "Mine is too." After Jake was done eating, both of them left the restaurant and went their separate ways. When Jake got home, he had a lot to think about. He thought about how the kingdom of the antichrist would be covered in darkness, and that people who had the mark would curse God, even though He was using the tribulation to bring more people to Himself. He opened his Bible and turned to the book of Revelation. **Revelation 16:1–2** read, "And I heard a great voice out of the temple saying to the seven angels, Go your ways, and pour out the vials of the wrath of God upon the earth. And the first went, and poured out his vial upon the earth; and there fell a noisome and grievous sore upon the men which had the mark of the beast, and upon them which worshipped his image." He turned on the television and watched TV until it was time for him to go to bed.

The next day, Jake met up with Jack and told him what he and David had talked about the other day, and he said, "I put it on Christbook." Jack said, "That's good. We got twenty new active accounts, and forty people had liked your status." Jake said, "That's good. I want as many people to know about this. I want to give everyone a fighting chance to accept Jesus as their Savior because God is willing that no one should go to hell but that everyone should come to repentance." Jake said, "Yeah, well, keep me informed on Christbook," and Jack said, "Okay."

In history class, Jake was learning about Adolf Hitler and World War II. His teacher said, "We went through World War II and the Holocaust because we didn't learn from history, and they say those who don't learn from history are doomed to repeat it." The teacher continued. "Adolf Hitler came to power because of World War I. World War I had bankrupt Germany. Everyone needed food and basic needs, and he promised to restore them. Hitler came as a man of peace, but he bathed the world in blood. Some people saw the writing on the wall, and they tried to stop him, but most people were oblivious to what he was doing, or they helped him accomplish his evil objectives, like the Holocaust. I said earlier that I would go back to the Holocaust. The Holocaust took place during World War II, and what happened was that Hitler and his Nazis drove the Jews out of Germany and every country that they occupied. They took them from their homes, then they took them to the gas chambers and killed them. That's why I tell all of my students to be better than the generation that preceded them. And with that, class is over."

After class ended, Jake went to the computer lab. He took some of his notes from class and put them together, comparing Hitler to the antichrist. He uploaded what he wrote to Christbook, then he went to his next class. In his English class, he was talking to Jack and David about how he took the notes from his history class about Adolf Hitler and compared him to the coming world leader who would be the antichrist. Both Jack and David said, "That's good. Some people will see what we wrote and will believe it and some won't believe it until the rapture, and most won't believe it at all." David said, "I prayed that our site will stay active even through the tribulation so that people will see that we saw what was going to happen before it happened." Jack said, "What we should do is make a video explaining the rapture and the beginning of the tribulation and the mark of the beast."

Jake and David both said, "Okay, we can use the video equipment in the computer lab after school once everyone is gone," and everyone agreed. After school, everyone met in the computer lab, and they wondered, "How are we going to start the video?" Jake said, "We can do it like this," and he gave everyone their lines.

After they rehearsed what they were going to say, Jake hit the record button, and David said, "Good morning, good afternoon, and good evening, depending on the time zone you are living in right now. Something life-changing has just happened. Millions of people have just vanished off the face of the earth, and we're three of the millions of people who have vanished off the face of the earth. We knew this event was going to happen, and we know that you are looking at us trying to figure out how we knew that this event was going to take place." Jake started talking. "We knew that this event was going to happen because this event was prophesied thousands of years ago in the Bible. If you have a Bible, turn to **1 Thessalonians 4:16–18**. It reads, 'For the Lord himself shall descend from heaven with a shout, with the voice of the archangel, and with the trump of God: and the dead in Christ shall rise first: Then we which are alive and remain shall be caught up together with them in the clouds, to meet the Lord in the air: and so shall we ever be with the Lord. Wherefore comfort one another with these words.'"

Jack picked up where Jake left off. "After the rapture, the world will be in chaos, and every explanation imaginable will be put forward to explain what the Lord Jesus has just done, and everything from UFOs and invasions from outer space to evolution will be speculated, but the one thing that won't be believed is that Jesus Christ has come back in the clouds of glory to take all believers to heaven. **First Thessalonians 5:2** says, 'For yourselves know perfectly that the day of the Lord so cometh as a thief in the night.'"

Jake started talking. "For a while, there will be chaos and confusion. And in the middle of this chaos and confusion, a man will rise, and he will appear to have all the answers. He will speak to every nation as a friend, and he will tell the world to come together in the name of peace and unity, to put away all their racial, political, and religious differences, and the world will believe him because he signs a seven-year peace treaty with Israel, and this will show the world the commitment of peace that this man represents. **Daniel 9:27** says, 'And he shall confirm the covenant with many for one week: and in the midst of the week he shall cause the sacrifice and the oblation to cease, and for the overspreading of abominations he shall make it desolate, even until the consummation, and that determined shall be poured upon the desolate.' Also, **Daniel 11:21** and **Daniel 11:23–24** explain that this man will come in peace. **Daniel 11:21** says, 'And in his estate shall stand up a vile person, to whom they shall not give the honour of the kingdom: but he shall come in peaceably, and obtain the kingdom by flatteries.' **Daniel 11:23–24** says, 'And after the league made with him, he shall work deceitfully: for he shall come up, and shall become strong with a small people. He shall enter peaceably even upon the fattest places of the province; and he shall do that which his fathers have not done, nor his fathers' fathers; he shall scatter among them the prey, and spoil, and riches: yea, and he shall forecast his devices against the strong holds, even for a time.'"

Jake picked up where Jack left off. "After this treaty, the world will follow this man, and at this point there will be no mistake who this world leader is. When he arrives on the world scene, everything in you will tell you to follow this world leader." Jake continued. "His promises will seem tempting, but you must resist him. **Revelation 13:4** says, 'And they worshipped the dragon which gave power unto the beast: and they worshipped the beast, saying, "Who is like unto the beast? Who is able to make war with him?"' Also, **Revelation 13:7–8** says, 'And it was given unto him to make war with the saints, and to overcome them: and power was given him over all kindreds, and tongues, and nations. And all that dwell upon the earth shall worship him, whose names are not written in the book of life of the Lamb slain from the foundation of the world.'"

David started talking again. "The world will celebrate this peace, but when everyone says peace and safety then destruction will come upon them, according to **Jeremiah 6:14,** and **Jeremiah 8:11** says, 'For they have healed the hurt of the daughter of my people slightly, saying, Peace, peace; when there is no peace.' Lastly, we know that there will be people who will ignore this because we have made this video before the rapture, but if you do that, it would be the worst decision that you can ever make, because how do you know that you will live past today? Some people will decide to wait until after the rapture to choose rather than to stand for Jesus Christ, and that also will be a bad decision. Not only will you have to deal with the deception of the antichrist but you also might be one of those people who will receive the strong delusion that will make you believe the lie rather than the truth, and before David leads you in the prayer to receive Jesus as your Savior, I'm going to talk to you about the mark of the beast.

"When the time is right, the antichrist will force everyone to receive a mark in their right hand or forehead showing loyalty to him and the state. **Revelation 13:16–18** says, 'And he causeth all, both small and great, rich and poor, free and bond, to receive a mark in their right hand, or in their foreheads: And that no man might buy or sell, save he that had the mark, or the name of the beast, or the number of his name. Here is wisdom. Let him that hath understanding count the number of the beast: for it is the number of a man; and his number is six hundred threescore and six.' All those who take the mark will be sent to hell and they will be tormented day and night. **Revelation 14:9–11** says, 'And the third angel followed them, saying with a loud voice, If any man worship the beast and his image, and receive his mark in his forehead, or in his hand, The same shall drink of the wine of the wrath of God, which is poured out without mixture into the cup of his indignation; and he shall be tormented with fire and brimstone in the presence of the holy angels, and in the presence of the Lamb: And the smoke of their torment ascendeth up for ever and ever: and they have no rest day nor night, who worship the beast and his image, and whosoever receiveth the mark of his name.'"

David said, "Thank you, Jake. Before I lead you in the prayer to receive Jesus as your Savior, there will be one hundred and forty-four thousand witnesses who will be preaching the gospel. You need to listen to them. **Revelation 7:4** says, 'And I heard the number of them which were sealed: and there were sealed an hundred and forty and four thousand of all the tribes of the children of Israel.' In closing, I'm going to lead you through the sinner's prayer to receive Jesus Christ as your Savior. Look at me and repeat this prayer. Lord Jesus, I'm a sinner. I believe that You died for me. I ask You to come into my heart and be my Savior and wash away my sins. I receive You now, Lord Jesus. I pray this in Your name, Lord Jesus, amen. If you said this prayer and meant it, then congratulations, you have joined the kingdom of our Lord and Savior Jesus Christ during this time of great tribulation."

David kept talking. "Things are going to get worse because you are living in a time of divine judgment, but Jesus is still with you, and He will guide you trust Him. Share this video with everyone until we meet in paradise. This is Jack, David, and Jake signing off. Thanks for watching, and we wish you peace." With that, Jake went and turned the camera off. They all sighed when they were done and agreed that it was a lot of stuff to go through, but they did it. David said, "I'm going to go home and edit it before we upload it to Christbook. I'm going to add captions of each Bible scripture we mentioned so as we are talking, people can see the scriptures." And with that, everyone left the computer lab and went home.

* * * * *

The guard threw Cody into the room. His arm hit the wall, and he screamed out in pain. Paul hopped over to him and said, "Cody, are you all right?" Cody said, "I'm fine. I'm in a little pain, but I'm fine." Cody kept talking. "Paul, I'm so sorry that I got you into this. All of this is happening because of me. I should have never come back into your life." Paul said, "It's all right. We will find a way out of this. We have to trust God," and Cody said, "I do, and I know that He will get us out of this." After they had finished talking, they both went to sleep, and while they were asleep, Paul put his arm around his wounded leg.

After a few hours, the door opened, and a few of Robert's guards came into the room and said, "Wake up." They kicked Paul in his wounded leg, and he let out a scream. Two of Robert's guards picked him up and told Cody to follow them. As they took Paul to Robert, Cody followed them. He started wondering what Robert was going to do to him, and Paul started praying, "Lord Jesus, I ask You to help us find a way to escape from this warehouse without any causalities, in Jesus's name, amen." They went into Robert's office, and Cody was shoved into his office. Paul was dropped, and he landed on his right knee. Robert said, "I should kill both of you right now, but I'm going to give you a chance to make this right. You will work for me again, or I will have your brother shot and killed right in front of you."

Paul said, "Don't do it. I'm not worth it." One of the guards kicked Paul in the leg, and he screamed, but he continued talking, telling Cody not to rejoin Robert's gang. Robert took his gun and shot Paul in the other leg, and he screamed louder. As Paul was screaming, Cody said, "Enough, stop. I will rejoin you on one condition." Robert said, "What's the condition?" Cody said, "Let me take my brother to the hospital. You can even send one of your armed guards with us." Robert said, "No. Now take them back to their cell," and the guard said, "Okay." As Cody was helping Paul back to their cell, Cody said, "What's that over there?" When the guard looked, Cody dropped Paul and hit the guard with a low blow, then he picked Paul up, and they headed for the exit.

Once they were outside, they started looking for someone to help. Robert and his gang members came running out of the warehouse, shooting at them. Cody said, "We have to find a way to get help." As Cody and Paul looked around, they saw an abandoned car behind a building. Cody helped Paul to the car and said, "I'm going to find some help. Stay here until I get back." Paul said, "I'm not leaving you. We have to stick together no matter what." Cody said, "There's no time. I'm going to get some help, then I'll be on my way back as soon as I can. Do you trust me?" He said, "Yes, Cody, I trust you, and I know that you will come back for me."

Cody shut the door, then he ran as fast as he could for help. As he was running, Robert and his gang were chasing and shooting at him, but he managed to get away, and he hid on a side street by a gas station. Once he thought the coast was clear, he took off running toward the nearest police station. He kept looking around to make sure that neither Robert nor any of his gang members were around. About fifteen minutes later, he found the police station. He ran into the police station, went to the service desk, and asked to speak to someone.

The woman said, "What does this pertain to?" He said, "This man named Robert kidnapped me and my brother, and he held us prisoner in a warehouse, and we barely escaped, but my brother is in an abandoned car with two gunshot wounds to both of his legs." The woman said, "Where is your brother now?" He said, "He's by the warehouse where we escaped." The woman took out her walkie-talkie and said, "We have a 10-71. A young man has been shot. We need an ambulance and backup immediately. I'm going to take the gentleman in a squad car to where his brother is." After she got off her walkie-talkie, she told Cody to follow her to the back and that backup police officers would meet them once he showed her where Paul was.

Cody got in the squad car and showed her the car where Paul was. They both got out of the car, and Cody opened the door and helped Paul out of the car. The lady officer told additional police units where they were, and the other officers said, "We're on our way. Give us two minutes." As they were waiting, Robert and his gang members came back and started shooting at the lady officer, Cody, and Paul. All three of them ducked behind the abandoned car, and as gunshots were ringing all around them, both Cody and Paul started praying, asking the Lord to let them live through this. As they were praying, the gunshots suddenly stopped. The woman officer looked, then motioned for them to get up. They got up and saw that Robert and all of his gang members were in handcuffs, and the officers were reading them their Miranda rights as they were taking them away. Cody and Paul were happy that the nightmare was over. Paul used the police phone to call his parents; he told them where they were, and they said that they were on their way. When Paul's parents arrived, they ran to hug Paul. Cody was just standing there, then Paul's mother grabbed Cody and said, "You're our son too. You are a part of this family now."

Cody said, "Thank you. I really appreciate that." The father said, "Let's get you boys home." When they got home, they ate dinner, took showers, then lay down in their respective beds and went to sleep. A few days after the incident, the police came to the house and told Cody and Paul that Robert had been arraigned on charges of kidnapping and attempted murder. His trial was in two weeks, and the district attorney was going to subpoena both of them to testify. Cody said, "That's fine," and the officer left. Paul looked at Cody and said, "Everything worked out. We're home safe, and Robert and his gang are locked up. Thank You, Jesus." Cody said, "I couldn't have said it better myself." Later on, Cody started praying, "Lord Jesus, thank You for delivering us out of that situation, in Jesus's name I pray, amen."

Over the next few days, Cody and Paul relaxed around the house and talked about different things like their favorite food, what kind of video games they have played in the past, and what their plans were for the future. Paul said, "I want to own my own businesses. Some of them will be Christian businesses, and some of them will be non-Christian businesses, but they will still have the same values of a Christian business." Cody said, "That's good. I want to be a doctor because I want to help people. I also want to tell people about the goodness of Jesus. Also, I want people to know that their lives can be better with Him than without Him." Paul said, "That's good. And also, it's good that we both want to have jobs that are going to help people." Cody said, "After I graduate from high school, I'm taking a year off, then I'm going to medical school." Paul said, "I'm going to do the same thing with business school. I'm going for either my bachelor's degree or my master's degree. Also, I might find me a partner to help me with my companies." Cody said, "Who do you think will get to be your partner?" He said, "I don't know, but if being a doctor doesn't work out, you will always have a position in my future company," and Cody said, "Thank you, bro. I really appreciate this." Then Cody left.

As the weekend came around, Cody asked Paul what his plans were. He said, "I'm going to stay at home and recuperate. I'm still kind of hurt from being shot in the chest and both of my legs." Cody said, "That's fine. You need to recuperate. If you need anything, let me know," and Paul said, "Okay." Cody went to the park and walked around, taking in all the beauty that God had created. He said, "We don't take time to even take in the beauty that is all around us," and as he was taking in the beauty, he said, "I know what I'm going to say when it comes to the trial. I forgive him for everything that he's done to me, just as Jesus forgives me for all the evil that I've done." He left the park and went to get something to eat. He went to R&B's to get a triple bacon cheeseburger, some fries, and a chocolate cookie-and-cream milkshake. He sat down, and while he was eating, four people came into the restaurant, and one of the four people said, "This is a holdup. I want everyone to put all their money, jewelry, and other valuables in the bag, and we will be on our way out." Cody got up and walked over to them, and he said, "You people don't have to do this. Right now, you are just some petty thieves, but all you have to do is give everyone their belongings back and leave, and I promise that no one will report you to the police."

Another robber took the butt of his gun and hit Cody in the head, knocking him out. By the time he woke up, the robbers were gone, but everyone there told him how brave he was standing up to the robbers, and he said, "Thank you, but I was trying to do what was right." Cody finished his food, then went back to Paul's house and told Paul what happened. Paul said, "I should have been there to help you," and Cody said, "No, you were right where you were supposed to be—at home recuperating and getting stronger, so when I do need you, you can come help me." Paul said, "I understand. I'm going to get better as fast as I can, and even if I'm not at one hundred percent, if you need me, I will be there to help you," and Cody said, "Okay." Cody asked Paul about what he was going to say to the judge, and Paul said, "I'm going to ask the judge to forgive him for everything even though he deserves to go to jail. I don't want him to get the max, which might be fifteen years, but I will ask the judge to give him five years." Cody said, "That's crazy. When I was in the park, I was thinking about what I would say, and I said that I would forgive him too, just as Jesus Christ forgives us when we sin. **Matthew 6:14–15** says, 'For if you forgive other people when they sin against you, your heavenly Father will also forgive you. But if you do not forgive others their sins, your Father will not forgive your sins.'"

The week before the trial, they both went to the district attorney's office. They went over their testimony, and the district attorney said, "As long as you stick to the truth, Robert and his gang will be behind bars for a long time." Paul's mother said, "That's good. I hope while they are in prison, they will give their lives to Jesus and let Him guide their lives," and both Cody and Paul said, "Amen." After they left the district attorney's office, Paul's mother said, "What do both of you want to do now?" Cody said, "How about we go to the movies? Is it all right with you, Mom, if you don't mind me calling you Mom?" She said, "I don't mind if you call me Mom. We can go to the movies. I think that could get your minds off all the negative things that both of you have been through these past few months." Paul said, "Yeah, I believe that it will." They drove to the movie theater and bought tickets to see a movie called *Super*. The movie was about a kid who came to earth to save the world, but instead of using his powers to save mankind, he used his powers to destroy mankind. Once the movie was over, Paul's mom asked them, "How was the movie?" and they both said it was good; it had a lot of action, and the story was well written.

They both continued talking about the movie. It helped them take their minds off all the crazy things that had happened over the past few months. After the movie, they went to get something to eat, then they returned to the house to do some homework and get ready for school. They worked on a group project for their English class where they had to create a short story about anything that they wanted. They created a story about them creating a wrestling company, and how another wrestling company tried to put them out of business, and they had to get edgier in order to compete and not go out of business, and in the end, they bought the rival wrestling company that tried to put them out of business. After they finished their project, they watched a little television, then they prayed and went to bed. The next day at school, they turned in their school projects and met up with some friends for lunch, and they told their friends all about the crazy things that they had been going through the past few months.

When they were done, everyone said, "Wow, y'all have been through a lot," and Cody said, "Yeah, but God said in **Isaiah 41:10**, 'So do not fear, for I am with you; do not be dismayed, for I am your God. I will strengthen you and help you; I will uphold you with my righteous right hand.' **Matthew 28:20** says, 'Teaching them to obey everything I have commanded you. And surely I am with you always, to the very end of the age.'" Cody said, "The last scripture I'm going to use is **Joshua 1:9**, which says, 'Have I not commanded you? Be strong and courageous. Do not be afraid; do not be discouraged, for the Lord your God will be with you wherever you go.'" Paul started talking. "Even though I was shot three times in less than a few months, and we were both kidnapped, we still trust God to keep us, and we knew that He was going to get us out of that situation. Also, we both said that we forgave Robert and his gang for what he did. We're going to ask the judge to give him a light sentence of five years instead of giving him a max of fifteen years to life." One of their friends said, "That's the definition of a true Christian, to be able to forgive someone who tried to kill you and leave you for dead." Paul said, "**John 13:35** says, 'By this everyone will know that you are my disciples, if you love one another.'"

After lunch, Paul and Cody went to history class. They were studying 9/11, also known as September 11, when some terrorists hijacked some planes and flew them into the World Trade Center, killing over three thousand people and injuring hundreds more, but eventually, they were caught and brought to justice. Paul turned to Cody and said, "They were brought to justice, just like Robert," and at that point, the bell rang, and they went home to study.

* * * * *

A few days after the rally, Julia and Tommy were both nervous for different reasons. Julia was nervous because she wanted to be vice president so that she could help CROWN improve and so that the word of God could be spread to all the schools. Tommy was nervous because he wanted to become vice president so that he and Ultimate Light could destroy CROWN; he knew that failure was not going to be tolerated. He went to Jason and said, "As of right now, Julia is winning." Jason said, "I know, but I have a plan. We're going to set her up, so everyone will believe that she's still working for us and that we sent her into the group to take it down from the inside. We are going to make it seem like you are the perfect person to be the vice president of CROWN."

Tommy said, "Perfect, but how are you going to set her up? Everybody knows that she has given her life to Jesus." Jason said, "That's true, but everyone knows of people who say that they're Christians. **Matthew 7:15** says, 'Beware of false prophets, which come to you in sheep's clothing, but inwardly they are ravening wolves.'" Tommy said, "How did you know where that Bible verse was?" Jason said, "I started reading the Bible so that when those Christian idiots try to use the Bible against me, I can use it on them." Tommy said, "Okay, I was making sure that you haven't lost your nerve and turned your back on us." Jason said, "I will never lose my nerve. I will do everything in my power to make sure that Christianity and CROWN will be destroyed." Tommy said, "I have to go. I have to attend a meeting with Chris and Julia because the election is next week," and Jason said, "Okay."

The next day after class had ended, Chris met with Julia and Tommy, and he told them that at the next meeting, they would have one more chance to plead their case on why they should be elected as vice president of CROWN, then a few days after that, everyone was going to vote. After that, Chris would count up the votes, then at the following meeting, he would announce who the vice president would be. "But no matter who wins, I don't want to see any infighting among you two. Even though this is an election, we're all friends here, and one can help the other to make the group better." Julia and Tommy both said, "Okay."

Later that night, Julia prayed. "Lord, I want to win this election. I believe that I will be the best person for the job, but I surrender to Your will because You know what's best. In Jesus's name, amen." That night, Jason put his plan into action. He went and found all Julia's old papers that she had written about destroying CROWN, and he doctored the papers to make it seem like Julia was still involved with the group. He even changed all the time stamps. Then he printed them off. He thought, *Tomorrow, I'm going to put these papers in everybody's locker so that they will turn against her and elect Tommy as the vice president.* Jason went to school earlier than normal; he put the papers in every locker and taped the papers on every door in the school. After he was done putting up the papers, he quickly and quietly snuck out of the school before anybody could come into the school and learn that he was the one who put up the flyers. When the teachers and students were filing into the school, they saw the papers showing Julia talking about destroying CROWN and how she was going to send someone into the group to destroy it from the inside. The flyer even said, "I myself might go in and infiltrate CROWN to destroy them."

As everyone was reading the flyers, Julia walked into the building. She started reading the flyers and said, "I said this a long time ago before I became a Christian. Now that I'm a Christian, I want to spread the love of Jesus to everyone. I want to take CROWN to places it's never been before, not destroy it." As she was talking, people started booing her, and she said, "I'm telling the truth. I'm not the person that I was." But as she was talking, people started booing louder, and at that point, she said, "I have to find Chris so I can explain to him that these papers are who I was before I gave my life to Jesus, but this isn't who I am now." Julia ran, and she went throughout the entire school looking for Chris. When she found him, he was sitting in a classroom, waiting for class to start. She ran up to him and said, "We have a problem." Chris said, "I already know about the flyers and them saying that you are going to destroy CROWN from the inside, but the only thing I can do is pray. I would count today as a blessing because you have one last chance to convince the members of CROWN that you deserve to be vice president." Chris continued. "I believe that you have what it takes, but you will have to convince everyone else. Can you do it?" She said, "Yes, I can, and I will be the vice president." Chris said, "Okay. After class, all hands on deck. I expect you to do great. I'm rooting for you." Julia left and headed for class. The whole day, she kept getting weird looks from every member of CROWN, and she felt bad. She knew that was how she felt before she had found the love of Jesus. She started praying, "Lord Jesus, I pray that the truth comes out, and I pray that whoever did this will be exposed, in Jesus's name I pray, and I thank You, Lord. Amen."

During lunch, she sat down next to Chris and told him that she'd prayed that the truth will come out and that the person who did this will either confess or be exposed. Chris said, "He will remember **Isaiah 54:17**, which says, 'No weapon formed against you shall prosper, and, every tongue which rises against you in judgment You shall condemn. This is the heritage of the servants of the Lord, and, their righteousness *is* from Me.'" He continued. "Even if you don't win the election, don't let it worry you or make you doubt your faith. Like I said before, if you don't win, maybe the Lord has something better for you, like my position as president of CROWN." Julia said, "You're right. I'm not going to worry about this anymore. I'm just going to trust Jesus and accept the outcome."

Chris said, "That's good. I will see you after school," and she said, "Yes, you will." After she had talked to Chris, the rest of her school day went as well as could have been expected. Even though she kept getting weird looks from members of CROWN, she didn't let it get to her. She kept a positive attitude. After school ended, she went to where the meeting was being held, and before she went into the classroom she prayed. She said, "Not my will, but Your will be done, Lord," and she went into the classroom. Members of CROWN were still giving her weird looks, but she didn't let it bother her.

When everyone was seated, Chris stood in front of everyone and said, "Welcome to the final CROWN meeting before the vice presidential election. First, we're going to give our two candidates one final chance to talk to you and convince you to vote for them. The first person I want to introduce you to is Tommy." Tommy got up and walked to the front of the classroom. He said, "I still believe that I'm the best person to be vice president, and since I have experience from being the former vice president of No Light, I can bring that same passion to CROWN before I saw the light and became a Christian. I wanted to destroy this group, now I want to see this group not only survive but thrive, and I want everyone in every school to give their lives to Jesus. Thank you." Then Tommy went back to his seat. Chris got back up and said, "Now I want to introduce the second candidate, Julia." Julia got up and walked to the front of the classroom. She took a deep breath and started talking.

"Hi, everyone, my name is Julia, and I believe that I'm the best person to be vice president. I've been loyal to CROWN ever since I gave my life to Jesus Christ. My salvation is genuine, and I wouldn't do anything to hurt any of you." She continued. "Let me talk about the flyers that all of you have seen today. All the writings that you saw, I did write them, but I wrote those over a year ago before I found Jesus. I was planning on destroying CROWN from the inside, but once I found Jesus and gave my life to Him, He started to change my heart, and now I don't want to destroy this group. I want to help this group. Also, I didn't ask Chris to be your vice president. He came to me and told me that he was going to appoint me as vice president. I told him to give me a few days to think about it because I wanted to pray and be sure that I was the right one to help lead, and now I know I am. I just need for you to trust me. Thank you." Then she went back to her seat.

Chris got back up, clapped his hands, and started talking. "I would like to thank both candidates for giving us great speeches. Now it's on you to vote on which one you believe will best represent you as vice president. Now let's talk about the end times and the forgiveness of Jesus and rejecting it. The Bible tells us that anyone who hears about the forgiveness of Jesus Christ and rejects it is saving up a terrible punishment. Go to **Romans 2:5–6**. 'But because of your stubbornness and your unrepentant heart, you are storing up wrath against yourself for the day of God's wrath, when his righteous judgment will be revealed. God will repay each person according to what they have done.' Anybody who rejects Jesus or thinks to themselves, 'I will wait until the tribulation to decide to follow Jesus,' that would be the craziest thing to do, because how do you know that you will live another day? No one is guaranteed one more breath beyond the one that you are breathing now. Choose this day whom you will serve, Jesus or the devil. Before I let you go, I want to pray for everyone. Lord Jesus, I pray that anyone who hasn't decided to follow You will make that choice today. Also, I pray that this group will pick the best person to be the vice president and that the person they choose will do Your will, in Jesus's name, amen."

Chris dismissed the group but asked both Julia and Tommy to stay behind so that he could talk to both of them. When they were alone, Chris said, "Good job, both of you, and congratulations, vice president." He shook both of their hands and said, "I'm saying this because the next time we're all together, one of you will be the vice president of CROWN, and I know that either one of you will do the position proud." They both said thank you and left.

When Julia got home, she was worried. She wondered if anyone was going to believe what she said about being a genuine Christian and whether people would judge her based on what she did before she became a Christian. After about an hour of thinking about it, she said, "I'm not going to worry about it. I'm going to let the Lord's will be done." She opened up the Bible, turned it to **Luke 22:42**, and read, "Father, if you are willing, take this cup from me; yet not my will, but yours be done."

At the same time, Tommy was talking to Jason. Jason said, "The plan is working perfectly. Soon I will be vice president of CROWN, and we will start phase two of our plan. We will slowly destroy CROWN, and the best part is that no one will see it coming." Tommy said, "So far so good. I am the perfect candidate, and I've been very good at being a good Christian. I've read the Bible and learned to speak their language, so they can completely trust me." Jason said, "When you first get into office, you have to appear to be doing what's best for CROWN, and you have to attack us personally." Tommy said, "What are you talking about attacking you personally?" Jason said, "I mean you have to go to other schools that we control, and you have to convert people to Christianity." Tommy said, "No, I don't want to make CROWN stronger. I want to destroy them." Jason said, "Tommy, listen to me. The ultimate goal is to destroy CROWN, but it has to seem like you are working to make it better. It has to be like a virus. It has to get in so deep that before they know it, it will be too late to stop it." Tommy said, "I trust your leadership. You haven't led me wrong yet, and I know you won't lead me wrong in the future," then he left.

The next day, CROWN met in the room that they always met in, and once they were all settled, Chris got up and said, "Today is the day that everyone has been waiting for. Today is election day. Today, we will have a vice president elect, and it's going to be either Julia or Tommy." Chris continued. "What we are going to do is, one at a time, everyone is going to get up and write the name of the person they want to see be vice president, then everyone is going to put their paper in this box, and after everyone is done, I'm going to tally up the votes. Then I'm going to announce who the new vice president will be. I will be the first to cast my vote."

Chris cast his vote, then everyone in CROWN got up and cast their votes, and when everyone was done, Chris took the box so he could count up the votes. Julia and Tommy were nervous; they didn't know which way the election was going to go. Chris came back and said, "I've counted the ballots, and we have a winner. Your new vice president of CROWN is..."

10

On the last day of the retreat, Daniel, Jasmine, William, Eric, Brittany, and I went swimming, and we did archery, and we also went hiking, and while we were hiking, Eric started talking, and he said, "How's everyone enjoying the retreat?" and Brittany said, "I'm enjoying myself. I'm also enjoying nature." I said, "I agree. I'm enjoying nature, and I got to meet people from all over. Also another thing, I get to worship Jesus and get encouragement, but the best part is I get to spend time with William. We are growing closer as brothers because of this retreat. And lastly, I'm learning more about the Bible and what's going to happen during the tribulation."

William said, "I'm also enjoying spending time with you, and I'm learning more about your faith and what's coming according to your Bible." Brittany started talking as she looked at William. "The antichrist is going to do so much evil that one-third of the people who are left behind will be killed in seven years, and that's America eight times over. He's going to force everyone to take the mark of the beast, and without that, no one will be able to buy or sell, but it's not about buying or selling. It's about who you are pledging loyalty to, Jesus or the devil. Anyone who rejects the mark will be killed." She opened her Bible and turned to **Revelation 20:4** and read it. "And I saw thrones, and they sat upon them, and judgment was given unto them: and I saw the souls of them that were beheaded for the witness of Jesus, and for the word of God, and which had not worshipped the beast, neither his image, neither had received his mark upon their foreheads, or in their hands; and they lived and reigned with Christ a thousand years."

I started talking. "We're telling you this because after Jesus comes back, and the antichrist comes to power, he's going to force everyone to take his mark, and anyone who rejects it will be killed. Also, we are telling you this because we don't want you to be left behind to choose between taking the mark of the beast or getting your head cut off." William said, "What happens to those who take the mark?" I took the Bible, turned to **Revelation 14:9–11**, and started reading. "And the third angel followed them, saying with a loud voice, If any man worship the beast and his image, and receive his mark in his forehead, or in his hand, The same shall drink of the wine of the wrath of God, which is poured out without mixture into the cup of his indignation; and he shall be tormented with fire and brimstone in the presence of the holy angels, and in the presence of the Lamb: And the smoke of their torment ascended up for ever and ever: and they have no rest day nor night, who worship the beast and his image, and whosoever received the mark of his name." I continued. "There's one more scripture I want to read to you, and it's **Revelation 16:2**. 'And the first went, and poured out his vial upon the earth; and there fell a noisome and grievous sore upon the men which had the mark of the beast, and upon them which worshipped his image.'"

Eric took over the conservation. "Things are going to get so bad that two things are going to happen. One, during the tribulation, there will be silence in heaven for a period of thirty minutes. If Jesus didn't return seven years later, no one wowld be saved."

William said, "I'm going to seriously think about everything that you all have told me," and everyone said, "Okay." Later, Daniel and I went canoeing, and we talked about everything. Daniel asked me what made me give my life to Jesus. I said, "After you told me about Jesus, and I rejected Him, I kept feeling Him soften my heart until I finally surrendered to the forgiveness and love of Jesus. After that, He's been with me every step of the way." Daniel said, "That's good. I pray for William every day that he will see the light like you have and give himself over to Jesus. Also, I want your parents to give their lives to Jesus too because God is willing that no one will perish but that all will come to repentance." I said thank you, then we got out of the canoe.

We met with everyone for lunch, and we had pizza and salad, and while we were eating, we were talking about next year's event in California. "I was talking to the pastor, and I was telling him that it would be nice to have the next event in California, so we can all have a chance to get out and experience life outside the city." Everyone said, "That sounds like a good idea if we do it. We should have a fun time." Later that night, we had the final concert to close out the retreat, and halfway through the concert, the rap artist Michael said, "Before we go any further, I want to stop to tell everyone something. I know we're having a good time praising Jesus, but I wouldn't be all right with not giving anyone an opportunity to receive Jesus Christ as their personal Lord and Savior. **John 3:16–18** says, 'For God so loved the world that he gave his one and only Son, that whoever believes in him shall not perish but have eternal life. For God did not send his Son into the world to condemn the world, but to save the world through him. Whoever believes in him is not condemned, but whoever does not believe stands condemned already because they have not believed in the name of God's one and only Son who is Jesus Christ.'"

Michael continued. "Anyone who wants to accept Jesus as their Savior, repeat this prayer. Lord Jesus, Savior of the world, You died for me. You were beaten to take away my sins. Today, I ask You to come into my heart and be my Savior. Cleanse me of my sins. I pray this in Jesus's name, amen." I looked around and saw people praying with Michael to receive Jesus as their Savior. I looked at William and saw that William wasn't praying, so I started praying that he would receive Jesus as his Savior. Once everybody was finished praying, Michael started playing his music again, and William looked back at me and asked me whether I was praying, and I said, "Yes, I was," and William said, "Why were you praying? You're already a Christian." I said, "I was praying for you. I'm always praying for you. It's a part of my job as your older brother to always look out for you and protect you, and that includes praying for you."

William started crying, and he hugged me, and he said, "Thank you so much, brother. I love you." I said, "I love you too. I'm so happy that you came to this retreat," and William said, "So am I." We enjoyed the rest of the concert, and after the concert was over, everyone went back to their cabins to pack and get ready to go home in the morning. After I finished packing, I started praying, and said, "Lord Jesus, thank You for allowing William to attend this retreat. It was a life-changing experience. In Jesus's name, amen." Then I lay down and went to sleep.

The next day, I had a hard time getting out of bed because I didn't want to leave this beautiful site I'd been at for the past few days, but eventually, I got out of the bed and woke William up, then we got dressed, ate, and put our belongings in the car. Then we met up with the gang. Everyone was talking about all the fun they had had at the retreat, then William said, "Before we leave, can we pray that everyone will have a safe journey, and can I be the one to pray?"

Daniel said, "Sure," and William started praying, "Lord Jesus, thank You for bringing all of us together, and I thank You for allowing Antowon to bring me here to this retreat. I learned a lot about You. I pray that we have a safe ride back to our homes until we have the next CROWN meeting, in Jesus's name, amen." I said, "Amen," and I hugged William. Everyone went to their cars, and when William got to the car, he looked at me and said, "Why did I volunteer to pray, and why did I pray in Jesus's name?" I said, "I guess the Lord used you to pray for us all. I guess that was the Lord trying to reach you. Maybe He's saying that you will give your life to Him before you die," and William said, "Okay." As we were driving home, I said, "William, I'm very proud of you," and William said, "Why?" I said, "I'm proud of you because you came to an event that was totally out of your element. The majority of the people there were Christians. You were maybe the only Muslim there, but you didn't let that stop you. You went, and you had a good time. Also, the Lord used you to pray for us so that we all would get home safe."

William said, "Thank you." I said, "Before we go home, let's go get some ice cream, then we're going home to watch TV and relax." We stopped and got some ice cream. William got chocolate, and I got cookies and cream, and while we were eating, I was staring into the sky. William noticed me staring into the sky. He said, "What are you staring at?"

"Nothing, I was thinking."

"About what?"

"Nothing, it's not for you to know."

"What is it?"

"I was thinking about the return of Jesus. When He comes back, I will be raptured."

William said, "What are you talking about, you will be raptured?"

"When Jesus comes back, all those who have given their lives to Jesus will be called to heaven to be with Him." I grabbed my Bible and turned to **1 Thessalonians 4:16–18** and I read, "'For the Lord himself will come down from heaven, with a loud command, with the voice of the archangel and with the trumpet call of God, and the dead in Christ will rise first. After that, we who are still alive and are left will be caught up together with them in the clouds to meet the Lord in the air. And so, we will be with the Lord forever. Therefore encourage one another with these words.' Also, **1 Corinthians 15:52–54** says, 'A flash, in the twinkling of an eye, at the last trumpet. For the trumpet will sound, the dead will be raised imperishable, and we will be changed. For the perishable must clothe itself with the imperishable, and the mortal with immortality. When the perishable has been clothed with the imperishable, and the mortal with immortality, then the saying that is written will come true: "Death has been swallowed up in victory."' When this happens, all those who haven't decided to give their lives to Jesus will be left behind. Also, when this happens, it will be invisible to the nonbeliever. That's what I meant when I said before that there will be mass chaos, and everyone will be trying to figure out what happened. The antichrist will use this event to unite the world under his one world government. He's going to tell the world that this event might happen again so they will follow him, and most people will follow him right to hell. This is the reason I'm telling you to receive Jesus as your Savior. The tribulation will be a time of delusion and deception, and even the lines of good and evil will be blurred in your mind."

I kept talking. "I don't want you to fall for his deception and take his mark because that will doom you to hell forever. Also, those who refuse the mark will have a hard time surviving and having a normal life." William said, "I have a question. What is the point of the tribulation?" I said, "The point of the tribulation is to judge unbelieving Israel and the world. It's also to bring repentance so people will know that Jesus Christ is Lord." William said, "That does make sense, but I'm still not turning against Allah and Islam." I said, "I understand. I don't want you to go through the tribulation, but you might have to experience the tribulation so you can experience the love and wrath of God." William said, "No, I won't because Allah will protect me. So when this antichrist character comes, if he comes, I will be protected." I sighed and said, "Okay, let's go home and relax." I drove us home, and when we got home, our parents asked us about our weekend, and we said, "We had fun." Our mother said, "Did you convert them to Islam?" William said, "No. We did try, but they said that they were loyal to Jesus," and the mother said, "Okay, at least you tried." I went to my room and unpacked my stuff. Then I went and lay down and went to sleep.

A few days later, I was watching TV when father burst into my room, and he was screaming, "What is this? What is this?" I said, "Dad, what are you talking about?"

"You have turned your back on Allah and Islam to follow Jesus Christ."

"Yes, I have, because Jesus died on the cross for my sins."

My father was filled with so much rage, he slapped me across the face hard, then he said, "Jesus isn't God. There's only one god, and his name is Allah. I want to hear you say it. Allah is the only true god."

I said, "No, Jesus Christ is the only true God."

My father slapped me again and screamed, "William, get in here now." William came into the room, and our father said, "Did you know about this?" Before William could answer, I got up and said, "Leave him alone. He doesn't know anything," and our father said, "Shut up," and slapped me across the room again. William said, "Father, stop. This is your son and my brother." Our father said, "He's no son of mine, and he's not your brother. He turned against us and our religion, and now he must die." Our father pulled out a gun and pointed it at me, but William stepped in front of me and said, "No, I'm not going to allow you to kill my brother." Our father pushed William out of the way and said, "He turned his back on the one true god, so now he must die."

William got in front of me again and said, "I knew Antowon had become a Christian, but I told him that I would have his back to the end, so if you want to kill him, you're going to have to kill me too." Our father kept pointing the gun at both William and me. He had so much rage in his eyes, but eventually, he put his gun down, grabbed me by my shirt, and dragged me out of my room and down the steps. Then he opened the door and threw me out of the house. I hit my head on the ground. William ran down the steps as our father was dragging me down and throwing me out of the house, and when I hit the ground, William ran out of the house toward me. But our father grabbed William's arm and said, "No, you're not going to help him." William pulled away from our father. He ran to me, helped me up, and said, "If my brother isn't welcomed here, neither am I. I'm going with my brother." He gave me my car keys and said, "As Father was dragging you out, I grabbed your keys, wallet, socks, and shoes, and your cell phone."

I said, "Thank you." I put my socks and shoes on, then said, "William, let's go." William helped me to my feet, and as we were leaving, our father kept screaming, "William, get back here. Get back here now or you will regret it." As our father kept yelling, we walked to the car and drove off. Once we were far enough from the house, I started crying, and William looked at me and said, "Antowon, it's going to be all right. I'm with you." I said, "I know you are, and I appreciate it. I knew this was coming, but I didn't think it would be as bad as it was. I didn't think he would pull a gun on me and drag me down the steps and throw me out, but he did." William said, "I'm sorry about it. It's my fault. He found the Bible in my book bag, and when he questioned me, I told him that it wasn't mine, so he knew it had to be yours. I'm so sorry. It's my fault," and William started crying. At that moment, I stopped the car and turned to William, and I said, "It's not your fault. I knew he was going to find out eventually. I was ready." Then I started the car again and kept driving.

William asked me where we were going, and I said, "To Daniel's house. Call him and tell him that we're coming." William said, "Okay," and called Daniel. Once he got off the phone, he said that he talked to Daniel and explained to him the situation; also, he told him that we were on our way, and Daniel had said, "We will be ready for both of you when you get here." I said, "Okay." When we got to Daniel's house, we both explained to Daniel and his parents what had happened, and his mom and dad told William and me that we were both welcome to stay with them as long as we wanted. Both of us said, "Thank you," and Daniel said, "Follow me." We both got up and followed him, and we went to his room. He already had sleeping bags and pillows out for us. William and I picked out which sleeping bag we wanted. I prayed, then I, William, and Daniel went to sleep.

The next day, Daniel woke William and me up, and he told us to come downstairs because his mom and dad had a surprise for us. We both got up and went downstairs, and we saw that Daniel's mother had made us breakfast. She had gone to the store and had bought us some clothes. William said, "You didn't have to do this for us. Just having us here is enough." Daniel's father said, "It's no problem. After all you two have been through, we wanted to show you both the kind of love that Jesus has for us all. It's unconditional love. No matter what you have gone through, you both will have Jesus, and you will have all of us." At that moment, my problems went away, and a large weight came off my shoulders.

* * * * *

Cierra's mother stayed in the hospital for a couple of weeks before she was released. Cierra was relieved. She drove her mother home, put her in bed, and left her to sleep. She called Jenny and told her what happened, and Jenny said, "Oh my goodness, is she all right?" Cierra told Jenny that she was fine. "She's resting in her room, and I'm going to be working in the house and doing all the chores until she is well enough to get back on her feet." Jenny said, "That's good. If you need any help with doing that, please let me know, and I will help you." Cierra said, "Thank you, I will let you know."

"Okay, I will talk to you later. I have to help my mom take care of some things, but if you need help, don't hesitate to call me, and I will help you." Cierra said, "Okay," and hung up the phone. She went to check in on her mother and saw that she was still asleep, so she closed the door and went to her room. She turned on the TV and watched *Hero*, an action TV show until she went to sleep.

She woke up periodically to check on her mother. Everything was fine, so about three o'clock in the morning, she finally went to bed. She woke up at 1:00 p.m. and went to her mother's room to check up on her, and her mother wasn't in her room. She said, "Mom, Mom, where are you?" She went down to the kitchen and saw her eating a sandwich, and she said, "Mom, why didn't you ask me to fix you the sandwich?" Cierra's mom said, "You looked very good sleeping, and I didn't want to wake you up." Cierra said, "Don't worry about me. If you need something, don't hesitate to wake me up, and I will take care of it." Her mother said, "Thank you." Cierra went to get a bowl of cereal. Twenty minutes later, she went to the mall, but before she left, she told her mother, "I'll be back as soon as I can," and her mother said, "Okay." Cierra went to a few stores and bought her mom a few things. She thought, *I'm going to surprise her with these.* She stopped at a restaurant and got her mother some food, then she went home.

When she got home, she called for her mother, but she didn't get a response. Cierra started getting frantic. She put the food on the table and started running through the house, opening every door, screaming, "Mom." Finally, she found her on the couch.

Cierra went to her mom and said, "Mom, Mom, are you all right?" Her mother woke up and said, "What is it, Cierra? I was sleeping." And Cierra said, "I was calling for you. I brought us some lunch, and I also brought you something else. Close your eyes."

Cierra's mother closed her eyes, then Cierra took out the present that she had bought, then said, "Mom, open your eyes." She opened her eyes, and when she saw the dress, she squealed. She grabbed the dress and got off the couch. "I love this dress. You got my favorite color, red. Thank you so much, Cierra. I really truly appreciate this." Cierra said, "You're welcome. I also went through the drive-through and got you some chili and some chicken nuggets. I also bought you some cookies and cream ice cream. I hope this helps you feel better and recover quickly," and she said, "So do I, Cierra, so do I." They both ate their food, then Cierra said, "I'm going to my room to take a nap. Also, I'm going to take the phone with me so no one disturbs you." Cierra's mother said, "Okay, but before you go, thank you again for buying me the red dress, and for buying me lunch." Cierra said, "You're welcome," then she went to her room, got in her pajamas, and turned on her music. While she was listening to her music, she fell asleep, and as she slept, she had another nightmare. She woke up screaming in a cold sweat.

She said, *I have to stop having these nightmares.* She started screaming, "God, Jesus, leave me alone. Stop sending me these nightmares. I will never serve You, so stop torturing me." Then she went back to sleep. When she woke up in the morning, she went to the kitchen and smelled sausage, pancakes, and freshly brewed coffee. She said, "Mom, what's the occasion?"

"I wanted to say thank you so much for what you did yesterday. I really, really appreciate it. So I decided to wake up early and surprise you with food just like you surprised me with food and a dress." Cierra sat down, and her mother fixed her a plate, then she fixed herself a plate and sat down. They had a nice talk and bonded over a hot breakfast, then they went to the living room and watched a few movies. They enjoyed relaxing at home watching TV and movies all day. The next day, Jenny came over to check on Cierra's mother. She knocked on the door, and Cierra answered the door. Jenny said, "Hi, Cierra, how are you doing?" Cierra said, "I'm doing good. How are you doing?" She said, "I'm doing good. How is your mom doing?" Cierra said, "She's fine. We ate breakfast together yesterday and watched TV and movies all day, which we both enjoyed." Jenny said,

"It's good that you both bonded. Both of you have been growing apart for a long time."

Cierra said, "Yes, we were."

Jenny said, "I've been praying that both of you would become close again. I also prayed that she would recover, and she did." Cierra said, "Thank you, thank you so much for your prayer," and Jenny said, "You're welcome." Cierra said, "Do you want to come in?" Jenny said, "Sure," and she walked into the house. They sat down in the living room, and Jenny asked Cierra, "Have you had any more dreams since the last time I talked to you?" Cierra said, "Yes. Yesterday, I had another dream that I had died and I went to hell. I saw fire and flames everywhere, and I smelled the smell of burning bodies, and the smell was horrendous." Cierra continued, "I heard screams, and this ugly-looking creature grabbed me and started pulling me toward the gates, and then a bright light penetrated the darkness, and the ugly creature let me go, and I started ascending back to earth. This happened four times, then the final time when the creature grabbed me, he wouldn't let go, then I heard a voice say, 'Let her go,' and the entire place shook like an earthquake, and the creature let me go, then I ascended back to earth."

Jenny said, "That was Jesus. He's trying to warn you to repent and turn to Him while there's still time." Cierra said, "I don't believe it. There must be some rational explanation as to why God is doing this, if God is doing this." Jenny said, "The only rational explanation is that He's showing you what hell looks like, and what's waiting for you if you choose not to follow Jesus. If you turn your back on Jesus, you will be destroyed."

Jenny continued. "Every opportunity to accept Jesus as your Savior should be grabbed because one day the rapture will come, or one day you will die, and dying without Jesus will mean complete and total damnation. A few years after the rapture, when the antichrist comes back from the dead, he's going to force everyone who's left behind to take the mark, and all of those who refuse the mark will be killed, and the question that baffles me is why people reject the way of escape when the choice is to either escape by accepting Jesus as their Savior or facing the antichrist. I wouldn't want to be in a situation where I would have to choose between accepting the mark of the beast and going to hell, or standing for Jesus and potentially getting your head cut off. Also, you should want to escape the judgment seat of Christ." Cierra said, "What's the judgment seat of Christ?" Jenny said, "It's when everyone who hasn't given their life to Jesus will be judged and sent to their final destination. **Second Corinthians 5:10** says, 'For we must all appear before the judgment seat of Christ, so that each of us may receive what is due us for the things done while in the body, whether good or bad.' **Revelation 20:11–15** says, 'Then I saw a great white throne and him who was seated on it. The earth and the heavens fled from his presence, and there was no place for them. And I saw the dead, great and small, standing before the throne, and books were opened. Another book was opened, which is the book of life. The dead were judged according to what they had done as recorded in the books. The sea gave up the dead that were in it, and death and Hades gave up the dead that were in them, and each person was judged according to what they had done. Then death and Hades were thrown into the lake of fire. The lake of fire is the second death. Anyone whose name was not found written in the book of life was thrown into the lake of fire.'"

Jenny kept talking. "Cierra, I care for you like a sister, and I don't want you to go through the tribulation, and I don't want you to go to hell, and neither does God. The final scripture I'm going to use is **2 Peter 3:9**, which says, 'The Lord is not slow in keeping his promise, as some understand slowness. Instead, he is patient with you, not wanting anyone to perish, but everyone to come to repentance.'" Cierra said, "I don't want to get my head cut off, but I still won't follow Jesus," and Jenny said, "I won't bring this conservation up anymore," and Cierra said, "Thank you." Then Jenny went home.

A few days later, Cierra went to the gym and worked out for a few hours. A few of her classmates from school came by, and they said, "Hey, Cierra, how are you doing?" Cierra said, "I'm fine. I needed to get some exercise. With all the food I've eaten due to stress, work, and school, I'm tired, and I'm gaining a whole lot of weight." One of her friends said, "That's good. You need to use whatever you think is necessary to get your mind off this stress." Cierra said, "Thank you.

I'm about to put my headphones on and finish my routine." They said, "Okay," and left.

Cierra spent the rest of her time working out and lifting weights, then she got in the car and went home. She went to her room, lay down, and went to bed. Cierra woke up a few hours later and went to check on her mother; she found her resting. Cierra went downstairs and ordered a sausage, ham, and pepperoni pizza, and then she went on her computer. She was surfing the Internet, and an article read, "Breaking news: Iran has attacked Greece in an unprovoked attack, and Greece has retaliated. Now Iran and Greece are at war. We will keep you updated as this situation develops." At that point, she was like, "We are closer to World War III." She kept searching the Internet and kept seeing sites reporting the incident between Iran and Greece. A few hours later, she went back on the Internet and looked for updates on the conflict between Iran and Greece. The reports said that Iran had invaded Greece, and the army of Greece had retreated to the capital. One-fourth of the country was now under the occupation of Iran, and the government of Greece was struggling to regroup.

Cierra said, "Dang, one-fourth of the country is now under Iranian occupation." The site said, "We will keep everyone updated as this situation continues to develop." Cierra got off the computer and called Jenny. She told Jenny about what happened in Greece, and Jenny said, "I'm surprised that it was Greece and Iran, but it doesn't surprise me that one country invaded another, because in the last days, the whole world will be filled with violence, and there shall be revolutions in every country." Jenny continued. "I do hope Iran doesn't conquer any more countries or territories." Cierra said, "I hope everything goes back to normal soon." Jenny said, "So do I, because soon, every country will be merged under a one world government, and one man will control the one world government." Cierra said, "I hope you're wrong because I don't think I could live under a one world government."

Jenny continued, "The same thing that brought Adolf Hitler to power in Germany will bring the antichrist to power over the world. **Revelation 13:7** says, 'It was given power to wage war against

God's holy people and to conquer them. And it was given authority over every tribe, people, language and nation.' The antichrist will use terrorist attacks to stay in power, and he will blame anyone and everyone who refuses to follow him as the reason his world peace isn't working. He's going to make it seem right that those who don't follow him are narrow-minded and enemies of the state, and that his followers should kill them."

Jenny kept talking. "I bet Iran will conquer Greece and maybe some other countries too." Cierra started talking. "Do you think this is the start of World War III?" Jenny said, "Yes, I do believe that this is the start of World War III. The Bible says in the last days the whole world would be filled with violence, and I believe that this along with the economy crashing will be everything that the antichrist will need to rule the world. **James 5:1–3** says, 'Go to now, ye rich men, weep and howl for your miseries that shall come upon you. Your riches are corrupted, and your garments are motheaten. Your gold and silver are cankered; and the rust of them shall be a witness against you and shall eat your flesh as it were fire. Ye have heaped treasure together for the last days.'" Cierra said, "Well, I will talk to you later," and Jenny said, "Okay." Then they both hung up the phone.

Jenny kept praying for Cierra, that she would see the writing on the wall, and that she would give her life to Jesus. A few days later, Cierra was on the phone searching the Internet, and she received a notification saying, "Breaking news: Iran has conquered Greece, and now they have attacked Israel. Israel is fighting back and pushing Iran out of the country. The Iranian army is struggling to regroup their forces for a counterattack." Cierra turned on the television and turned to the NNN network. The anchorman Michael said, "As last reported, Iran has conquered Greece and have attacked Israel, but they have been pushed back to Greece, and Israel is now setting up more defenses. We will keep you up to date on the latest information as this situation continues to develop. Tune in to the NNN Network and the NNN app." Cierra said, "We are in trouble, and we are next."

* * * * *

A few days after David, Jack, and Jake made the video explaining the rapture and the mark of the beast, David took a few hours to edit the video, then he emailed Jake and Jack the video and told them to let him know what they thought. Jake and Jack both responded to David, telling him that they loved the video and believed that everyone on Christbook would like the video too. David uploaded the video to Christbook, and in the description, he wrote, "This is a video that explains what is going to happen to millions of people soon, and what's going to happen now, and what you can do now that you have been left behind." He added, "Share and tell us what you think. If we get enough good feedback, we will do more," then he hit the publish button. After publishing the video, he started outlining the next video, talking about the seven seals, the seven trumpets, and the seven bowls that will be poured out during the tribulation and how a person can avoid these judgments. After he wrote the outline, David decided to split the seven seals, trumpets, and bowls into three separate videos if they did another one so they could do the videos in depth to explain what each seal, trumpet, and bowl is, explain the significance of each one, and explain how long each judgment was going to last.

Monday, when David was at school, he met up with Jake and Jack and told them about the next video. He also told them that depending on how much positive feedback they got, they would make more. "Whether we get positive feedback or not, I believe that we should make as many videos as possible because the truth about everything will be hidden about the rapture, the antichrist, the mark of the beast, and everything in between."

Jack said, "I like the sound of that, but if we do, then we are going to have to do a lot of research. I don't want to give anyone fake or misleading information." Jake said, "Okay. The next video will be about the seven seals, and we are going to do the video in depth so that there will be no mistake or misunderstanding about what's going to happen during the tribulation." Jack and David said, "Okay, let's do some research during lunch and after school." They agreed and went to class. During lunch, Jake, Jack, and David quickly ate their lunch, then they went to the computer lab, went on the Internet, and searched the first seven seal judgments. The first thing that came up was **Revelation 6:1–12**. Jack clicked on the link, and it took them to a site that explained the first seven seals and how the first four seals were the first Four Horsemen of the apocalypse. Jack, Jake, and David kept reading.

The first seal represents the antichrist, and he goes forth conquering and conquering. The second horse is red, and he has the power to take peace from the earth. The third horse is black, and he will have the power to cause a worldwide famine. They kept reading and learned about the fourth horseman, and how death and hell followed this horseman. Jack said, "I don't want to be left behind after the rapture," and Jake and David said, "Me neither, especially because the first four seals are just the beginning of the tribulation." They read the rest of the site explaining seals five through seven, then they closed the site, and Jack said, "I'm going to write out what we are going to say for the next video during my study hall period, then after that, we're going to go over what everyone is going to say. Then tomorrow after school, we can go into the studio and record the next video." David and Jake said, "Okay." Then they all went to class.

While in class, Jake and David kept thinking about what they had read on the computer. Jake turned and looked at David and said, "God has told us what's going to happen in advance, but people won't believe it." David said, "In the last days, people will say, 'Where is the promise of Jesus's return because we haven't seen anything.'" David opened his Bible and turned to **2 Peter 3:3–5**. "Knowing this first that there shall come in the last days scoffers walking after their own lusts, and saying where is the promise of his coming? For since the fathers fell asleep all things continue as they were from the beginning of creation. For this they are willingly ignorant of that by the word of God the heavens were of old, and the earth standing out of the water and in the water." David continued talking. "People are ignorant because people choose to be. With all of this technology, people can't say, 'We didn't know about the rapture, the tribulation, or the mark of the beast.'"

Jake said, "You're right. That's why I'm praying for my friends and family, that they will see the light as we have before the rapture happens or they die. Dying without Jesus will be the worst thing ever." Jake kept talking. "The worst thing the Lord can say to me is 'Depart from me.'" He turned to **Matthew 7:21–24** and read, "Not everyone who says to me, 'Lord, Lord,' will enter the kingdom of heaven, but the one who does the will of my Father who is in heaven. On that day many will say to me, 'Lord, Lord, did we not prophesy in your name, and cast out demons in your name, and do many mighty works in your name?' And then will I declare to them, 'I never knew you; depart from me, you workers of lawlessness.' Everyone then who hears these words of mine and does them will be like a wise man who built his house on the rock.'" David said, "So you are telling me that there will be people who think that they are Christians and that they are doing what's right, but their heart will be so full of corruption that when they die, they will think they are going to heaven but they will go to hell." Jake started talking again. "Yes, they will be going to hell because they never truly gave Jesus their heart, and they are going to say, 'Didn't we cast out demons and do miracles in your name,' and Jesus is going to tell them, 'I tell you the truth, I don't know you.'"

David said, "I do not want to hear that from the Lord. I want to hear, 'You have done good, my faithful servant. Come enter the kingdom prepared for you since the foundation of the world.'" After class ended, Jake and David met up with Jack, and he showed them the script for the next video, and Jack said, "This video will be an hour long because we have so much to discuss in this video. I want to make sure that everyone gets equal time in this video. We might go over, and if we do, that's fine. Lastly, I want to do a dramatization before we start talking so people can visually see what's going on before they hear us." Jake and David both said, "That's a good idea."

Later on that night, Jack prayed and said, "Lord, none of us knows exactly how the tribulation will take place, but I pray that You will use these videos, if not now, please use these videos during the tribulation, in Jesus's name I pray, and I thank You, Lord. Amen." When Jake got home, he got on the Internet and researched videos of current events, Bible matches, and how current events will lead to the events that would happen after the rapture. Jake prayed that the videos would be used to reach and warn people. "And if these videos don't reach a multitude of people before the rapture, that they will reach a multitude of people during the tribulation. In Jesus's name, I pray, amen." The next day at school, all three of them met up before class and talked about the new video they were going to make, and David said, "During lunch, we should talk to some of our friends about being a part of the dramatization. We can film that after we do the video, then we can add them together, so the video might be either an hour and a half or two hours, depending on how long the dramatization will be."

Jack said, "Okay, good idea, but let's figure that out after we finish filming the video of us talking." Then Jake said, "I will work on the script for the dramatization. We need a person to be the antichrist and the false prophet, and we need people to be citizens. We need three other people to be the red, black, and pale horses of the apocalypse, and lastly, we need some people who will be killed during the tribulation." David said, "I agree we need all the extra people we can get." Jack said, "We can ask other schools if they want to participate in the dramatization. I already know that all of us want to be in the video too." Jake said, "I will play the antichrist or the white horseman." David said, "I will play the red horse," and Jack said, "I will play the black horse, but we still need one more person to play the pale horse of death, and also, we need a director who knows how to put this all together." Jake said, "We could ask the drama teacher to direct the video since he's used to directing plays." David said, "Okay, I'll ask him after school today."

After school, Jack, Jake, and David went to the drama room and went up to Mr. Bradford. They told him about the video they were doing and asked him to be the director of the video. He said, "Okay, I'd be honored. I'm open to direct anytime you need me. Just let me know twenty-four hours in advance, just in case someone asks me to do something." After they left, they went to the hallway and prayed. Jack started the prayer. "Lord Jesus, we thank You for everything that You have done in our lives and everything that You will do. We pray that these videos will be used for Your glory and that people will give their lives to You. In Jesus's name, we pray. And we thank You, Lord. Amen."

The next day after school, Jake told David and Jack, "Tomorrow's the day we are going to start working on the video. We are going to do the speaking part of the video, and over the next few weeks, we are going to do the dramatization part of the video. Then I'm going to edit the video. I might do it where we speak for a few minutes, then show a clip from the dramatization, or I might do it where the dramatization goes first, then we talk, but I haven't decided yet how I'm going to do the video."

Jack said, "Just pray and ask the Lord, and seek His face and His glory," and Jake said, "I agree." Then they went to class. As they went to their respective classes, they helped spread the word about their video. They said, "If you want to be an extra in the video, please let us know ASAP so we can get people's schedules together and start filming the video. In a month, we are going to put this video on our Christbook so everyone can see it."

Two days later, Jack, Jake, and David met in the recording studio at school. They got in their positions, and Jake grabbed the remote, hit the record button, and started talking. He said, "Good morning, good evening, and good night, depending on where you are right now. Last week, we made a video discussing the events that have just happened called the rapture. Today, we are going to keep talking about the events that are either taking place now or will take place. Jack is going to start us off with the first seal that will be opened and what will happen." Jack said, "My name is Jack, and I will be talking about the first seal and the first horseman. In Revelation 6, the Bible talks about a man that will come to power, and he will come conquering and to conquer. **Revelation 6:1–2** says, 'Now I saw when the Lamb opened one of the seals; and I heard one of the four living creatures saying with a voice like thunder, "Come and see." And I looked, and behold, a white horse. He who sat on it had a bow; and a crown was given to him, and he went out conquering and to conquer.'" The first horseman is the antichrist, and by now you should have a pretty good understanding of who this person is. There will be no misunderstanding as to who he is and what's he's doing or going to do." Jack said, "Next, David is going to explain who the next horseman is and what he's going to do."

David started talking. "The next horseman is the red horse, and this horseman will take peace from the earth so that mankind will kill one another, and I believe this means that even places that are peaceful will be violent to the point that people will be dying in the hundreds of thousands. **Revelation 6:3** says, 'When He opened the second seal, I heard the second living creature saying, "Come and see." Another horse, fiery red, went out. And it was granted to the one who sat on it to take peace from the earth, and that people should kill one another; and there was given to him a great sword.'" David said, "Next, Jake is going to talk about the third horseman and what his purpose is." Jake said, "The third horse will cause a worldwide famine. Also, the price of food will triple. **Revelation 6:5–6** says, 'And when he had opened the third seal, I heard the third beast say, Come and see. And I beheld, and lo a black horse; and he that sat on him had a pair of balances in his hand. And I heard a voice in the midst of the four beasts say, A measure of wheat for a penny, and three measures of barley for a penny; and see thou hurt not the oil and the wine.'" Jack came back and said, "The last horseman is the pale horse of death. I believe that this horse will bring hell on earth, and more people will die. **Revelation 6:7–8** says, 'And when he had opened the fourth seal, I heard the voice of the fourth beast say, Come and see. And I looked, and behold a pale horse: and his name that sat on him was Death, and Hell followed with him. And power was given unto them over the fourth part of the earth, to kill with sword, and with hunger, and with death, and with the beasts of the earth.'"

David started talking again. "The fifth seal shows all the people that will be killed for their testimony of the word of God. **Revelation 6:9–11** says, 'And when he had opened the fifth seal, I saw under the altar the souls of them that were slain for the word of God, and for the testimony which they held: And they cried with a loud voice, saying, How long, O Lord, holy and true, dost thou not judge and avenge our blood on them that dwell on the earth? And white robes were given unto every one of them; and it was said unto them, that they should rest yet for a little season, until their fellow servants also and their brethren, that should be killed as they were, should be fulfilled.'" Then Jake spoke. "The next seal will cause a massive earthquake known as the 'wrath of the Lamb' earthquake, and this earthquake will be so strong that the entire world will fill it at the same time. **Revelation 6:12** says, 'And I beheld when he had opened the sixth seal, and, lo, there was a great earthquake; and the sun became black as sackcloth of hair, and the moon became as blood.' The mountains will be removed from their places, and the mighty men are going to ask God to let the rocks fall on them to hide them from the wrath of the Lamb of God. **Revelation 6:14–17** says, 'And the heaven departed as a scroll when it is rolled together; and every mountain and island were moved out of their places. And the kings of the earth, and the great men, and the rich men, and the chief captains, and the mighty men, and every bondman, and every free man, hid themselves in the dens and in the rocks of the mountains; And said to the mountains and rocks, Fall on us, and hide us from the face of him that sitteth on the throne, and from the wrath of the Lamb: For the great day of his wrath is come; and who shall be able to stand?'"

Jack said, "The final seal will cause a period of silence for thirty minutes because the people in heaven will be so starstruck about everything that is happening on the earth that it will literally take their breath. **Revelation 8:1** says, 'And when he had opened the seventh seal, there was silence in heaven about the space of half an hour.' This will be the worst time to be on the earth because of all the evil and judgments that are going to happen." Jack continued, "Even though you are going through the tribulation, you can still give your life to Jesus by repeating this prayer. Lord Jesus, I believe that You died for me. Today, I ask You to come into my heart and be my Savior, in Jesus's name, amen." David said, "This concludes this video. We will continue to post videos to explain the tribulation. Bye for now." And Jake turned the camera off. Jack said that he was going to edit the video, then after they finish the dramatization, he was going to include clips of the dramatization and show the video in its entirety. A few days later, they talked to their respective classes and instructed everyone who wanted to be in the video to meet outside on the football field after class.

After class, they went to Mr. Bradford and told him that they were going to start filming after school, and he said, "You didn't give me a twenty-four-hour notice, but luckily for you, I don't have anything to do after class today, so I will be happy to direct for you after school," and all three of them said, "Thank you." After school, everyone met on the football field, and Mr. Bradford came on the football field and lined up everyone where they needed to be. The first thing they filmed was Jake talking to all the students, telling them that after the mass disappearances, "We all need to come together in the name of peace and put aside all our hate, bigotry, and selfness. And we have to work together. That's the only way for us to make this world better." And the crowd cheered.

After that, David and Jack portrayed the red and black horse respectively, but after they finished filming, they realized that they didn't have a person to portray the pale horse of death. One of the extras came up and said that he would play the pale horse of death. Jake asked him what his name was, and he said, "My name is Eugene. I'll play the pale horse of death. Just tell me what I have to do." David told him what he had to do, then they filmed the pale horse scene. They filmed the rest of the dramatization, and Mr. Bradford said, "Great job, everyone," and Jack said, "I'll go home and finish editing the video." Over the next few weeks, Jack edited the video, and when he was done, he said, "This is the best video we have made yet." After he finished editing the video, he published it on Christbook, then he lay down, prayed, and went to bed.

* * * * *

In the days leading up to the trial, Cody and Paul were nervous. They had never testified in front of a judge or a jury, and to make matters worse, some of Robert's former gang members were sending them death threats, telling them that if they testified against Robert, they were going to kill them. Paul's mom took them to their attorney to show them the notes. At the attorney's office, they asked to speak to Mike, and the receptionist at the desk said, "Give me a few minutes to see if he's available." She went to the back, and while they were waiting, they pulled out their cell phones and started researching different things. As they were on their phones, their attorney Mike came out and said, "I'm ready to see you now."

They went to his office and showed him the notes. He said, "I'm going to call my friend at the police department, and I'm going to ask her to put all three of you in witness protection until after the trial." But Paul protested. "I don't want to be put in witness protection, and it's not because of ego. I'm not afraid of Robert and anyone in his gang. If they want to come after us let them. I'm tired of running and being shot and hiding. I'm ready to fight them head-on." Cody said, "No, that's not the way we should do things. We need to do things the right way, and considering that you have been shot three times in the past few months, I really understand that you are feeling this way, but we can't let our emotions dictate our actions. We still have to do what's right in God's eyes, and to quote President Obama and First Lady Michelle Obama, 'When your enemies go low, we go high.'"

Paul said, "You're right, Cody. It's just hard because I'm tired of being attacked and hurt, but I can't beat my enemies by attacking them low, so I'll go into witness protection." Cody said, "I'm glad. I don't want to lose my brother. It was your faith during the tribulation and everything that you had gone through that convinced me to give my life to Jesus, to leave my old life behind, and to forge my life for Jesus, so if I don't give up, then you can't give up either." Paul said, "Okay, I won't give up." Mike said, "Give me a few minutes while I make this call." He left the room, and Paul turned to Cody and said, "Thank you for saying what you said. Even though everything that happened to me led you to Jesus, I was still fighting my own demons, and I still am. It's still a struggle for me. Every time I do something good, it comes back to bite me in the butt."

Cody said, "Remember **Romans 12:21**: 'Do not be overcome by evil, but overcome evil with good.' Also, **Psalm 37:27** says, 'Turn from evil and do good; then you will dwell in the land forever.' The last scripture I'm going to use is **Galatians 6:9**, which says, 'Let us not become weary in doing good, for at the proper time we will reap a harvest if we do not give up.'" Paul hugged Cody and said, "Thank you," and Cody said, "No problem."

Mike came back into the room and said, "I talked to the detective at the department, and he said tomorrow all of y'all will be put into witness protection, including your husband," and Paul's mother said, "Thank you." Mike said, "I'm going to accompany you to your house so you can get your stuff, then I'm going to take you to my house for the night. There will be armed police officers posted around the house twenty-four hours, then after that, we're going to take you to a hotel until the trial." They left Mike's office and went back to the house. They got enough clothes to last them the entire month, then Paul's mother called Paul's father, and she told him where they were going. She told him that armed police officers would be at his workplace to escort him to where the family would be. They would be escorted somewhere else the next day and held at a hotel until after the trial. Paul's father said, "Okay," and hung up.

After she hung up, she informed the police officers and Mike of her husband's consent, then they went to Mike's house. At Mike's house, he told them to make themselves comfortable and that one of the police officers would be going out to get them some food. He asked them what they were in the mood for. Paul said he wanted some tacos, Cody wanted pizza, and Paul's mother wanted chicken. Mike told the police officer what everyone wanted, and he said, "Okay," and left. While they were waiting on their food, Paul's mother talked to the boys, encouraging them and telling them that everything was going to be all right. Cody said, "I know, but I'm just ready for all of this to be over so that we can return to our normal lives." Paul said, "I am too, but like you told me earlier, we have to be patient and trust God. He knows what He's doing, but we have to trust Him. He knows where all the pieces are going to fit."

Cody said, "You're right," and Paul said, "I know what you are thinking. You thought once you gave your life to Jesus, everything was going to be smooth, and that all of the things you'd said or done were going to disappear." Cody said, "No, but I didn't think that I would struggle this much, and I didn't think that I would even doubt the Lord's plan for all of this." Paul's mother started talking. "We all have doubt sometimes. Our flesh will never totally die until we go to heaven, and that's why the Bible says, 'Help my unbelief' in **Mark 9:24**." As they were talking, the police officer came back with the food. He gave Paul's mother, Paul, and Cody their food, then they prayed and ate their food. Then they relaxed until the police brought Paul's father to Mike's house. When he got there, he asked everyone how they were doing. Everyone said that they were fine, but they couldn't wait until the trial was over so they could return to their normal lives and not worry about someone trying to kill them.

Everyone agreed. They finished their food, then turned on the TV and watched the news. They saw that Iran had invaded Greece. When they saw this, they all said, "Jesus is coming back soon. I want to be ready when He comes back," and everyone said, "So do I." As they were watching the news on the NNN network, they heard that Iran had moved farther into Greece and was closing in on the capital. As they turned the TV off, Cody said, "Wow, the Bible does say in the last days there will be wars and rumors of wars and revolutions, and there shall be wars in diverse places." Paul said, "I believe that Iran is going to conquer the country and move to other countries. Eventually, they might have a hold on Europe and Asia soon if they keep attacking and conquering territories."

The next day, Mike woke everyone up and said that they would be leaving soon. The police officers and the SWAT team would transfer them to the hotel ready for them. Paul's father woke up and said, "Which hotel are we going to be at?" Mike said, "It's called the Gold Paradise Inn. The police are already there securing the place, checking everyone who leaves and enters the hotel. Anyone who's even related to Robert's crew won't get within twenty feet of the hotel. We're going to treat all of you like the first kids, the first lady of the United States, and the president." Mike continued. "We are going to transport you in the bulletproof car. We're also going to have snipers outside when you leave and when you get to the hotel."

Paul said, "Thank you so much for everything that you are doing," and Mike said, "No problem. When it's time for trial, you will see me again." Once they left Mike's house, they got in the car and said bye to Mike. He closed the door, and they headed for the hotel. As they arrived at the hotel, one of the police officers opened the door and said, "Follow me." They got out of the car, and as they headed toward the building, they heard gunshots, and the SWAT team said, "Move, move now," and they rushed Cody, Paul, and his parents into the hotel. The SWAT team got Cody, Paul, and his parents into the hotel and rushed them into their room. Everyone relaxed but was told not to leave the hotel room for any reason. "Don't open the door unless a police officer is at the door," said a detective. "Stay away from the windows, and do not open the blinds. I put the phone number of Officer TJ in Paul's phone. If you need anything, call or text him. I put armed police officers outside the hotel, in the hotel, and outside your hotel room." Paul said, "Thank you."

After the detective left, they turned on the TV and the streaming services, and they spent the next few days watching TV shows and movies. Over those few days, Mike came in and told them that Monday was the start of the trial and that the police would be there at 8:00 a.m. sharp. "The trial starts at 10:00 a.m., but we want to make sure that we get you into the courtroom early so that all of you are safe." Paul said, "Okay, and thank you so much for everything that you have done for us." Mike said, "You're welcome. I'm happy to help." Over the next few hours, Mike went over Cody's and Paul's testimonies; he prepped them to be cross-examined by the defense attorney and the possible questions that the defense attorney might ask them. A few hours later, Mike left the family relaxed. They started watching shows on the streaming app, then they ate some food. It was their routine until they went to bed.

Cody and Paul woke up at 6:00 a.m. and were ready by 7:00 a.m. Paul's parents got up at 7:00 a.m. and got dressed. Everyone was ready by 7:55 a.m., and at 8:00 a.m., the police were there to pick them up.

At eight, the police knocked on the door, and Paul's father asked, "Who is it?" The police officer said, "It's the police," and he showed his badge to the door. Paul's father opened the door, and the officer was standing in the hallway with about sixty SWAT police officers. One of the SWAT team members said, "We're ready to go when you are." Paul's mother said, "We're ready to go."

When they arrived at the courthouse, the police surrounded the car. One of the police officers opened the door. Paul was the first person to step out of the car. Everyone piled out of the car behind him, and the police told them to follow. The police led them into the courtroom. An officer said, "Be seated. We have metal detectors set up, and we have armed SWAT officers that will be with you at all times during the trial, and I'll be here with you too." Paul's father said, "Thank you so much." After the officer left, they prayed and asked the Lord for His protection and His guidance in Jesus's name. Around 9:45 a.m., everybody began to enter the courtroom. The police were patting them down, and they also had to go through metal detectors and full-body scans. As that was going on, the armed officers watched them. When everyone was in the courtroom, the correction officers brought Robert in. As Robert was walking in, he looked at Cody and Paul and growled at them. He stopped and growled at them again, and the guard pushed him and said, "Keep moving." Robert kept walking.

Paul's mother looked at Paul and Cody and said, "Are you two alright?" Paul said, "I'm nervous, but I'm fine," and Cody said, "I feel the same way." Paul's father said, "Just relax, trust God, and do the best that you can." Cody said, "Okay, Mom and Dad, we will." His Mom said, "I know you will, son." The judge entered the courtroom, and the clerk said, "All rise. Docket number 05-16-28-32, the People vs. Robert McDowell on the charges of kidnapping, attempted murder, and attempted murder of police officers. Judge Lance presiding."

Judge Lance said, "Mr. Robert, how do you plead?" and he said, "Not guilty, Your Honor." The judge said, "I would like to hear the prosecutor on bail." The prosecutor said, "Mr. Robert is a flight risk, and there have been multiple attempts on Mr. Cody's Mr. Paul's life. They have received notes from members of Mr. Robert's gang that told them that if they testify, they will be killed." The judge said, "Bail is denied. Please reprimand the defendant to lock up until after lunch." Paul sighed and said, "This is going to be an ugly trial, and I already know that our personal lives will be targeted, but I believe that we can take it, and we will thrive." Everyone shook their heads. Paul said, "I'll be right back. I have to go do something." He left, and one of the officers followed him. He went to the bathroom and started praying.

He said, "Lord, why me? Why is it that every time I do something good for Cody, I end up suffering for it? I went to convince him not to sell drugs and to stop being a part of a gang, and I get shot. Then we get kidnapped, and I get shot again. Lord, is this a test? Are You trying to test me with all of these tribulations, or do You have something in store for me? I pray in Jesus's name, amen." Paul went back to the courtroom. The trial was starting up again, and the prosecutor said, "The first witness I want to call is Cody." Cody got up from his seat and went to the witness stand. The bailiff said, "Do you swear to tell the truth, the whole truth, and nothing but the truth, so help you, God?" and Cody said, "I do." The prosecutor said, "Please state your name for the record," and he said, "My name is Cody." Then the prosecutor said, "How do you know the defendant?" Cody said, "I used to be a part of his gang, and then I left his gang thanks to my brother." The prosecutor said, "What happened after you left the gang?" Cody said, "The first time, one of his gang members shot Paul when the bullet was meant for me. The second time, Robert kidnapped me and my brother and tried to force me to rejoin his gang, and when I refused, he shot Paul in the leg, then he tried again to get me to rejoin, and I said no again, then he shot Paul in the other leg."

The defense attorney said, "Objection," and the judge said, "Overruled." The prosecutor said, "How did you escape?" Cody said, "We escaped because one of his members came in, planning on killing us, but I jumped him, and we escaped. Then I helped Paul into the car and went to the police station for help. Then Officer Sarah and I went to where Paul was. Paul, Officer Sarah, and I were being shot at, then the police stopped him."

After that, Paul was called as the next witness, and the prosecutor asked him to state his name for the record. "My name is Paul." The prosecutor said, "According to Cody, you were shot by accident, and then shot again when Mr. Robert tried to get Cody to rejoin his gang. Is that correct?" Paul said, "Yes, sir." Then the prosecutor said, "Why did you go after Cody that night?" Paul looked at Cody, and

Cody nodded his head. Paul said, "I had suspected that Cody was selling drugs. One night, I decided to follow him to see where he would lead me, and he led me to his gang. I told Cody that he didn't need to be in the gang because he had us, but his gang members came up to us, and he pointed the gun at me. I was trying to deescalate the situation, and that's when one of the gang members tried to shoot Cody. I jumped in front of him and took the shot." The prosecutor said, "What happened the second time?" Paul said, "Cody and I were hanging out when we were kidnapped, and Cody told you the rest of what happened to us and how we escaped." The prosecutor said, "Thank you. I have no further questions for the witness." The judge said, "Does the defense wish to cross?" and he said, "Yes, Your Honor." The judge said, "Okay."

The defense attorney said, "I'm very sorry for what happened to you, but how do you know that it was my client's fault when you said yourself that Cody was a part of his gang?" Paul said, "Because I had talked him out of the gang. Cody and I were hanging out every day after I got out of the hospital, and Cody kept apologizing to me for being shot, and he even said that he would never do it again, and he never did." The defense attorney said, "Couldn't Cody have been lying, telling you that he was done with the gang life but secretly still in the gang life?" Paul said, "He wouldn't have done that to me, and you can't get me to turn against my brother." The defense attorney said, "I have no other questions for the witness," and the judge said, "You may step down." Paul went back to his seat and apologized to Cody, and he said, "It's fine."

The prosecutor said, "Lastly, I call Officer Sarah to the stand." Officer Sarah came to the stand, and she testified on what happened, then the judge sent the jury back to talk and render a verdict. During the deliberating, Cody and Paul prayed and said, "Lord, please let them find Robert guilty, and let him pay his debt to society, but we also pray that he will give his life to You, in Jesus's name, amen." An hour later, the jury came back, and the judge said, "Have you reached a verdict?" and they said, "We have." Then the judge said, "Please read it." The lady said, "When it comes to the People vs. Robert on the charge of kidnapping, we find the defendant guilty. On the charge of attempted murder, we find the defendant guilty. And on the charge of attempted murder of multiple police officers, we find the defendant guilty."

Judge Lance said, "Thank you, jury, for your service. You are free to go. Please reprimand the defendant until sentencing. We are adjourned." Then he left. Cody, Paul, and their parents hugged each other. The boys said, "It's finally over," and the parents said, "Yes, it is."

A few weeks later, Cody, Paul, and their parents were coming back home from eating out. When they were pulling the car into the driveway, the house exploded into flames. Paul said, "Robert's gang members tried to kill us," and Paul's mother said, "Yes, they did. And now it's time for us to move away from here."

* * * * *

Chris came back and said, "I've counted the ballots, and we have a winner. Your new vice president of CROWN is Tommy." Tommy acted surprised. He turned to Julia and extended his hand to her, and she shook his hand and said, "Congratulations, Mr. Vice President," and Tommy said, "Thank you." He continued, "I thought you were going to win, so I had a concession speech ready to concede the election to you, Julia." Julia said, "I had a victory and a concession speech ready, no matter the outcome." Julia stood in front of the group and said, "I wanted to be vice president because I believed that Chris and I could take CROWN and the message of Jesus to every school that we possibly could and that the Lord would use us to bring as many people to Jesus as possible, but the Lord must have had other plans for me. The group has spoken, and you have chosen Tommy as the vice president. As a faithful member of the group, I pledge my support to the goals and purposes of CROWN, and I also pledge my support to help President Chris and Vice President Tommy in any way that I can." Then Julia walked to her seat.

Tommy said, "Thank you, Julia. As a gesture of goodwill, I want to offer you the position of advisor to the vice president, if that's all right with you, Mr. President," as he turned to Chris. Chris said, alright "That's fine with me, but I was going to offer her the position of chief of staff to the office of the president." They both turned to Julia, and Chris said, "What's it going to be? Do you want to work for me or Tommy?" Julia said, "I don't know right now. Let me pray and think about it, and I will give you my decision by the end of the week." After Chris prayed, he dismissed the group but asked that Tommy and Julia stay behind so that he could talk to them for a few minutes.

After everyone had left, Chris said, "Julia, I really appreciate the way you handled the election. Even in defeat, you acted like a winner. I didn't know that Tommy was going to become vice president, but I knew that if you didn't become vice president, I still wanted you in the administration." Julia said, "Thank you, I appreciate it. I will tell both of you my decision on Friday." Chris said, "Okay," then turned to Tommy and said, "Congratulations on becoming vice president of CROWN. I look forward to working with you to make our group better and bring the message of Jesus Christ to everyone." He put his hand out for Tommy to shake. Tommy shook his hand and said, "I look forward to working with you too." Chris said, "That's it for this week. I'll see both of you in class tomorrow," and they both said, "Okay," and left.

Tommy went to Jason's house and told him that the plan worked out perfectly. "CROWN voted me as the vice president, but we have a problem. I had to do something that I didn't want to do but had to," and Jason said, "What did you do?" Tommy said, "I had to offer Julia a job as advisor to the vice president." Jason said, "*What?* Why did you offer her a job as your advisor when we are trying to destroy CROWN?" Tommy said, "I did it as an olive branch since we destroyed her chance to be vice president. It was a way to show her that we are on the same side." Jason said, "Okay, just as long as you don't lose sight of the objective to destroy CROWN." Tommy said, "I haven't. I have more news. Chris offered Julia a job as the chief of staff to the president." Jason said, "What did she say?" Tommy said, "She hasn't given either of us an answer yet, but she will give us an answer on Friday." Jason said, "You have to get Julia to side with you to strengthen your power in the group. Also, you need to keep up the charade that you want to do what's best for CROWN." Tommy said, "I will talk to her tomorrow and try to convince her to side with me over Chris." Then he went home.

He thought to himself, *Everything is going according to plan. I'm the new vice president of CROWN, and soon I will have Julia at my side as a stepping stool to overthrow Chris and become president of CROWN. Then after that, I will eventually destroy CROWN and Christianity and free everyone.* When Tommy got to school the next day, he went looking for Julia. He found her in the library. He walked up to her, sat down in the chair next to her, and asked her how she was. Julia said that she was fine. Tommy kept talking. "Have you talked to Chris today?" Julia said, "Yes, I'm supposed to meet with him here in about ten minutes. He wants to talk to me more about the offer of being chief of staff to the president." Tommy said, "Okay. I want to talk to you about my offer of being advisor to the vice president. I still want you to be my advisor. I think that both of us can make some serious progress. We can take our group to places it's never been before." As he was talking, Chris walked over and sat down at the table. He said, "How is everybody doing?" and they both said, "We're fine." Chris said, "Julia, I have wanted you to be a part of my administration since the beginning, that's why I asked you to become vice president before Tommy asked to be vice president, but when you didn't win the election, I decided to offer you the position of chief of staff to the president." Chris continued, "I believe that your salvation was genuine and that you want the very best for CROWN. Also, I have another surprise to tell you. The position of chief of staff is the position that will succeed me as president of CROWN." Julia said, "What? I thought the vice president is the person who becomes president?" Chris said, "Typically that is the case, but since I'm the president, I can decide which person will succeed me as president, and I want it to be you, Julia. I want you to be President Julia of CROWN. What do you say?" Julia said, "I will let you know my decision tomorrow or by Friday at the latest," and Chris and Tommy said, "Okay."

Julia went to class, and on her way, she started praying. "Lord Jesus, I don't know what to do. I want to show that there are no hard feelings about me losing the election, but I do want to take Chris up on his offer to become chief of staff and eventually become president of the group. Lord, please show me what to do, in Jesus's name, amen."

Tommy met up with Jason after school and said, "We have a major problem," and Jason said, "What's the problem?" Tommy said, "The position that Chris is offering Julia, the position as chief of staff to the office of the president. He told her that if she accepts the position, then when Chris steps down or graduates, she will become president of CROWN." Jason screamed, "*What?* The vice president is supposed to succeed the president if he steps down or graduates." Tommy said, "Chris told Julia that since he's the president of CROWN, he can decide who will succeed him as president." Jason said, "Do you have anything to offer her if she accepts your position?" and he said, "No, I don't." Jason said, "Since you don't have a counteroffer, we need to come up with another plan to destroy the group and Christianity." He continued, "Give me a few days to come up with a plan. In the meantime, if you come up with anything, let me know."

Friday came around, and Julia went looking for both Chris and Tommy. She found them in homeroom, and both of them said, "What's your decision?" She said, "I will tell both of you my decision during the CROWN meeting," and they said, "Okay." The rest of the day, Chris and Tommy kept thinking about what Julia's decision was going to be.

At the end of the day, Tommy, Chris, and Julia met in the classroom, and Chris told Julia that she could announce her decision after he was done talking about the topic for the meeting, and she said, "Okay." Chris got settled and prayed, and when he was done, all the members of CROWN were in the room in their seats. Chris went to the front of the classroom and said, "Welcome to CROWN. Today we will be discussing the mark of the beast, and what it means, what will happen to those who take the mark, and those who reject the mark." Chris continued. "As I've mentioned before, when the time is right, a world leader will come to power, and even though he will say that he comes in peace, he will bathe the world in blood. This man will be called the antichrist, and for the first three and a half years, he will work to unite the world under a one world government, currency, and religion. During the middle of the tribulation, he will be killed. **Revelation 13:3–4** says, 'One of the Beast's heads looked as if it had been struck a deathblow, and then healed. The whole earth was agog, gaping at the Beast. They worshiped the Dragon who gave the Beast authority, and they worshiped the Beast, exclaiming, "There's never been anything like the Beast! No one would dare go to war with the Beast!"' After the antichrist is killed and brought back from the dead, he's going to proclaim himself God, and he's going to force the world to worship him and to take the mark of the beast."

Chris kept talking. "As we discussed before, the antichrist is going to kill anyone who refuses to follow him, and all those who follow him will go to hell. **Revelation 19:19–21** says, 'I saw the Beast and, those who assembled with him, earth's kings and their armies, ready to make war against the One on the horse and his army. The Beast was taken, and with him, his puppet, the False Prophet, who used signs to dazzle and deceive those who had taken the mark of the Beast and worshiped his image. They were thrown alive, those two, into the Lake of Fire and Brimstone. The rest were killed by the sword of the One on the horse, the sword that comes from his mouth. All the birds held a feast on their flesh.' It will be very bad for anyone who's left behind, especially for those who take the mark of the beast because they have sold their soul to the devil, and they will have no hope of any salvation. I was going to also talk about the battle of Armageddon, but I will do that another time. Before I dismiss the meeting, I'm going to turn the group over to Julia, who has an important announcement to make."

Julia got out of her seat and walked to the front of the classroom. She began, "At the last meeting, I lost the election for the vice presidency. Vice President Tommy offered me a position as advisor to the vice president, but then Chris offered me the position of chief of staff to the president. I didn't know which position to take, so I prayed about it and asked the Lord for His guidance, and I finally made up my mind." She continued. "I'm going to take Chris up on his offer to be his chief of staff. Together, we can take CROWN to places it's never been before. We can take back some of the schools from No Light/Ultimate Light, and spread the message of Jesus to all the schools. Who's with us?"

Everyone clapped their hands, and each one said, "I am." Chris said, "With that, I dismiss everyone. I'll see all of you at the next meeting." Then everyone left. Chris went to talk to Julia and said, "Thank you for accepting my offer to become the chief of staff." Julia said, "You're welcome. To be honest, I didn't know whose offer I was going to accept. Both of your offers were good, but I prayed about it, and the Lord told me what to do, so I decided to take your offer." She turned to Tommy and put her hand out. Tommy shook her hand and said, "No hard feelings." Then he left.

Tommy went to see Jason and told him that Julia had accepted the position as Chris's chief of staff. Jason was furious, and he said, "Give me a few weeks, and I will come up with a plan that will start the downfall of CROWN and Christianity." Tommy said, "Good," then went home. At home, he thought, *CROWN is getting too powerful. I must use my position as vice president to bring them down. If Jason doesn't come up with a plan, I will, and I'll destroy CROWN and Christianity myself.* Then he went to bed.

The next day, Tommy went to Harriett Tubman Middle/High School and approached some people whom he knew were on the fence about whether they wanted to receive Jesus as their Savior. He said, "Hi, my name is Tommy," and the kids said, "We know who you are. You're the vice president of No Light, the Christian-hating group that wants to destroy the group CROWN." Tommy said, "I'm not a part of that group anymore. I've given my life to Jesus. I'm now the vice president of CROWN, and now I want to spread the message of Jesus to every school and get more people on the right path." The guy said, "My name is Albert. Why should I believe that your God is the only way when every religion says their god is the only way?"

Tommy said, "As you already know, I was the vice president of No Light under Jason and Julia, but after Julia left No Light and joined CROWN and Christianity, I really wanted to destroy her, CROWN, and Christianity. But one night, I was watching TV, and a pastor was preaching. At first, I thought he was just talking about the goodness of Jesus to get some money, but then he said, 'I'm not doing this for money, and I don't want any of you sending me money.' The pastor said, 'If you accept Jesus as your Savior, I want you to tell everyone that you know that you have accepted Jesus as your Savior, and I want you to tell them what He's done for you.' At that moment, I wanted to give my life to Jesus."

Albert said, "That's interesting. How can I give my life to Jesus?" and Tommy led Albert through the sinner's prayer to receive Jesus as his Savior, and once he was done, Albert said, "Thank you," and Tommy said, "You're welcome." Then he left.

A few days later, Chris walked up to Tommy and said, "Is it true?" and Tommy said, "Is what true?" Chris said, "Have you been playing us all this time, and sabotaged Julia's campaign in order to become vice president?" Tommy said, "No, why would you think that?" Chris said, "I received a letter saying that you did, and until I get the truth, I'm suspending you as vice president and appointing Julia as acting vice president." Tommy said, "No," and Chris said, "I have spoken." Then he left to find Julia. He found Julia outside and told her what had happened. She was sad and mad at the same time, and she said, "Why would he do that?" Chris said, "It was a plot to destroy CROWN from the inside. Until this matter is resolved, I'm appointing you as acting vice president, and you are also keeping your position as chief of staff. I'm calling an emergency CROWN meeting after school to discuss it," and she said, "Okay."

After school, all the CROWN members met in the classroom. Chris explained what happened and told the group that he had appointed Julia as acting vice president until the truth came out and also that she was keeping her position as chief of staff to the president. "I told her that she will be pulling double duty, but I believe that she can do it." Everyone acknowledged this and went home.

To be continued.

EPILOGUE

For by works of the law, no human being will be justified in his sight, since through the law comes knowledge of sin.

For by grace are ye saved through faith; and that not of yourselves: it is the gift of God: Not of works, lest any man should boast **Romans 3:20** and **Ephesians 2:8-9**